M000072781

JESUS AND

MAGDALENE

João Cerqueira

For Carlota

Author's Note

The film *Jesus of Montreal* by Denys Arcand inspired me to try and create a novel in which a contemporary Jesus relives the most important episodes of his former life.

My reading of the Bible made it clear that the path would have to be a different one.

Recent social and political events illuminated the way to go.

In the end, He won't be the one on the cross.

Statement of interests advised for moral reasons: The person writing these lines is a Christian. Not in the religious sense of the word, but in its etymological, philosophical, ontological, and other meanings. Although I do tend to punch and kick more than I turn the other cheek, I consider the message of peace, of love among men, and of forgiveness to be the greatest gifts ever granted to mankind.

Statement of interests advised for environmental reasons: I was born on a farm. I lived with the beasts of the field such as hens, ducks, turkeys, oxen, cows, pigs, snakes, centipedes, worms, wasps and cockroaches; I killed rats with sticks, drowned bees, and shot sparrows (acts which at the time delighted me, but which today I regret somewhat). That doesn't make me an environmentalist. Still, not only do I admire those who defend nature, but I also see ecology's place as a world priority to be vital for human survival.

Statement of interests advised for reasons of race: Being Portuguese, according to recent genetic research, I should have genes from Caucasian, Jewish, and Arab populations. And so, whether for DNA reasons or for reasons of conviction (faith), I would like all peoples, ethnicities, and *races* to be able to live as one—and if they have to shoot anything, then let it be sparrows.

Patriotic statement of interests: I have the utmost regard for all emigrants, independent of the dialect they speak

João Cerqueira

This book is a work of fiction. Names, characters, places, and incidents are the product of the author's imagination or are used fictitiously. Any resemblance to actual events, locales, or persons, living or dead, is coincidental.

JESUS AND MAGDALENE Copyright ©2016

Line By Lion Publications
318 Louis Coleman Jr. Drive
Louisville, KY 40212
www.linebylion.com

ISBN: 978-1-940938-77-6

All rights reserved. In accordance with the U.S. Copyright Act of 1976, the scanning, uploading, and electronic sharing of any part of this book without the permission of the author is unlawful piracy and the theft of the author's intellectual property. If you would like to use material from the book (other than for review purposes), prior written permission must be obtained by contacting the publisher. Thank you for your support of the author's rights

"And God saw that the wickedness of man was great in the Earth, and that every imagination of the thoughts of his heart was only evil continually. And it repented the Lord that he had made man on the Earth, and it grieved him at his heart."
Genesis 6:5-6

"Therefore, when I reflect on the wise and good constitution of the Utopians, among whom all things are well governed and with so few laws, where virtue hath its due reward, and yet there is such an equality that every man lives in plenty - when I compare with them so many other nations that are still making new laws, and yet can never bring their constitution to a right regulation; where not withstanding every one has his property, yet all the laws that they can invent have not the power either to obtain or preserve it, or even to enable men certainly to distinguish what is their own from what is another's, of which the many lawsuits that every day break out, and are eternally depending, give too plain a demonstration."
Thomas More, Utopia, p. 38

PROLOGUE

**(or good reasons for Jesus not repeating the events
of the first coming to Earth)**

For reasons unknown, Jesus has returned to Earth.
But he won't be going down the same path as last time,
either because he likes to be original, or because times
are different now, or maybe just because he has learned
his lesson.

For example, he won't have to be born from a virgin
by the work and grace of the Holy Spirit, in a
reproductive feat attributed to a dove. At the time this
fact may have raised a few eyebrows, provoked a
frown from some, insults from others, but now, in a
world where paternity tests are commonplace, it would
be too risky to use the same method to come into the
world. If, instead of the Holy Spirit, genetic profiling
proved he had another father, it would cause a scandal.
And because you can't twist the logic of the epiphany,
i.e., have a virgin father instead of the mother, for this
reason, even when you take low birth rates and the

aging population into account, it's better not to be born again.

After all, his relationship with his progenitor wasn't exactly the best. He once addressed her as "woman" at a badly organized, wine-less wedding, and on another occasion he failed to recognize her, or his so-called siblings, in the middle of a crowd.

And so, in not being the offspring of a winged father, and a mother who did not *know* her husband, he wouldn't have to endure embarrassment similar to that of Joseph, who preferred to go and saw wood than to stay at home and nail together thoughts that might explain the mystery.

Nor would he have to dream about angels, who could be very convincing in their virginal explanations, but understood little of the delicacies of matrimonial carpentry.

On the other hand, in the absence of a birth, the Three Kings wouldn't come, laden with gifts, following a star—the name given to comets at the time. Nowadays they would be inspected at customs. The guards would open their luggage and find frankincense, gold, and myrrh—the favored presents of any child. The gifts would be confiscated and the Three Kings, given their dark skins and turbaned heads, would be detained on suspicion of terrorism.

For the same reason, there would be no massacre of the innocents, and no flight into Egypt. Hardly a recommendable destination, given that ever since gods with the heads like jackals and falcons had been banned and a new faith imposed, religious diversity has no longer been tolerated. As a result, the flight would be as dangerous as being exposed to the madness of Herod.

Continuing in this vein, it's only natural that there would be temptation, but none identical to the first one, initiated by the guidance of the Holy Spirit himself—such mysterious behavior, as shouldn't the Holy Spirit avoid temptation instead of leading pure souls, like Jesus, into it? On the other hand, even the devil comes off badly in this story set in the desert, where it is suggested that he needs a middleman to choose his victims, a task he should be quite capable of on his own.

Fasting for forty days and forty nights wouldn't be repeated either, as it would be excessive, even for the son of God. Not even the craziest anorexics would go to such extremes. If in this difficult test he decided to test his limits once again, given how easy it is to call for a pizza, his fasting might have been broken on the first day.

And he wouldn't consider that looking is a form of adultery, nor would he suggest the radical method of plucking out your eyes or cutting off your hands to refrain from immoral deeds because mankind would be crippled, but nonetheless still able to sleep around.

Nor would he take a stance on delicate matters such as the wealth of the Catholic Church or how it condemns contraceptives or homosexuality. Just imagine if he decided to knock on the Vatican door to introduce himself.

"Good morning, I'm Jesus Christ and I'm here to talk to the Pope."

They probably wouldn't take him seriously, they'd refuse him an audience and the Swiss guards might even drive him out. And then Jesus, making his way once again to the masses, in a sermon that would pass from the mount to the media, would be able to give an interview to the newspapers, criticising the opulence of the Church, and once again say that heaven is no place for the rich, advising the Pope and the cardinals to renounce their wealth, sell their properties, shares, works of art, cellars of French wines, high-octane cars, and even the popemobile, and then hand out these billions of dollars to the miserable of this world. Just as in the film *The Shoes of the Fisherman*, in which Anthony Quinn is revealed as the best Pope ever, being Soviet and American at the same time.

As there is no Sanhedrin to put him on trial, or Pilate to condemn him, there would be yet another scandal. The Holy Father and the cardinals would not like to be forced to become Franciscans and, feeling their bare feet on the cold stone floor and the three-knotted cords constricting their kidneys, they would call their lawyers, their accountants, and their tax-haven managers and all meet up in the Sistine Chapel. Under the reproachful gaze of those biblical figures who have never used checkbooks or credit cards. And white smoke would be the last thing to come out of that meeting.

However, in a sudden bout of contrition, they may even try to reach an agreement with Jesus:

"You arrive as if from another world, without any warning, and want us to become poor overnight?"

"I suppose I have the moral authority to raise the matter with you."

"You had authority back then, but nowadays the financial authority is much more important than any morals."

"Listen, it was back then, too, and I could even have become rich, but I resisted temptation."

"And wasn't this your obligation," they would say, "to resist temptation? With such a backward world and such ignorant people, you couldn't give bad examples."

"Well, the Romans had a grandiose civilization," Jesus might say.

"Exactly, and we are the Roman Catholic Church, and so it's only natural that we would be grandiose, too."

"Spiritually grandiose, yes," Jesus would say.

"Come on, be reasonable, there must be another way we can come to an agreement, we already have so many people causing us trouble..."

"Are you referring to the behavior of certain priests?"

"The problem isn't the priests, it's the newspapers and the television," they might say.

"Are you saying you tolerate the abuse of the clergy?"

"Don't come now and lecture us, when the fault for what has happened is yours, too."

"Mine?" Jesus would ask.

"Yes, yours, because if you had married Magdalene nobody would be obliged to be celibate and none of this would have happened."

Other cardinals would enter the discussion.

"Here you have the truth. You didn't marry her, you didn't assume your responsibilities, and now you are surprised that there are these scandals," the first cardinal would say.

"After all, if the disciples were married, why did you stay single?"

"Do you have anything against marriage?"

"Very well, gentlemen, I'll bother you no more," Jesus would say.

Relieved, the Curia vented its emotions when Jesus had turned his back.

"Man, some people just don't know when their time is up. God help us!"

Then a new rift between the faithful would probably develop: the Schism of Property.

Some would support Jesus and his appeal to abandon all worldly goods, while others would remain true to the Pope. Catholic columnists and atheist columnists would contribute to further fan the flames of faith; many people would be excommunicated and banned from entering churches.

To begin with nothing would be heard from the other religions, then prudent, vague declarations calling for tolerance, and finally, when they realize that something similar could happen to them, unconditional support of early religious power, with veiled recommendations to teach them a good lesson.

With the world and mankind like that, it wouldn't be worth getting involved in major endeavours, and much better to take care of minor quibbles — problems that are less complex, but nonetheless difficult to resolve.

8 - Cerqueira

1

CORN

«Beware of false prophets, which come to you in sheep's clothing, but inwardly they are ravening wolves. Ye shall know them by their fruits. Do men gather grapes of thorns, or figs of thistles? Even so every good tree bringeth forth good fruit; but a corrupt tree bringeth forth evil fruit. Every tree that bringeth not forth good fruit is hewn down, and cast into the fire. Wherefore by their fruits ye shall know them.»
Matthew 7:15-20

Rumors had been flying for some time that farmers in St. Martin were planting genetically modified corn on the quiet. It all started with an email making the rounds, followed by a reply with Google Earth images, and then finally, both text and images being posted on Facebook. As a result, the environmental organization *Green Are the Fields* decided to investigate. Trucks driving by at night, an allusion to progress, made by the Minister for Agriculture, and the broadcast of an episode of *The X-Files* erased any doubts. Simple-minded and ignorant, the farmers had been easy prey for the voracity of the gene manipulators.

An action posted on *YouTube* by a French environmental group, previously praised by *Greenpeace*, showed them how they should act. Dressed in clothing imitating skeletons and skull-like masks, their colleagues invaded a farm planted with mildew-resistant onions, doused it with gasoline, and set light to the crop. Filming the operation themselves, before escaping they left a green flag in the ground, to show that the land had been cleansed of genetically modified plants. In the end, by way of a threat, they warned that no farmer of genetically modified organisms would be safe in any part of the world. And then they vanished.

However, to ensure the successful switch into Direct Action, Judas thought it best to beef up the training of the colleagues.

"Our comrades have done mankind a great service. If they had not acted, thousands of consumers would have put food with altered genes into their bodies, pregnant mothers would have passed them onto their babies, and many malformed children may have been born. Experiments on animals have proved the risk of mutations, sterility, premature aging, weakening of the immune system, allergies, tumors, cancerous diseases, and unexplained deaths. The same consequences are probably already happening to human beings without doctors associating them with genetically modified food. As the bacteria in the digestive system absorb the toxic genes, the consumer is transformed into a poison factory, which slowly kills him…"

At this moment, Magdalene felt the need to intervene. "This has yet to be proved by scientists. We have to be thorough."

"Don't interrupt! In a capitalist society the media are dominated by groups whose interests extend to all lucrative activities. Anyone who sells newspapers can sell onions, too. As a result, freedom of information doesn't exist, the truth is distorted, and citizens end up not knowing what's happening. And at the same time as they keep the public in the dark, the system demonizes its enemies. Thus began the defamation of eco-terrorism, with the manipulation of nature complemented by the manipulation of consciences."

"That's true, but there are some excesses that are harmful to the cause—"

"Let me finish! The gene manipulating researchers are the real terrorists and the repressive state that sets its stormtroopers and dogs on demonstrators. And we can only respond to violence with more violence. Any attempt at political reform is useless because the system is flawed. Unfortunately, many swap freedom for servitude. But, even though society is anesthetized, we won't just sit there and watch. While the lambs march towards the slaughterhouse, we will bury our teeth into the jugular of the butcher."

"You're only saying this as a figure of speech, of course?"

"No, I'm not! It was through violence that major changes in history were made and the greatest conquests of mankind achieved. If Louis and Antoinette hadn't lost their heads, liberty, equality, and fraternity would have remained nothing more than a theory. But, in practice, what we are left with is globalization, tax havens, and the destruction of the planet. So it's our turn to guillotine the enemies of nature. All the rest is playing the capitalist system and ending up embracing it."

When the lecture was over, despite the unanimous support for Direct Action, the props used were in need of repair. Two onions were tossed at the French.

"These skeleton disguises contribute to the loss of rural identity that the environmental cause also aims to preserve. It is a subjection to mass cinema, to consumer culture, to capitalist marketing. The ethics of ecology are not compatible with this mockery. I refuse to wear them," Simon protested.

"Me, too. If ecology is transformed into a spectacle, it will end up for sale, like a commercial product. For the symbolism of the action to be reinforced we should wear regional costume or country clothing," Mary suggested.

"Regional costume? No way! I suppose you have no idea that folklore is associated with poverty and the ignorance of the old regime? It's bad enough with fashion designers ripping off traditional costumes and the artisans who have made them," replied John.

Following the lack of enthusiasm in the initial suggestion and the disinterest shown in the subsequent one, the props were put away. In jeans and trainers the Greens were ready to destroy the genetically modified corn.

The following day they entered St. Martin at two in the afternoon. The sun was peeping through the clouds and the wind blew listlessly. From the top of the dirt track they saw the village for the first time. Magdalene opened the car window and gazed at the village as if watching a television documentary. First she saw the hills, fields, olive groves, and granite houses, then granaries topped with crosses, huge threshing floors, old people sitting before their front doors, children running around, farmers pulling oxcarts; finally dogs, sheep, loose hens, and swallows in the skies. Everything was foreign to her. As they approached the farms, the scent of the ploughed earth grew more intense.

"Don't show your face," Simon told her.

After a few rounds of the village, making their way down cobbled alleys and muddy dirt tracks, they stopped their cars close to a farm that looked suspicious to them: green gate, whitewashed wall, large area. As there were no villagers in sight, they got out of their cars, softly shutting the doors, and made their way in silence towards the property. Carefully stepping along the ruts left by oxcart wheels and kicking off the weeds that grabbed at their feet, they searched for an opening close to the brambles against the wall.

They were exploring the land when a brown hedgehog passed before them. It was the size of a rat, had a pointed snout, and looked as if encrusted with thorns. It resembled a huge chestnut, still in its burr. Frightened, the animal curled up on itself, forming a ball of spikes.

"That is one damn ugly critter," Mary commented.

"It's harmless and feeds on the insects that are harmful to agriculture. Farmers like to have them nearby. As it hibernated during the winter, it must be starving," Simon explained to her.

"It must carry tons of diseases," muttered Mary.

"You're right. Careful you don't catch AIDS," Magdalene replied.

And everyone laughed, except Mary.

Forty meters further on they discovered an opening in the tangle of brambles. The whitewash of the wall interrupted the dark green of the bush. They smiled at each other in satisfaction. James and John high-fived. A lizard warming itself in the sun scuttled off down a crack between the stones.

"This one will do, but we'll only go in if no one's about," Judas ordered.

Supporting each other, with hands and shoulders serving as steps for feet, they climbed the stone wall. A few shards of broken glass weren't going to put them off. Gloves and a hammer sufficed to remove this basic attempt at protection. In less than ten minutes the twelve members of the environmental group had scaled the barrier separating them from the GM crops. At their feet, tiny pieces of glass glistened like emeralds.

From the top of the wall they could see the field of corn. Verdant, leafy, lush. Nature had never created such prodigy. Corn like this, with such high stalks, with cobs that fat, and orangey beards, could never have resulted from earth fertilized with manure, spring water and the sun's rays. The sap of capitalism was flowing through those plants: greed, deception, toxicity.

This could be no other than the sinister *Bt*-corn, manipulated with the toxic gene of the *Bacillus thuringiensis*[1] to resist corn borers and armyworm pests. A genetic aberration. Producing a protein that inhibits the absorption of food and destroys the digestive system of insects, *Bacillus thuringiensis* supplied an insecticide for the creation of pest-resistant hybrid corn. There, in St. Martin, their *delta endotoxins* would be lethal for *Lepidoptera* (moths and butterflies), *Diptera* (flies and mosquitoes), and *Coleopteran* (beetles), leading to an environmental catastrophe from which humans would not be spared.

"This guy is a scoundrel!" Mary said.

"He chose the easiest path, crop rotation is too hard for him,"Judas said.

"And he hasn't the slightest idea of the consequences," James said.

---

[1] *B. thuringiensis* was first discovered in 1901 by Japanese biologist Ishiwata Shigetane, and in 1911 was rediscovered in Germany by scientist Ernst Berliner. *Bacillus thuringiensis*, also known as Bt, is a naturally occurring soil bacterium. Bt bacteria produce proteins that stop specific target insects in their tracks while being safe for non-target animals. One of these proteins, produced from the gene *Cry1Ab*, targets corn borers. The tools of biotechnology were used to insert the *Cry1Ab* gene into Bt corn, providing a solution for protection of corn from corn borer attack. Source: Syngenta.

"He must think that genetic engineering is like witchcraft," Magdalene said.

"But he's messing with the food chain," John said.

"Before long the insects will be dying," Simon said.

"And then the hens," Mary said.

"We have to teach him a lesson!" James said.

"This is the only language these people understand," John said.

"They say they put wine in their baby bottles..." Judas said.

From up on the wall they could see the field of corn. The area was larger than they had thought. Resistance to pests had strengthened the plants, multiplying the heads of the Hydra.[2] Suddenly a breeze shook the stalks, sending out a rustle. The monster was becoming restless in defiance. In this moment, a mutation took place in the Greens' feelings of disgust, transforming them into fury. With their mood genes now modified, they jumped down into Mister Joe's farm and began to destroy the crops. Some kicked the stalks until they broke, others ripped them from the earth — all thoughts of gasoline were forgotten. The Herculean work of the environmentalists created clearings in the crops, without causing the Hydra to regenerate. However, when it seemed that nothing could stop

---

[2] Hera's creation, the Lernaean Hydra was a snake-like water monster with many heads. For every head cut off, it grew three more. It had poisonous breath and blood - even its tracks were deadly. The Hydra was killed by Hercules as the second of his Twelve Labors.

them, with verdant victory in their sights, something unexpected happened.

Awoken halfway into his siesta by the noise, Mister Joe, accustomed to purloiners of fruit and foxes, rose from his bed. The wardrobe mirror reflected his back, as he bent over to pull on his boots, and the sudden rotation of his torso and his left side as he left the room. He passed along the sunny corridor, opened the door, crossed the vine-covered veranda, and descended into the courtyard. He went into a storeroom. He studied a pitchfork, a stake, and an axe, before choosing the stake. And he ran in the direction of the noise.

What on earth could be happening? Thieves were usually much quieter, the neighbor tended to hit his wife behind closed doors, and those weren't the sounds of hens having their throats slit. As he was pondering possible explanations, farmer Joe came across a troupe of masked people destroying his corn crop. He'd already seen women kissing each other on television, and a priest who didn't believe in the miracle of Fatima, but nothing that compared to this. That they would steal from him, or divert his irrigation water, he could understand; thieves and jealous neighbors would always exist. But that someone would raze a field of corn, without profiting from it, was totally beyond him. Nature's bounty was a blessing for the men who worked it. Sacred. Destroying a corn harvest was like setting fire to a church.

His fat-fingered, calloused hands tightened around the wooden stake. Tight tendons emerged on his wrists, and hardened muscles flared on his arms. Sweat rolled down the wood. With his cudgel at the ready, Mister Joe entered the cornfield to hunt down the intruders. As he advanced, his face became distorted, revealing a silver canine tooth. A predator was on the loose in St. Martin.

Busy with destroying the corn, the environmentalists didn't even notice his arrival. Appearing from between the stalks, farmer Joe surprised the nearest intruders with three brutal whacks. John, Simon, and Mary were out of the battle. Their cries caused the others to interrupt the corn destruction. As some of them were more than fifty meters away, they couldn't see anything, but those who were closer discovered their fallen colleagues and a stranger with a club in his hand. They'd never seen something like this on *YouTube*. And by the time they realized that there were enemies out there more lethal than corn, Mister Joe was already wielding his stake.

They still tried words first, "Wait, calm down, we're here to protect you," but the farmer didn't hear a word, moved by a fury similar to that of the environmentalists when they were destroying the field of corn. And just as the corn was unable to talk, to tell them it was as much modified as they were, the farmer, too, was unable to hear what they were saying about genetic experiments and health dangers — as deaf as an ear of corn.

Like a riot policeman, Mister Joe now pursued the environmentalists with steely determination. Making the most of the group's dispersal throughout the farm, he threw himself onto single trespassers, away from the pack. The victims of the rural constabulary tried to escape down tracks in the cornfield, only to be trapped in deadends of impenetrable greenery. And so a violent threshing began. Powerful blows on the back, on arms and legs: haematomas, contusions, and broken ribs. However, when the environmentalists managed to regroup, they began to fight back. Armed with the plants they had intended to destroy, they started to throw heads of corn and stalks at their assailant. Their great aim, gained through much practice on policemen, forced him into retreat. A well-placed cob got him right on the forehead, stunning him. Mister Joe finally lowered his stake. The environmentalists then began to circle him, getting ready to restrain him.

But then Madame Grace appeared, Joe's wife and mother to their three children, who had emigrated to Paris. A woman toughened from tilling the land and caring for cattle, thrifty, devotee of Saint Martin, for her farming wasn't just sacred: she had inherited the farm from her parents.

The farmer's wife had been hanging out the laundry in the bleachery when she had been surprised by the shouting of strange voices. "Pilferers! Help!" she cried at the neighbors. Armed with a rake, she set off towards the cornfield, dragging her clogs, her flaccid flesh wobbling. Her straw hat flew from her head and her plait of blonde hair flapped like a mule's tail, mad with fury. When she saw her man rolled up like a hedgehog to protect himself from the blows, she bucked in anger.

Like a modern-day Molly Pitcher, she revealed the strength of a woman who doesn't paint her nails or wax her armpits. In the meantime, the neighbors came running in, multiplying the stakes and rakes. The Hydra of St. Martin didn't need to regenerate, with so many Heras of farmers to come to its rescue. The bodies of the defenders of the corn now suffered violence comparable to corn popping. Resisting the impact of the cobs and the blows from the stalks, Grace lambasted six of them.

When the fray came to an end, the farming couple's bodies were macerated with cuts and bruises, but they felt triumphant. They had taught the intruders a good lesson. After wiping the sweat from his face with his shirtsleeve, fumbling a swelling on his forehead and assessing the extent of the damage, Mister Joe broke the stick of the green flag, fallen between the stalks, and called after the fleeing intruders, "Dare to come back and you'll leave with lead in your britches!"

As for Madame Grace, after putting down her rake and dabbing at the blood from her cut lip with her apron, perhaps inspired by a new saint, this time Joseph[3], she opted for the educational reprimand. "Go find some work, you good-for-nothings!"

Of all the environmentalists, such words, more painful than sticks and stones, stung the most for Magdalene.

*

When Father Justin found out about the attack on Mister Joe's farm he was hardly surprised. The world was increasingly dangerous and it was only a matter of time before crime reached his parish. The Pope had warned them about the loss of moral values in society: the lack of religion in homes, attacks on the family, materialism, debauchery, and the excess of freedom — all this had made human beings weak to the temptations of the devil.

He had known of these temptations and their consequences from an early age. At twelve, when

---

[3] Joseph is the patron saint of workers.

trying to steal some jam from the seminary kitchen, he had been spanked by the cook, the gatekeeper to paradise with plump arms instead of wings. "It may have been the devil tempting you, but you're the one who'll get it," the aproned defender of justice told him — thus corroborating the teachings of the priests about the association between pleasure, sin, and suffering. Through personal experience, he understood that man is vulnerable to temptation — paying dearly for boldness. Getting a hiding wasn't the same as being expelled from paradise, but in the struggle between man and the devil, giving in to temptation turned apples into jam.

The temptation to steal corn was as old as mankind. Fortunately, the method of punishment had remained unchanged. What was new was that the miscreants took revenge on the heads of corn and destroyed the crop. The world was getting worse and worse.

*

Jesus returned to Earth by walking down the middle of the road, without anyone noticing his reappearance. Just another man among the hurrying passersby, with the only difference being that his face didn't look anxious or morose. On the contrary, he was smiling. He was smiling like someone without a worry, without a cross to bear.

This phenomenon of appearing out of thin air in the middle of a city without anyone noticing shouldn't be considered a miracle, just an inexplicable trick, just like those when an illusionist disappears in a puff of smoke in front of the audience. After all, if he had been accused of practicing magic, he could have cashed in on his talent.

Looking at him — tall, slim, long hair, dressed like a bargain hunter from a Zara sale — if having to guess his age, people might have estimated at somewhere between thirty and thirty-three years old. Some evildoers would have said that he was someone who had been under the knife to look younger and had blood transfusions to feel rejuvenated. Others would be categorical in their belief that he was a foreigner, from who knows where.

Two students playing hooky took him for a mature student. From her balcony, spying down on the urban bustle, an old dear had no doubts that he was just another carefree youngster, sponging off his parents. For the taxi drivers, who stared at him below the holy virgin hung from the rear-view mirror, that hippy looked a bit suspicious. And who knows what an effeminate old man who winked at him was thinking.

It was all very different from the last time he had been here. However, his amazement didn't stem from the changes to urban planning or to technology, but rather from his discovery of the city's inhabitants. The people were taller, fatter, hastier, and they no longer wore tunics or sandals (at least the majority); there were still people of every color, many single women, and unaccompanied children. They all seemed strange to him, bizarre, exotic, almost another race and from another planet.

A few questions then occurred to him: would it all have turned out differently if instead of other people from the past, he had met these? How would these beings react, so different from those he had known two thousand years ago? Would he manage to attract a group of faithful here, too, and from time to time some crowds, who would follow him everywhere, but in the end, just as they had before, end up betraying him, abandoning him, and even denying him before the rooster crows? Would the whole city turn against him again, the authorities arrest him, the judges condemn him, their hands washed of guilt, and the mob exult his death? Or, on the contrary, would it all be different: a euphoric reception, or total disinterest in his message? What would these mysterious men and women do confronted with a new *Good News*? Would they practice Good henceforth and as if nothing else interested them in life? Or would they do exactly the opposite, and engage religiously in Evil? Or, and probably the most probable, would they continue to watch television, drink beer, and send text messages without paying him much attention?

In the middle of all this amazing urban wildlife, where there was no shortage of dogs more ferocious than any Roman mastiff, the only thing that seemed familiar was a group of longhaired, bearded hippies, dressed in purple and selling jewelry. These entrepreneurs whom the state would never support, whom liberals refused to embrace, and whom conservatives ignored in their resistance to change may have been the only ones to recognize him, because when he approached they immediately said "peace and love" to him—a modern, floral, and hallucinogenic version of "peace be with you."

There were other things that made this return to the world of men who had treated him so badly, this shock caused by the modern world, seem less strange: beggars, cripples on the ground, madmen screaming, prostitutes, pickpockets, trash, and spitting in public.

*

Jesus first saw Magdalene next to a stall where she was selling books and magazines on ecology, pots with trees for transplanting, t-shirts, soybean cookies, and tofu empanadas.

Although the other members of her group supported fundraising and promoting the green cause, most of them tried to get out of having to spend a day on the street behind a stall. Magdalene, however, took pleasure in her mission. Convinced she was contributing to a better world, she always volunteered to replace unenthusiastic colleagues. Her belief in fighting for a noble cause, without asking for anything in return, filled her with pride. In such an unequal and unjust world, there was no lack of causes for which to fight, but the environmental cause seemed the most important to her.

Men and women considered to be saints helped the disadvantaged, the International Brigades battled against fascism, and environmentalists defended nature and therefore mankind. Ever since she had organized a protest against racial discrimination at university, a hunger for activism had grown in her and had become part of her identity.

Jesus approached Magdalene, intrigued to see someone who appeared to be a vendor from former times, when wheat was exchanged for olive oil, and olive oil for wine; when there was no need for invoices and tax declarations; when the police were Roman and the thieves were crucified. The stall was all that separated them. The girl intrigued him even more when he discovered a scar on her arm, the mark of a recent wound.

Magdalene looked him in the eyes and saw a color that she was unable to define: sky blue, lemon green, poppy purple. And so she remained still, staring at him in silence for several seconds. Seven demons did not leave her body, and neither did a single word pass her lips.

To anyone else who came her way, she would have said, "Good afternoon, would you like to know about our work preserving nature and protecting life?" Or, in the case of those wise guys who accused her of hindering progress and insinuated that she was crazy, "You are being manipulated by disinformation campaigns by the multinationals. I would advise you to buy one of these books to discover the truth."

On hearing the voice of Jesus asking her what she was doing, Magdalene turned. She could see herself reflected in his luminescent irises. Then, timidly, like a marigold beginning to open up to the sun, she explained that she was raising funds for an environmental group. Jesus was intrigued, he wanted to know more about those who considered the lilies of the field. Saving souls, saving plants, saving the planet, maybe it was all related. Ashes to ashes, dust to dust.

Minutes later, her petals fully opened, Magdalene was chatting with him as she would a friend. It was more important to explain her ideas than to earn half a dozen dollars. After all, it wasn't often that she met someone interested in listening to her. But when she began to put away her stall, Jesus noticed that the board holding the books and ecological products was wonky — the work of an amateur.

"Do you have a hammer?" he asked her.

"Here," Magdalene replied, passing him her small toolbox.

In a flash, he pulled out four nails, straightened the board, and nailed it back. The bench was now perfectly straight.

"My goodness, you're really good at that." Magdalene thanked him for repairing it, and put the stuff in a bag.

"My father worked with wood," he replied, with a sheepish grin.

The conversation then continued. It was Jesus' turn to listen to a sermon on the contemporary world, almost always in silence, as you would expect of a layman. The sermon began with Magdalene protesting that the gap between the rich and the poor was immoral; her new interpretation emphasized the impossibility of serving two masters.

"If wealth is concentrated in the hands of the few it is because others have created it. Demand for cheap materials means that millions of human beings are exploited every day. In addition to being deprived of their natural resources, they work for a price close to slavery. Take chocolate for example. Third world workers pick cocoa in exchange for miserable salaries, while the multinationals make huge profits. All fortune is based on a crime."

Admitting his own failure to encourage fair distribution of wealth, Jesus nodded, reflecting, however, that without chocolate consumers there would be no exploitation.

From social injustice, Magdalene moved on to pollution. "Besides being immoral and unjust, this economic model has poisoned the oceans and the atmosphere, decimated forests, and caused the polar icecaps to melt, leading to the extinction of many species. Every day a new ecosystem is put in danger. The planet is running out of resources, and is unable to regenerate. Even so, no one respects the Kyoto Protocol, and disasters like Chernobyl, Bhopal, and Exxon Valdez will happen all over again. Sooner or later, capitalist depredation will bring about a cataclysm capable of exterminating mankind itself."

Although he agreed with the premise, Jesus doubted Magdalene's prophecy — not even the Great Flood had been able to do that.

The struggle against genetically modified organisms came next. "Genetically modified organisms are a good example of the threat hanging over mankind. Instead of ending famine by improving traditional farming methods and eliminating protectionism of western farmers, they unleash mutations in pests and make them resistant to pesticides, triggering the collapse of world agriculture."

Faced with a subject that he had never commented on, Jesus felt less responsible for the matter. But he continued to think that his friend's warnings were exaggerated. As Matthew had said, he really did trust in providence.

The moment of greatest disagreement was when Magdalene suddenly turned against religion. "In a fairer world, religion would end up disappearing. Men created it to deal with death, inventing another life after this one because nobody could cope with the idea of dying. Fairy tales comfort children, religious promises comfort the adults. In fact, religion only serves to hinder scientific advances, to oppress women, and to divide men. Christians were persecuted for their faith, then they warred with Muslims, massacred the Jews, and finally killed each other at the Saint

Bartholomew's Day massacre. Many centuries down the line, the Jews still proclaim to be the chosen people in a kind of religious apartheid, and many Muslims now want to kill anyone they consider an infidel. Do you think there is anything positive in this succession of intolerance and violence?"

This time, despite not feeling well represented on Earth, Jesus felt the need to counter. "Perhaps you've never thought that without religion, the boundary between good and evil might disappear for the majority of mankind, since for billions of human beings, religion is the only moral reference they have. Where else would men have found a model to live as a community? What other laws could they obey? And to which principles would they have applied justice? Wouldn't there be even more violence in a world without belief to counterbalance instinct?"

This was a discussion Magdalene had encountered before; in similar situations she would have immediately refuted, countering that Stalin had been a seminarian, Hitler had mystical beliefs, and the Vatican had helped Nazis escape to South America. But, without knowing why, this time she didn't go down that path.

It then occurred to her to return to the matter of defending life and human dignity, condemning the death penalty as a barbarous crime — a position with which Jesus was in total agreement. Yet something quelled her spirit. She was reminded of a discussion she had once had about abortion, during which she had stated that the owner of the womb should be able to do as she pleased without having to consult whoever had watered her seed. Immediately, she had heard the same accusation from others, who also proclaimed to be advocates of life, in vociferations closer to someone who venerates the devil than someone who invokes God.

And that discussion had ended with a slap.

*

Magdalene felt she had met an activist able to join her on the group's next struggles against genetically modified organisms. He seemed to match the profile of a true environmentalist. Not the kind that knows everything, publishes scientific articles, and takes part in conferences but doesn't do anything. No, he was more like her: practical, eager to act and to settle accounts with capitalism. The world needed men like this, able to sacrifice themselves for their fellow man. And what's more, he was a good carpenter. Together they could do extraordinary things.

*

After the attempt at destroying Mister Joe's corn, the Greens had learned things the hard way: they would never go on environmental raids again without preparing first. Courageous and worthy acts they may be, but hardly intelligent and definitely lacking in efficiency. Direct Action required research, organization, and prudence.

"The *YouTube* video may even have been financed by the multinationals to besmirch the environmental cause and discredit ecologists. Real environmentalists would never have worn those ridiculous disguises," ventured Mary.

"We need to be careful, because there are people who want to sabotage our struggle. There are many undercover agents out there," James warned.

"It's true, the environmentalist movement is full of wolves in sheep's clothing," agreed Simon.

And so it was decided that from then on the planning of each environmental operation would be more rigorous. They would need to know the places where they were going to destroy genetically modified organisms, as well as the customs and mentality of their victims — so that they would not become the executioners of those who wanted to protect them.

They should first talk with the peasants, go to their bars, drink their wine, dirty their own hands in the earth, help when the pig is slaughtered and when inspecting the fertility of hens. Maybe they should wear rural clothing. And only then, when they had won the trust of the yokels, would they be able to warn them of the dangers of genetic engineering and teach them about modern ecology. Yes, this effort in rural empathy was necessary, instead of venturing into unknown territory inhabited by ferocious and barely sympathetic creatures. If you do what the Romans do when in Rome, then surely you should do what the rednecks do, when in the country.

As they didn't suspect the planting of genetically modified organisms elsewhere, they discussed returning in three months to St. Martin. To start with some of them were reluctant.

"I never want to set foot there again," James said.

"Those people are dangerous. This time someone could die," Mary cautioned.

"If I go, I'm taking a rattle and nunchucks. I have debts to settle with those guys," warned John.

"Take it easy. The rural reeducation project to teach them to respect nature is a peaceful one. There will be no more confrontation, or violence. Isn't this what we agreed?" Judas replied.

"Camping in the hills for a few days to watch what's happening in the village isn't a bad idea. One or two of us could even approach the locals, with caution of course, but if we all showed up together, they're going to recognize us," warned Magdalene.

"No one will recognize us. We always have our faces covered. The police have already filmed us on various occasions and have never been able to identify any of us. For the locals we'll be visitors like any others. Rural tourism is all the rage and there must be loads of people asking them about farming. So they won't suspect a thing," Judas said.

"Yes, they might not recognize us, but it's not so clear if they'll accept us into their community. The romantic image of countryfolk welcoming outsiders with open arms is the stuff of 19th-century literature. With these brutes it'll be difficult to arouse any empathy," warned Simon.

Judas shrugged. "Nobody said it was going to be easy."

"I'm not sure this strategy is going to work, either. I've never heard of any similar experiment that has stopped GM crops from being farmed. It'll be a waste of time," James added.

"A waste of time?" yelled Judas. "If that farmer has planted modified corn, the others must have done the same. The whole village must be contaminated. Either we try to do something, or we might as well disband the group. There are already enough 'couch' environmentalists."

This threat silenced any malcontents and skeptics. No one wanted to be accused of having destroyed the environmental group, or of preferring the couch to Direct Action. The rural reeducation project would begin the following week.

*

The members of *Green Are the Fields* had planned to camp in the hills around St. Martin, next to a watercourse surrounded by vegetation. However, after a long and arduous climb, what they found was an arid heap and a dry creek. The virtual images didn't correspond to the geographic characteristics of the landscape, and the reference to biodiversity proved to be just as untrue. The ground was stony and scorched and they couldn't see a single bird.

Although exhausted, they did not contain their frustration.

"This is horrible, there's no life here. I have never been in a more depressing place," said Mary.

"It makes you think of deforestation in the Amazon, it's so bleak. But if the fields are fertile, why is the mountain deserted?" asked James.

"When there is no water in the soil, nature becomes sterile, and there are also natural agents that cause surface erosion of the earth. The mountain slope doesn't help, but this does not exclude that human responsibility lies behind this desertification. Maybe they had been burning the land and caused fires," ventured Simon.

"No, this is the result of global warming and of the destruction of the ozone layer. The rising temperature leads to drought, followed by excess rain, which takes away the minerals from the soil. There are similar cases in Al Gore's documentary. Anyone skeptical about climatic change should be forced to spend a week in these places," said John.

"There is no place safe from pollution. They have globalized the destruction of the planet. And these people don't understand that the long-term losses will be greater than immediate profits," said Magdalene.

"Enough whining now!" shouted Judas.

And everyone looked at him.

"Listen. We are here to prevent any more ecological assaults from taking place in this land. Not for complaining ourselves. And facing adverse conditions contributes to forging a true environmentalist. The plan was changed, but the end result will still be put on YouTube. This ecological victory will bring us fame and recognition from Greenpeace. And that is as important as ending the transgenic maize. Do you understand? So, stop talking and let's find a better place to pitch our tents," ordered Judas.

The mountain seemed like a lunar landscape to them. It did, however, allow them to observe their surroundings. About to cross the moon, the sun carried their gaze from where they were located to the cornfields. In this downward path, the light began to gild the rocks and then finally to cause the crops to sparkle; in between, dragonfly wings shone with iridescence and the hairs on the bees glowed yellow. The sun's last rays of the day also modified the genes of reality. And the crops looked stunning.

Among golden buzzing and hot stones, they ended up settling for the wasteland they had discovered. Some of them noted that they had never breathed air so pure. Others experienced a rare sensation of freedom. And they all discovered that silence was an unknown melody.

What's more, Chomsky[4], Foucault[5], and Singer[6] would take on new meaning if discussed far from any sofa.

---

[4] Noam Chomsky was born in 1927 in the United States. He is a linguist, philosopher, essayist, and political activist. Chomsky criticises the capitalist system and American foreign policy, proposing a political model of libertarian socialism. Defender of civil disobedience and of nonviolent direct action, he supported the "occupy" movement.

[5] Michel Foucault was born in France in 1926. He was a philosopher who, among various fields of knowledge, studied power relations. Foucault established a comparison between the prison system and the treatment given to the insane, to ethnic minorities, and to homosexuals.

[6] Peter Singer was born in Australia in 1946. He is considered a philosopher of morals and ethics. In his book *Animal Liberation*, 1975, he states that the same ethical principles existing between human beings should also be applied to those between humans and animals.

However, just when they had placed one foot in the forge, a snake suddenly appeared. A snake like the ones you see on television, greyish, with scales, and almost a meter long. Appearing out of the blue, the reptile came to a standstill in front of the camp, sticking out its forked tongue at the environmentalists. With hair-raising hisses it claimed its stake on the territory. The environmentalists tried to shoo it away by shouting and stamping their feet on the ground, but the snake would not be moved. Instead it stared at them with hypnotic eyes, as small as they were frightening.

They had landed on an unknown planet that appeared uninhabited, but it was actually home to life. Hostile, predatory, and tough. The experience of facing the police with helmets and batons, or farmers armed with stakes, was of no use before such a strange creature. During their last demonstration in front of parliament, they had managed to cross the security cordon, weaving among the agents trying to grab them and almost made it to the entrance door. Now the roles were switched, with them having to prevent a space from being occupied. But the uniform that bars access and repels revolts didn't work for them.

Suddenly the animal moved. John tried to lift it with a stick — just as he had seen on the *Discovery* channel — and toss it far away, but the reptile managed to escape him and slid a few centimeters closer. After a series of nods, it raised its head as if preparing to attack its prey.

"It's a viper," Simon said.

"And by its color it looks venomous," James warned.

"They get inside sleeping bags and attack when you're asleep," Mary said.

Scared voices spoke of the lack of antidotes and the piercing pain of those attacks: death by suffocation and death by haemorrhage.

It was then that the venom of instinct bit their hands and a shower of stones hailed down on the creature, crushing it. The uniform had, after all, the mysterious ability to fit to any body.

For some seconds they stood frozen, staring at the squashed snake flesh.

Mary was surprised.

"The flesh is so rosy ... looks like a ..."

"A rabbit?" asked James

"Yes, a rabbit."

An owl flew over them and launched a shrill peep. They now knew the bitter taste of the fruits of evil. Until Simon redeemed them from the fall.

"That's what life in the country is all about. Farmers remove the animals that threaten their crops or come into their homes. Whether with sulphate, with traps, or with a stick, they never tire of killing animals. And nobody is sorry about it. If we're here to try and understand them, it's only natural that we act as they do."

Mary rounded off the environmental reasoning.

"And by killing the snake, we've saved other animals. So then the creature's remains will serve as food for insects and fertilize the earth."

The mention of the theory of natural selection helped ease their guilt for having taken part in the process of the survival of the fittest. They could continue without sin in the wild garden of St. Martin. After all, corn was more important than the damn snake.

Once the body was buried without ceremony — in nature nothing is lost, everything is transformed — they continued with setting up their tents on the hill. The moon appeared on the horizon.

After giving a few instructions to his colleagues, Judas began to pitch his tent below the only tree that offered shade. Even though one of the group's rules was that there were no leaders, he felt responsible for the operation. He had chosen the location, proposed the date for attacking the GM crops, and now he was organizing the camp. There might not be any leaders, but a coordinator was vital. He had stood out in the planning of actions of civil disobedience and resisting authority for some time now. The threat of disrupting the parliamentary debate on GMOs was down to his reckless tactics; and he had also been the one who broke into the laboratory of the university pharmaceutical department to free the rabbits and guinea pigs, as well as the only one brave enough on the following day to set fire to the rector's car. The ideas of his colleagues inflated enthusiasm at meetings, seemingly able to lift them from the confines of the world to rip out modified plants or to save guinea pigs, as quickly as they suddenly deflated when touched by the pin of a remark. Without his commitment, would they have ever made it to St. Martin? Would they be so close to an environmental victory? Would *Green Are the Fields* even exist?

Nevertheless, hardly had he buried the first tent peg when a colleague grabbed his arm. James had disagreed with the rural reeducation plan and had not changed his mind. Direct Action with gasoline was the only way to put an end to GM corn. *Greenpeace* had used machines to destroy modified wheat in Australia, but nothing was as good as flames to exterminate the GM crops. They would appear at dawn, drench the farm from the top of the wall, light the fire, and flee. The whole crop might not be destroyed, but at least the farmers would be given a warning. A warning from the hell awaiting them if they were to continue sowing GM corn. Talking with these broncos wouldn't lead anywhere. And the sooner they were away from this wasteland, the better.

"Hey, this place is mine! Didn't you see I'd left my backpack there?" It was James, who wanted the space where Judas was setting up his tent.

Judas shot back. "What?"

"Yes, I spotted it before you and put my bag there so nobody would take it. Go on, look for somewhere else, there's plenty of room on this craphole of a hill."

A kernel of corn had entered Judas' ear. After so much dedication to the cause, fighting with the police and snakes, this imbecile comes along to shoo him away? Hidden below his clothes, the buttons burst on his uniform.

"You're more worried about your comfort than about nature. You should have stayed at home, comfy on your couch!"

"And you think that you're in charge, that you can give orders and decide what happens and what doesn't. But who gave you the right? Just who, exactly?"

From the outset no one dared intervene. Now it wasn't the corn, but the rocks supplying the material for the words being formed.

"Seeing as up till now you've done nothing for the environmental cause, you should keep quiet!" Judas said.

"And what have you done, apart from take the money we've raised?"

"Repeat what you just said!" Judas was now just inches from James' face.

"Why has no one ever seen the accounts?"

"He's right," John interrupted.

"You stay out of this! I have nothing to hide," Judas said.

"When we get back, you'll have to show us all the bank statements and all the receipts for expenses you've had," James insisted.

"I'll rub them all in your face!"

Before the blows could cause any damage, the other environmentalists put an end to the feud, reminding them of the reason why they were there and of the cause that united them. Simon made a suggestion, to calm things down.

"The mountain is everyone's and belongs to no one person. Let's draw straws to see who goes under the tree and the matter will be sorted."

Simon had tossed a flower instead of a stone, and everyone wanted a go.

"In that case, I want to draw straws, too," complained Mary.

"I do, too," said John.

"And me..."

Pitching your tent in the shade of a tree was the right of any environmentalist in combat. Neither snakes, nor riot police, nor the theories of Darwin could prevent it. Judas wasn't hanged from a fig tree, but at that moment he didn't have thirty pieces of silver of authority.

However, there was no agreement as to how they would decide who got the pitch. The draw could easily be manipulated: the coin toss falsified, the names in the hat marked, and whoever it was hiding the stone in their hand could make signals. There were many ways to cheat. With the draw in doubt, the spiked language returned. Everyone saw everyone else as a police officer blocking their right to occupy a public place.

It was then that Magdalene cut short the dispute.

"What is this? You want to defend nature and you're arguing because of a tree? Aren't you ashamed of yourselves? What if someone had been filming all this? What image would this give our cause? Have you already forgotten that the Earth is being destroyed and that GM crops have reached this village? Pull yourselves together, comrades!"

An acid rain poured down on their heads. Embarrassed as if they had been caught eating at McDonald's, they dispersed, lost in thought, inattentive to the pebbles tripping them. A uniformed woman demands even more respect than a man.

In the meantime, Magdalene began to pitch her tent under the tree, under the shade of disagreement. And it all appeared so natural, as if now nobody had the right to occupy that space, that neither Judas nor James dared open their mouths.

At this, the sun disappeared behind the hill and the wind picked up. The small tree began to shake, its leaves and branches rustling. The owl let out sharp cries. A mosquito plague began to fall upon the camp.

Even though sceptics doubt it, nature sometimes becomes enraged. Deforestations, oil spills, radioactive leaks, global warming, and slaughtering snakes can leave her furious.

*

That night Magdalene dreamt about Jesus.

She was wearing a green overall and gloves, her hair was protected by a plastic cap, and a mask covered her mouth. She was in a large laboratory, looking through the lens of a microscope. All around her there were similarly dressed people — some sitting, others standing, each engaged in a different task. All of them were concentrating intently, and no one spoke.

She worked for Monsanto. The evil gene-manipulating, pesticide-and-defoliant-inventing multinational. But, weirdly enough, Magdalene was happy. Absorbed in her work, as if nothing else existed other than that experiment in genetic alchemy. Like a goddess about to create a new species, more perfect than all the others she had engineered, Magdalene the scientist took delight in her experiments. However, as is always the case in *lucid dreams*, the awareness of this pleasure disturbed her.

There was a project: to create a new kind of fast-growing corn that would be immune to all known diseases and would let off an odour that would repel predatory insects. This extraordinary plant would do away with the use of toxic herbicides, nitrogen fertilizers, chemicals that pollute groundwater; it would not raise CO_2 emissions, or require great amounts of watering. Such a grain would represent a miracle far greater than nature's abilities — showing how nature represents a past of deprivation, while genetic engineering heralds a future of abundance; it would be a super-food designed to deal with population growth and put an end to famine. And only the biotechnology of Monsanto could produce this future. The Brave New Agricultural World, with only Alpha corn — even better than Bt.

Expectations from the scientific community and from consumers were high. Newspapers speculated that this was one of the greatest discoveries of mankind, the radio said the same. On the news

Cristiano Ronaldo was shown with two Swedish girls — "they like me because I'm rich and handsome," he said. This and other information were part of the dream, like the text shown in some film scenes to set the time and place.

Other companies were trying the same feat, but it was Magdalene and her colleagues who had lifted the veil on the secrets of the genes, mapping them, decoding them, manipulating them — and coming closest to the finish line. Within Monsanto itself, Magdalene was heading the research, with the other scientists forming a team that followed her lead. They were just spare parts in a whole she controlled. As such, she closely watched the results of the latest tests, feeling that the chimera was edging closer and closer.

In truth, Magdalene, when awake, knew almost nothing about genetics and less still about the technological processes behind their manipulation. She had read stuff in the papers, browsed websites, watched documentaries, listened to layman conversations, and these scraps of information had provided the tattered rags with which she had sewn together her short patchwork blanket of scientific knowledge. Put another way, she didn't know diddly-squat about the matter. But that didn't stop her from dreaming that she was the greatest geneticist, about to invent a plant resistant to everything — pests, mice, environmentalists — and saving mankind from famine.

Even if we lose our identity, dreams enable us to reach for the stars, to walk in the clouds, to play with a magic wand that transforms frogs into genetically perfect princes. And so, radiant dreamer Magdalene was testing the magical powers of her wand, and her corn prince was almost ready.

Suddenly, the dream changed.

Preceded by the crash of the door as they broke it down, Judas and his green militia stormed into the laboratory, shattering test tubes, pipettes, beakers, funnels, flasks, stirrers, centrifuges, microscopes, tables, chairs, and computers. Everything went flying. The muscles of a choleric triumph twitched on his face and a rage yet to be quenched roared in his eyes. Eager to raze Monsanto to the ground, Judas even managed to hit his comrades with the equipment he was tossing against the wall, and to cut his hands on the glass he broke. It was in this blood-soaked form, like a beast that corners its prey after the chase, that he made his way towards Magdalene, the traitor. Holding a chair above his head, Judas was going to crush her as he would a GM crop. In Magdalene's wide eyes, the color of terror was blue.

It was then that a door opened and Jesus appeared, stopping Judas in his tracks. He was wearing a white tunic and his hair and beard were longer than before. The serene physiognomy Magdalene knew had gained an expression of authority. He seemed taller and endowed with superhuman strength, omnipotent and omniscient. Nothing could oppose him. If she hadn't have been terrified of Judas, she would have been intimidated by Jesus. Just as the others were.

The cold light of the laboratory had disappeared before the glow coming from Jesus' body, forcing both intruders and scientists to cover their eyes with their hands. Only Magdalene kept her eyes open, immune to his radiance. Very slowly, everyone began to recover from the impact of the light and headed towards Jesus, with no difference between assailant and victim. Defenders of nature and its researchers walked side by side, as if they had discovered that they were heading towards the same destination.

Only Judas stood still, but he lowered his chair.

Magdalene had finally shed her fear and freed herself from anxiety. There was now an agreement between the feelings of the woman who was sleeping and the woman in the dream. Genetics and nature had become reconciled. Jesus had not only protected her from Judas' blow, but had also freed her from the guilt of being a gene manipulator — far from being a miracle, this was no small thing.

However, when everyone was gathered around Jesus and waiting for him to offer words of wisdom, to give good advice, to explain what he was doing there, the saviour pulled up one of the few remaining intact chairs and sat down. He then crossed his legs, took out a cigarette, tapped it a couple of time against the back of his hand, and began to smoke, peacefully — a behavior that irritated the scientists as it violated safety rules and disturbed the environmentalists, who suspected that it contained GM tobacco.

One puff, another puff, and nothing. Not a word. Just grey smoke, very unhealthy.

Even Magdalene started to become intrigued. A saviour appears for gene manipulators attacked by gene defenders, avoids a blood bath and astronomical damage, puts everyone in a daze, and then sits down for a smoke? It didn't seem right. A few words were required, an explanation, a telling off.

But Jesus rarely did what was expected of him.

He observed the bewildered men and women in front of him, waiting for the right moment to start his peacemaking speech. He was enjoying the cigarette, so he would finish smoking it. And what a shame one of those little machines couldn't make coffee, or that there was no cognac or port wine in those test tubes. The bad thing about scientists was that they didn't know how to appreciate the good things in life. In the meantime, researchers and intruders were becoming desperate. But Jesus was now entertaining himself, blowing smoke rings. It was a small punishment for those who wanted to play at gods, just as it was for those who wanted to destroy temples.

Finally he put out the butt in an intact flask, shifted his gaze from face to face, lingering on Magdalene's, and then spoke, with Judas in his sights.

"Judge not, that ye be not judged. For with what judgment ye judge, ye shall be judged: and with what measure ye mete, it shall be measured to you again. And why beholdest thou the mote that is thy brother's eye, but considerest not the beam that is in thine own eye?"[7]

*

Perhaps influenced by the dream, maybe for reasons that only her heart knew, or merely to annoy Judas, Magdalene decided to introduce Jesus to her environmentalist friends. Faced with such an important operation, it would be negligent to disregard this ally. And so, pretending she had forgotten to bring any underwear, first thing in the morning she went down the mountain.

---

[7] The Bible, King James Version, Matthew 7:1-3.

It was a sunny day and the light made the colors all the more bright, just as the rain seemed to fade them. The world was blue, green and yellow, with dashes of red. To Magdalene it seemed that the very earth was radiating light and thus coloring the sky and causing the sun to glow. As if it had a life of its own, as if, every now and then, it wanted to introduce itself to mankind in stunning beauty to remind them of the treasure they had been given. The Earth was a woman and only women could understand it, Magdalene daydreamed.

Confident that nobody would recognize her because she had been wearing a woolly hat and had covered her face the last time she had been there, she walked the cobbled lanes of St. Martin without fear. Narrow, irregular, and winding, barely had these lanes revealed a series of façades before they hid them, directing you to another place. The village retained its modesty, never revealing itself entirely to strangers, with only the exercise of memory being able to discover it. And the inhabitants also seemed to want to hide, as Magdalene didn't see a soul. An intense aroma of baked cornbread was the only sign of human presence.

She finally saw someone in the next lane. An old lady dressed in black was seated on a bench at the door to her house. The scarf covering her hair caused her withered face to stand out, her swollen hands ended in short, gnarled fingers, her feet were stuffed into wooden clogs. She could have been sixty or a hundred, thought Magdalene. The woman had a hen on her lap, its legs tied, a knife in her right hand, and a bowl at her feet. She was about to kill it. The hen struggled in vain, submitted to the fat claw of the peasant woman. She placed its neck on the edge of the bowl, put the blade on it, and began to saw away with vigorous strokes. The cartilage cracked. A jet of blood spurted out onto the stones of the lane and onto the old woman's skirt. The bird writhed, letting out the moans of a grieved soul. Then, in gushes, a dark torrent began to fill the bowl. Even when headless the hen struggled on. Finally, it used up its resources in a last spasm, stretching out its leg.

Stopping to watch, Magdalene received a smile from the bloodied biddy. The bird's death seemed to have filled her with life; suddenly Magdalene felt giddy, as if someone had hit her, and when she saw the amount of blood in the bowl, paste-like and steaming, she almost vomited. Did people really eat that? Disgusted, she barely managed to return the greeting, before fleeing, not wanting to witness the hen being plucked.

Fortunately she hadn't witnessed a pig or a calf being slaughtered. Reconciling animal rights with human needs caused her to become distracted on her journey. She continued in this frame of mind, absorbed in her thoughts, when it occured to her that if the hen had eaten modified corn, something could happen to the old woman and her family. This possibility roused a slumbering ghost in her: she could have eaten GM produce herself, without realizing it. Did she have *Bacillus thuringiensis* in her body? After all, for years nobody cared about reading labels on food packaging. If she had never been shown images of guinea pigs deformed because of genetic experiments, she would never have become an environmental activist.

As she brooded over the matter, she turned into an alley that led her once again to the center of the village. The smell of bread brought her to her senses. She looked around and realized that she had come back on herself. As the houses and lanes all looked the same, she hesitated as to which direction to take. She looked towards the windows in search of assistance, but all she saw was a child, pointing a slingshot at her. The kid couldn't have been more than ten years old, but he had the strength to fully stretch the rubber device that hurled stones. Uncertain as to whether this was part of a game or if she was about to be hit, she quickly descended a slope. The asymmetric rocks and loose stones required her full attention, lest she twist her ankle, a greater threat than any ghost.

Magdalene was half way down, eyeing an unexpected hole in the ground, when she came across a girl who was coming up the slope. She was tall, thin, and had long black hair. Panic-stricken, she climbed the slope with the agility of a goat. Magdalene had to lean back against the wall of a house so as not to be knocked down. Seeming not even to see her, the girl passed by without saying a word and disappeared into the next lane. Not everyone submitted themselves to a slow pace of life in St. Martin.

She was still listening to the steps of the runaway girl, when she discovered an older woman, also climbing the slope with great effort. She was short, fat, and had gray hair. If the first had appeared frightened, this one seemed furious, screaming, "You're gonna get a hiding when I catch you!" and brandishing a switch of birch. And the faint sound of tiny little feet in flight disappeared under her pachydermic steps.

Magdalene quickly understood what was happening. A mother was chasing after her daughter to give her a beating, in the rural fashion. She had received a few spanks when she was small, not always with just cause, but she had never been thrashed. Such brutality! Civilization and human rights had not even made it to this lost hamlet.

Did they solve problems only by resorting to violence? They really had put wine in their feeding bottles! After all, what on earth could the poor girl have done to deserve such punishment? Had she painted her nails? Was she taking the pill? Maybe she'd just given her boyfriend a kiss.

The reasons for them being in St. Martin were becoming more justifiable by the minute. And these victims of rural savagery would be the first to understand the environmentalist message.

On the rest of her journey, all the way to the bus stop, the images of the hen struggling and of the girl fleeing her mother pained Magdalene. She hoped the girl would find somewhere to hide on the hill until her mother's fury had abated. After the dead hen, enough blood had been spilled already.

To help her forget the incident, during the bus ride she picked up her favorite book, *Utopia*, by Thomas More, and reread an underlined paragraph.

"Bound by the ties of good-nature and humanity to use our utmost endeavours to help forward the happiness of all other persons; for there never was any man such a morose and severe pursuer of virtue, such an enemy to pleasure, that though he had set hard rules for men to undergo, much pain, many watchings, and other rigors, yet did not at the same time advise them to do all they could to relieve and ease the miserable, and who did not represent gentleness and good-nature as amiable dispositions."[8]

With great lucidity, Thomas More had understood that a more just world could only be built by respecting

---

[8] *Utopia*, Thomas More, p. 70.

the laws of nature. The environmental struggles would also lead to equality among men, to an end to barbarous punishment, and would perhaps also diminish the suffering of poultry.

Admittedly there were slaves in utopian society and religion played an important role, but, when seen in the context of its time, the work had been the first to propose the construction of a more just and fraternal world. It was no wonder therefore that business moguls hated good literature and the true masters, satisfying themselves with airport books, other books that taught them how to make even more money, and *Playboy*. Their Utopia had already been achieved. And they defended their golden-egg-laying hen with more than just sharpened knives and birch switches.

This realization, through the association of ideas, brought to mind the creatures of medieval bestiaries, the demons of Hieronymus Bosch, and the beings depicted in books from the time of the discoveries, which described the fauna and the inhabitants of unknown lands: men with animal heads, endowed with a single, giant foot and their face in the place of their chest. Would genetic tomfoolery, at the hands of scientists even more deranged that those of the modified corn, end up bringing similar monsters to life? For them to appear in amusement parks or on reality-TV shows. Would the island of Doctor Moreau become reality? Hadn't science managed to achieve almost every dream and delirium of men in the past, such as the desire to fly, immediately transforming the invention into profit?

But, when the vehicle came to a halt, the struggle between Utopia and Dystopia faded.

*

Magdalene searched for Jesus and she found him. Not in her heart, but in the same place that she had first met him. Perhaps because she had chosen this place as one where she might see him again, or maybe because he had stayed there waiting for her. As soon as he caught sight of her, Jesus walked towards her and embraced her. Initially surprised, Magdalene soon relaxed in his arms and pressed her face against him. They remained like this for a few seconds, before parting, somewhat embarrassed. Magdalene then made her invitation.

"I would like you to come with me to our camp so I can introduce you to my environmentalist friends. Someone like you will be made very welcome."

Jesus did not seem surprised about the invitation, but humbly expressed his doubts as to his worth.

"Do you really think I could help your cause?"

"Of course, you'd be a great help. There are so few people interested in our cause."

"Can I ask you a question?" Jesus said.

"Sure..."

"Why are you so committed to trying to change the world? Why do you risk helping people you don't know and who could even turn against you? I have met few people like that."

"What I don't understand is that the majority of people couldn't care less. They just shrug their shoulders and don't want to know, despite all this misery around them. Do they have a clear conscience when they sleep at night? They turn on the TV, see children dying of hunger, and then just switch channels, thinking nothing more of it. I just can't do that. I'm young, I have the energy, and I have the duty to do something for others. Cynics say that people like me are lunatics, utopian, but for me, that's the only way life makes sense. What does it mean to be human, after all?"

"That's the big question," Jesus said.

"Being human is being supportive. If even animals help each other and cooperate, how can we only stare at our own navels? Ants build communities of millions of individuals and don't let anyone die of hunger. They don't have culture, or science, or religion and still they are more supportive than us."

"The human being is imperfect, but you have to believe in the future."

"Have you seen the film *Blade Runner*?" Magdalene asked.

"No, I haven't."

"The film shows what the future will be like if we do nothing. The Earth has been destroyed, major companies dominate what remains, and men have lost humanity. This wasn't science fiction, rather, it was a glimpse of what reality would become. The devastation of the planet gives rise to a totalitarian system controlled by predators, something that was already happening. And the most disturbing thing is that creatures designed by genetic engineering to be slaves are the ones who fight for freedom, are capable of love and of being altruistic. They are not human beings. These have been definitively transformed into money-making machines or police of the system."

"I have to see this film..."

"You'll understand better because it is imperative to try and change the world," Magdalene said.

"It's an almost impossible task, but someone has to try."

"We share many ideas, don't we?"

"Yes, some," Jesus said.

"It's true that we've only known each other a short time, but I'm usually right when it comes to judging people. Like me, you want a better and fairer world. I feel there is love in you." She looked at his eyes; there really was something there.

"I think the same about you."

"Will you come, then?" Magdalene said.

"I'll come. When do we leave?"

As they were waiting for the bus, Jesus noticed that in the group of people at the stop, there was a man with a limp. With the help of a crutch, he dragged an inert leg along, this effort triggering ungainly movements traveling up from his hips, through his torso, and ending in a wobble of his head. Each step was activating a malfunctioning mechanical system where a missing part caused the others to clash. Nevertheless, the owner of the machine had found a way to make the most of the damage, using the involuntary movements to find his balance and, after a few steps, to move almost effortlessly. The mechanism thus wound itself. However, when the bus arrived and the waiting passengers were required to climb two steps, the machine was confronted with an obstacle for which it wasn't prepared. The man hesitated before the door and went no further. Some people tried to help him, but they succeeded only in hurting him.

"Get off me! I can do it on my own," he ordered in fury. And everyone moved away from him.

"Can you let me get by, please," Jesus asked the people waiting to get on. Then he entered the bus, turned around to face the disabled man at the bottom of the steps, and stretched out his hand to him. The driver, who was protesting, became quiet. The man was perspiring and trembling. He didn't react to the help being offered to him, in order to protect himself from further humiliation. Then Jesus spoke to him. The other people drew closer, but no one could hear; the driver also missed the words. The disabled man breathed deeply, grabbed Jesus' hand, and climbed up into the vehicle. Seen in the rear-view mirror, the steps taken to reach his seat seemed to the driver to be those of a normal man.

During the journey, Magdalene decided to tell Jesus everything.

"There's something I have to tell you…"

"What is it?"

"As you've probably already heard, the environmental movement isn't monolithic. Everyone opposes the current development model, but there are many currents within the movement. One of them believes that it is more important to act than to talk. It is on the Earth itself that the struggle takes place, and not in the media. We don't oppose this discussion, and we are pro the defense of minority culture being included in the concept of ecology, but we prefer direct action."

"Direct action...carry your message to the people..."

"We do not expect others to solve problems, nor do we ask for license to act," Magdalene said.

"So that's why you set up camp?"

"Yes, our group set up on the mountain in St. Martin because we have an important mission to carry out. An environmental catastrophe is imminent, caused by GM corn planted by some farmers. If we don't act quickly a disaster will take place, due to the contamination of other plants, mutations in insects, and a series of unpredictable consequences—"

"And what are you going to do?"

"We're not going to destroy the corn, if that's what you were thinking. This method wouldn't work."

"That's what I would have thought."

"Yes, it could disparage the environmental cause," Magdalene said.

"And there is also the danger of causing physical damage to the farmers themselves or of hurting yourselves."

"The farmers aren't our enemies, but if we could, we would use a whip to drive out the merchants who brought them these modified seeds."

"These guys cause nothing but trouble," Jesus said.

"It all comes down to greed and profit."

"So what's your plan?" Jesus asked.

"With such country folk, the most intelligent route is educational and dissuasive action, which would bring them back to traditional farming. We're going to redeem them through the word."

"So you're going to be the good shepherdess," Jesus said. The bus came to a stop and Jesus grabbed the seat in front of him.

"And do you know anything about sheep?" Magdalene asked.

"So they say."

"What, as much as you know about films?" Annoyed, Magdalene got up and said she was going to the bathroom.

Jesus thus began to realize that she was professing some sort of faith, shared with other people. Apart from all the sects, nature itself now — or once again — had its worshipers, who were convinced that they should save the world. He then remembered that the first cult created by mankind was that of the goddess Mother Earth. Everything came from her and everything returned to her, in a cycle of permanent regeneration. Could there be anything in common between those who erected tombs that imitated a pregnant belly and those who nullified fertility with condoms?

In the meantime, Magdalene had returned to her seat and carried on explaining her plan.

"As I was saying, the educational awareness-raising of the country folk could involve screening films at the primary school, followed by a debriefing session and handing out natural seeds."

"If you sow a seed of mustard in the earth, a tree with great branches will eventually develop," Jesus said.

"But the most important thing would be to convince the farmers themselves to take part in actions defending agriculture aimed at fellow farmers. These people only understand the same language as their peers. For the message to be fully understood and accepted, you need a little cussing, some country music, moonshine, red tractors, and some potash nearby. Hypermarkets do similar marketing campaigns with country singers."

"If you did it like that, I'm not so sure the tree would grow."

"Do you think it would be better to advise them to surf the net in search of scientific articles written in English?" Magdalene said.

"No, but nothing is certain in this world, especially for shepherds."

"Hey, we're going to do all we can to stop them from planting GM crops, but we're no miracle makers."

"Me neither," Jesus said.

"So ..."

"So ...?"

"If the educational route fails," Magdalene said, "if nothing can dissuade them from planting GM crops, we would be left with no alternative other than destroying the fields of modified corn."

And not wanting to continue the conversation, Magdalene put in her earphones and turned on her iPod. Nick Cave sang the first track off the album *The Good Son*: "*Foi na cruz, foi na cruz que um dia meus pecados castigados em Jesus....*"[9]

Magdalene's confession had not surprised him. Wasn't violence a distinctive characteristic of the human species? Perhaps, twisted in a gene, it was part of their DNA. And maybe people who avoided it were suffering from a genetic error: the blessed meek who will not inherit the Earth. So — Jesus reflected — the task of scientists should be the discovery of this gene, to modify it. After all, he had embodied that role himself, that of genetic manipulator, in trying to correct human nature, straightening the wonky nail of this gene that woke for the first time when Cain killed Abel. However, men weren't Rubik's Cubes for which there was a solution, nor were they made of Lego. For a while he felt some sympathy for the enemies of his friend. Who knows, maybe when they've finished

---

[9] The chorus of *Foi Na Cruz*, the first track of the album *The Good Son* by Nick Cave & The Bad Seeds, is sung in Portuguese; in English it translates roughly to: "*It was on the cross, on the cross, that one day my sins were punished in Jesus.*"

dealing with healthy corn, they'll try their luck at the sanity of man?

In the meantime they reached St. Martin.

At the entrance to the village they met an oxcart led by a family of farmers. The father was pulling the animals by a leather strap tied to their horns and the mother was walking by his side; in the cart an adolescent sat and a child stood, entertaining itself by poking the oxen with a goad. Orange in color, the creatures looked old and exhausted; the hair on their loins was dried out and there were dung stains on their rumps. The team were tied to a yoke and they swished their tails incessantly at the swarms of flies. They lowed piercingly. The cart moved gradually forward, slowed by the roughness of the pathway. And this was in no way helped by the child bringing blood to the oxen's shoulders or by the father briskly jerking them. At a certain point, the mother sat down in the cart, too, making the animals work even harder. The wheel left deeper ruts in the ground now. And foam drooled from the mouths of the oxen.

Magdalene stopped to watch them: child labor, cruelty to animals, backwardness, and ignorance. That family probably drank its fair share of red wine, too.

Indignant, she questioned Jesus.

"Shouldn't those children be at school or out playing?"

"This is what life's like in the country. The kids go to school in the morning and in the afternoon they help their parents on the farm. They only rest on Sunday."

"That's not a normal childhood though, is it? They must work more than five hours a day. This is a kind of child exploitation like any other. How can they do well at school after this? How can they acquire the teaching that will free them from this life of serfdom?"

"It's a very hard life, but it's always been that way. Their parents and grandparents did the same. Farming requires work from the entire family if they want to subsist. That's why there is so much abandoned land."

"But they have farm machinery, tractors, harvesters..."

"Pollution not a problem for you all of a sudden?" Jesus said.

"Don't joke about serious issues. The problem here is the GM crops. And now, why don't you go try and explain to them that genetically modified seeds are a threat to their way of life. It costs nothing to try, does it?"

"I'm not sure this family even knows what that is."

Magdalene watched as the cart moved away, and continued watching as the country boy practised the art of spurring on lazy beasts. They carried on walking. Without the need for animal traction, the sun quickly advanced towards the mountain.

When they began to climb the slope they met a group of boys, squatting before a rocky outcrop. Covered with lichen and moss, the rock gave off a greenish hue that contrasted with the garnet sweater of one of the boys. Magdalene guessed they were between ten and fourteen years old.

"Look, these country kids can explore nature at their will. City kids know nothing of this fun and games in the open air," she said tenderly.

Jesus said nothing, but left the path to go to them.

Eager to establish contact with healthy youngsters who didn't need Sony PlayStations to have fun, Magdalene followed him. She could now tell that this was lively play, because she could hear laughter. As she approached, the guffaws increased. At that instant Magdalene wanted to be a child again, to join this group and twirl in the pine needles, to climb trees and explore caves.

Finally they reached the jokers, who, engrossed in their play, didn't notice their arrival. Magdalene then peered over their heads and saw the reason for their hilarity: the adolescents had caught a frog and had placed a lit cigarette in its mouth, hoping that the creature would burst like a balloon. After stealing eggs from birds' nests and catching bees in a bucket, they were now amusing themselves with a frog. As the frog had puffed up in defense — not because of the smoke — the boys were now convinced the creature was going to burst at any moment. And if it didn't burst from the smoke, it would burst under a hail of stones.

Magdalene got ready to give the boy closest to her a couple of slaps when Jesus placed a hand on her shoulder. "Don't do that." Her arm didn't even lift and her muscles relaxed.

At this moment the adolescents noted their presence and disbanded, fleeing through the sunflower field. They laughed again, as amused now as they were before they had been caught. The eldest, believing he was a safe distance away, turned and made an obscene gesture at them with his middle finger. "Screw you!"

When Magdalene looked back to see where the frog was, all she found was the extinguished cigarette. It had vanished in a puff of smoke. The mixed aroma of tobacco and moss made her nauseous.

The rest of the climb took place in silence. Horrified by what she had seen, she didn't utter another word; genetic modification, spanking, and child labor weren't the only problems in St Martin. He didn't speak, either. The example he had set of loving animals had not been successful and instead of coming to him, the children had run away. Half an hour later, they reached the environmentalist camp, as exhausted as if they had dehusked a whole cart of corn.

A stroke of cirrus spread across the sky; the sun was a flashlight with low battery.

At the camp, Judas had made the most of Magdalene's absence to recover his lost authority. The quarrel over the tent had strengthened the conviction within him that he was living in a dog-eat-dog world. Anyone could become an enemy, with the tiniest of conflicts able to ignite the fuel flowing from life. However, the best way to tame the beasts wasn't always the whip.

Judas spoke to his colleagues, who sat around him, in a tone close to yelling (not far from threatening, and a close relative to cursing). Because the fault, the most grievous fault for all these problems, according to Judas, lay entirely at their feet.

"...The huge failure of the initial plan can also be blamed on your attitude. You acted in a disorderly manner, some hampering others, wasting time and energy that could have been used to the clear the farm. And the gasoline? Where did the can of gasoline get to?"

Judas was passing sentence on his colleagues when Magadalene and Jesus arrived. The Greens' passage through purgatory had come to an end; they couldn't be entirely purified, but there wasn't time for more. It was time to reveal the new tactic for fighting GM crops, more evolved than the last one, but requiring other skills, brain instead of brawn, with words achieving what force was not able to obtain: the manipulation of the rural mentality. These beasts would be tamed, too, without need for a whip.

*

Magdalene introduced Jesus to her colleagues as a friend, who shared the same concerns for the future of the planet and the fate of mankind. Here was a man sensitive to contemporary problems, defender of the weak and the oppressed, who was not afraid of the powerful. In short, a comrade whom they could count on in the coming green battles.

Jesus was tempted to correct her, clarifying that he wouldn't be involved in any kind of battle, but he said nothing. Prudence was required with people who wanted to separate the wheat from the chaff, without letting it grow. After all, the awareness campaign for the country folks might lead to extensive organic farming.

Jesus' presence made Judas restless. "I've already met this guy somewhere," he said. Not required to kiss him, he didn't shake his hand, either. Where had it been? He greeted Jesus from a distance and stood watching him. "I've seen his face before." But, unable to remember where he had met him, Judas stopped paying him any attention, wrote him off as being just some idiot. He had more important things to think about. He called to his colleagues again and continued to explain the plan.

Convinced that the influence of the clergy in rural environments had changed very little since olden days, he proposed to make use of the priest of St. Martin to pass on the environmental message to the farmers during his sermons. It was therefore important to get to know the shepherd of this flock of snotty sheep in order to involve him in the transhumance against modified genes. The priest would be the intermediary between the environmentalists and the country folk, the bridge that would unite civilization to rusticity, the beginning of the rural reeducation program. In the end, something good would come from this evil GM business.

"Picture the scene: the bells are ringing, the church packed with people, the men with caps in their hands, the women with scarves on their heads, each of them fearing divine punishment, their heads bowed, but with some hope of receiving some form of blessing from above, repeating prayers without understanding their meaning, repenting the same sins as usual, and then, in a dramatic tone of voice, verging on the threatening, the priest begins to warn that the new corn they have planted is the work of the devil, and so anyone who continues to sow it would go to hell and roast there with the corn, and that it is a Christian's duty to only use plants that God has created and to destroy the others..."

James became even more skeptical. "You're wacko, bro. How many joints have you smoked today?"

"I may have exaggerated a touch, but everyone understood the idea. Only the priest will be able to convince them to abandon GM crops. Or would you prefer to go and talk to them?" replied Judas.

"I agree with the plan," Mary added. "The priest is one of them, he listens to their confessions, he knows them better than anyone. He will be able to persuade them to abandon GM corn. And at worst, he also takes a beating."

John spoke. "I don't trust priests, though. The church has always been the wrong side of history. It's becoming richer and richer, and I'm not surprised that it invests in shares of Monsanto, oil companies, and loggers destroying the rainforests. Why should we place the solution of such a serious problem in the hands of this guy?"

"Judas, didn't you just ask about the gasoline? I have more faith in a can of gasoline than in the entire clergy," James said.

"Let's set light to the corn, it's what they deserve!" cried John.

"They burn the land themselves to clear the soil of weeds and scrub. It's the environmental method preferable to pesticides. Fire is part of the traditional practices of agriculture," added Simon

"Do you want to burn down the whole village? Destroy the houses, kill animals and even people? In this case you can put on your skeleton disguises, which would ensure the appropriate fantasy."

Before the silence of his colleagues, Judas imposed his plan on them. "To reeducate the peasants and put an end to modified corn, we need neither fire nor scientific reports. Look at the example of liberation theology in Latin America. If the priests can pass on progressive messages to the people, they can also pass on environmental messages."

James tried to thwart him again, confronting him on the same religious grounds.

"Yes, but the majority of dietary prohibitions are imposed on meat and alcohol. Nobody is saying you shouldn't eat cereals. Millions of people have been taught that they couldn't eat pork, beef, and animal blood, but nobody has been told that it was a sin to plant and eat corn."

"Genetically modified corn," Judas corrected, "if the faithful accept abstaining from eating meat during Easter, then they'll also accept the ban on planting GM corn, for the same reasons of faith and fear in God. Doesn't the Pope condemn cloning and artificial insemination? He should also condemn GM corn, then."

With this statement, any combustible outbursts were extinguished.

Nevertheless, Simon found a spark. "The Vatican has already changed its views. The Pontifical Academy of Science, which as you should know expresses its opinion on questions of ethics, approves the use of GM crops in farming."

"Well, and you think that the priest of this parish is that well informed? As soon as he hears talk of genetic modification, he'll immediately think that these experiments offend the sacred character of life. We just have to direct the reasoning in this direction. This time we will be the ones undercover."

"Yes, you could be right. But we still need to define how we are going to approach this. Are we all going to talk to him? Or should only one of us go? The plan's success depends on his first impressions of us and we don't know what kind of person we're dealing with," Simon warned.

Magdalene raised her hand. "I'll speak with the priest. I went to Sunday school, I was forced to go to mass, I took moral classes, and so I know my way around them. They're all the same. It might be that these creatures will finally be of some use. None of you would be against that, would you?"

While Judas had been talking, she had anticipated the opportunity to introduce new themes in the transformation of the rural mentality: after making the priest aware of the threat of GM crops, she would broach the problem of child labor, children's rights, and animal rights.

"Take a bottle of wine with you," Mary suggested.

The improbable ally surprised Judas, but he soon sensed that the mission would be better undertaken by a woman. A woman's wiles could convince anyone, especially a priest, because the same words spoken by a man, when uttered by a woman entered the ears like a wet tongue, carrying other meanings and leading the male imagination to the wildest of fantasies. Bewitched by their own desires, however subdued or perverse they are, men yield droolingly to their requests. Was this not how Herod conceded the head of John the Baptist to Salome? Or how Holofernes lost his at the hands of Judith? As such, the priest, surely a nutter, accustomed to old dears with moustaches and varicous veins, will eat the corn out of Magdalene's hand.

The idea of turning religion against GM crops seemed a masterstoke to Judas. He had strengthened his leadership, avoiding having to drink with the locals or testing their hens' fertility. Being attached to a cord coming from Judas' hand, the puppet priest would pull the strings of the parishioners' wills. The puppets would thus be taken from the church to the cornfields, possibly stopping off at the bar on the way. And at the end of the puppet show, the puppeteer could throw the puppets in the trash and return to civilization.

*

When she left the camp, for once Magdalene was in agreement with Judas. She also thought it obvious that in a rural community the priest would continue to have a great influence on the parishioners, and that it made entire sense to go to him and get in his good books. The word of a cleric echoing throughout a church would acquire the value of a judgment proffered by Solomon himself. In this case, the corn wouldn't be cut in half, rather ripped out of the ground.

As to ingratiating herself with the priest, even without a gift of wine, it wouldn't be too difficult. How could the curate of the village, this cassocked oaf, resist her? Because his dream certainly wouldn't be the same as that of the Reverend Martin Luther King, Jr. Direct Action offered many possibilities, seduction being the most efficient.

No, in the end it wouldn't be country music, red tractors, and potash that would create the atmosphere conducive to the environmental conversion of the peasants. These were no better than a tire on a rope, put up in zoos for chimpanzees to exercise on. Equipment requires the collaboration of the user and sometimes not even farmers feel like listening to music, let alone chimpanzees capering about. The most elaborate of staging and the greatest effort can thus only end in failure. The one thing that would never fail, however, was religion; nothing instilled more fear in these country creatures, who spanked their children and tortured frogs.

When Magdalene and Jesus left the camp, she revealed to him her ruminations.

"Did you know that nature and the Christian religion have a great deal in common?" she said.

"Really?"

"Yes, the Bible shows this: the garden of Eden was an environmental paradise where you could eat organic fruit and no species was threatened with extinction; Noah saved all these creatures from the unexpected flood; Isaiah guaranteed that in the Messianic Kingdom the wolf shall dwell with the lamb, the leopard shall lie down with the kid, and the child will play by the cobra's hole; Ezequiel makes the leftover flood water healthy; and Daniel is well received in the lions' den."

"Thank God there were no chocolates back then."

"But adulteresses were stoned, also thanks to God," Magdalene said.

"Thanks to men…"

"Fine," said Magdalene, "but what is certain is that a Christian cannot ignore ecology. The main parables speak of nature and farming. Plants and animals were chosen to pass on moral messages. More than from mankind, virtue comes from the Earth and from its creatures. And the evangelists themselves then take on zoomorphic shapes. Lucas appears as an ox…"

"I see you've studied the Bible."

"You don't need to," Magdalene said. "It's all on *Wikipedia*."

"On paper it's something else."

"Sometimes you're a bit antiquated."

"The world changes so quickly."

"Listen, I discovered more," she said. "In the Old Testament there is a law prohibiting felling trees during war, another advising you not to maltreat oxen, and another still protecting birds when in the nest."

"I know," Jesus said.

"You know nothing, pay attention. And the first environmental activist was Saint Francis of Assisi, the patron saint of animals and the environment, whom he called brothers. He begged alms for birds and suggested the presence of animals in the liturgies. He considered himself the son of Mother Earth. And then there was Father António Vieira, who defended the Indians, the forests, and the seas in Brazil. One set free the birds and the other spoke to the fish. As much as I hate to admit it, the Christians played a very important role in the defense of nature."

"This *Wikipedia* is really interesting."

"Hey, maybe one day the Vatican will join forces with *Greenpeace* and there will be a green pope, bishops brandishing crosiers on the high seas against whale-hunting ships, novices scaling the United Nations headquarters to unfurl environmentalist banners, the faithful lighting candles for the Amazon..."

Jesus smiled. "So you do see a use for religion after all. Maybe you have more faith than you think."

"Faith in mankind, in nature, and in all living beings, yes," Magdalene said.

"Maybe that's all you need."

"Look, one day I'll die, my body will be buried, eaten by worms, dissolved into the earth, then some plant will feed on my molecules and a part of me will be transformed into oxygen. Finally some animal or person will breathe me and I will become part of that being. This will be my resurrection."

"I just hope you won't be breathed in by some gene manipulator," Jesus said.

Magdalene shot him a puzzled look. "So, I'll probably go to heaven and, at some point, I'll meet you there, too."

"Most likely."

"Everyone has their own version of Utopia, don't they?"

"The majority of mankind seems to believe in something more than chemical transformations," Jesus said.

"Have you ever known anyone to rejoice in death?"

"It's natural to have a fear of the unknown. Besides, death always causes suffering to family and friends..."

"Couldn't it be that they suspect there's nothing after that?" Magdalene asked.

"What's the point in living if you believe in nothing?"

"It makes entire sense, because it's all we have left," Magdalene said.

"And those who become ill and disabled? Should they give up on life?"

"I hope to live for many years, but if an accident or an illness leaves me in a vegetative state, like a plant you need to water to stop it from dying, I would ask them to give me something to make me fall asleep and never wake up. Would you be able to do that for me?"

Jesus paused. "As a proof of love?"

"Yes."

"And would you be able to pull out a plant that seemed withered to you? For the love of nature?"

"Fine, let's change the subject. What interests us now is convincing the priest."

"Fine."

Well aware of the difficulties of convincing others, Jesus placed little faith in Magdalene's mission. His experience having discussions with doctors of law did not motivate him to join Magdalene, although it was possible it would be different with this man whom they were about to visit. He would limit himself to listening to the arguments of both parties in this attempt to combine religion and ecology, to invent a new fault and create a new virtue.

*

The church of St. Martin stood between the village and the mountain, on the site where once stood a pagan sanctuary associated with worshiping fertility—Celts, Iberians, and Romans had made sacrifices in this place. Built almost a century ago, it was rectangular with an apse, featuring a single nave with a barrel vault, a portal with capitals imitating the Romanesque style, and an oculus; inside there were two carved wooden side altars and an altarpiece featuring a painting depicting the Stations of the Cross. The people believed that if infertile women went to pray there they would be blessed with pregnancy, a belief that attracted pilgrims from other places and a few curious minds. Father Justin didn't like this popular syncretism, believing instead that Saint Rita of Cascia[10] should suffice, but he saw himself powerless to contradict it. One thing he refused to tolerate, however, were offerings placed outside the church, and his infertile parishioners trying to get pregnant on a slab next to the temple.

---

[10] Rita was born in 1381 in Roccaporena, Italy, and died in 1457. After the death of her husband, she joined an Augustinian community of religious sisters, where she was known both for practicing mortification of the flesh and for the apparent efficacy of her prayers. She was canonized in 1900, and is honored as a patron saint of hopeless causes.

The priest was sweeping the yard when they spotted him. Magdalene had imagined a middle-aged man, ruddy and stocky, but the person they now discovered was older, pale faced and of normal stature—the only thing she'd gotten right was the roundness of his tummy. She hadn't expected him to be friendly, but she hadn't thought that he would be hostile, either.

However, on this afternoon, Justin had succumbed to the sin of wrath. Hours earlier a parishioner had come to him asking to have her confession heard, and what he heard had left him furious.

"Father, I have a great sin to confess," the parishioner began.

"Well, tell me what it is."

"For a few months now I have been stealing from the church collection bag. I put in a coin and pull out a note."

"What? And just how much is it that you have stolen?"

"Oh, around two hundred dollars, father."

"And you only repent now, you wretched thing?"

"It's just that God has punished me with a bout of sciatica, father."

"And was right to, to teach you not to steal from the church"

"And I wasn't the only one to be punished, because now my husband can't manage to do that."

"Do what?"

"That what a man and a woman do, Father."

"Just as well for him, too, because I'm sure he got some of the takings, too."

"Forgive us Father, we are very poor…"

"And you want me to stay poor, too?"

"I'll give all of it back, Father."

"Of course, you'll give everything back that you stole, you thief, with interest. And as penance, the pair of you will do parish work for a month."

Having discovered that members of his own congregation were stealing from him, Justin confirmed that the world was going from bad to worse. And of every temptation to which the human being could succumb, that of taking someone else's property, in the present as in the past, was the one that afflicted society the most.

Magdalene and Jesus saw his somber mood and hesitated. Justin ignored them and continued cleaning, sweeping the dirt in their direction as if he wanted to sweep them far from the church, too. A sudden gust of wind lifted the dust and caused it to fly back into the priest's face. Closing his eyes, he coughed and swore. As the sweeping had stopped, Magdalene took the opportunity to approach him.

"Good afternoon, Father, we would like to talk to you."

Father Justin held his broom in front of him to ensure they kept their distance. "If it's money you're after, you can leave!"

"We've come to ask for your help, nothing more. Help us to protect nature."

"Protect nature? I'm a priest, not a forest ranger! Nature knows how to protect itself, men are the ones who need to be protected from temptation."

Magdalene ventured to show him the link between ecology and religion. "If God created nature, is it not a Christian duty to take care of his garden? And wouldn't it be a great sin to try to correct his work, altering the genes in plants? Would this not be an offense to the Creator?"

Justin was surprised by Magdalene's logic and was at a loss for words. To gain some time, he retorted with a quotation from the Bible, "God spake unto Noah and to his sons: every moving thing that liveth shall be meat for you, even as the green herb have I given you all things."[11]

Magdalene used the priest's statement to reinforce her argument. "Ah, so you agree with us after all, because if you are saying that it was God who gave life

---

[11] Genesis, 9:1-3.

to the animals and to the plants, you also believe that man has no right to try to imitate him."

Father Justin felt as if he were caught in a trap of his own making. He dropped the broom, tightened his grip on the rosary he had in the pocket of his cassock, and looked dispiritedly up to the heavens in search of an angel to help him.

"One step at a time, young lady. It would be better if we continue this conversation inside the church."

For varying reasons, Father Justin, Magdalene, and Jesus came to a halt as soon as they crossed the door of the temple. For Justin, he took no pleasure in bringing into the house of God two badly dressed strangers with hidden intentions. For Magdalene, entering a church always left her upset, powerless to deal with feelings such as guilt and fear of death. And for Jesus, the discovery of a place where his tragic fate was celebrated, filled with iconography of suffering, brought disturbing memories racing to the surface.

In the shadows of the nave, far from the collection box, the conversation continued.

"If you don't want money, what the devil do you want?"

"As I was saying, nature is being destroyed by irresponsible people. It is our duty to warn people."

"Oh, is this about the Amazon…"

"You should know, Father, that in this blessed land the hand of God has already been amended by man. The farmers have been duped into planting seeds created by genetic engineering."

As a country man, born and bred, Justin thought that she wasn't right in the head. Maybe she was on drugs; that sparkle in her eyes was suspicious.

"Genetic engineering?"

"Yes, modified plants."

"Modified plants? Do you know what a graft is?" he said.

"This isn't the same thing, this is done in laboratories and is harmful to life."

"And has anyone died?"

"It's unknown if there are any human victims yet, but GM crops are a threat to mankind."

"And just where are these modified plants then?"

"In the cornfields. There is at least one farm nearby where they have planted GM corn."

Justin took a deep breath, closed his eyes, and ran his fingers through his bushy eyebrows. "So it's because of the corn that you've come to talk to me?"

"Yes, we're really worried."

"Worried about corn?"

"About the corn and about people, because, as I explained to you—"

"Now I see. Now I understand that you really do need help…"

"Yes, we need your support to explain the situation to the farmers and persuade them to go back to traditional farming. As you know, Saint Francis of Assisi and Father António Vieira defended nature, too."

Justin looked at her with pity. They wanted to teach the Lord's Prayer to a priest. "You want me to explain to the farmers, to tell them to go back to traditional farming?"

"Before it's too late, Father."

"Very well, I'll prepare a homily that will help you. Come to the midday mass on Sunday," Father Justin said.

Having remained silent in the gloom of the nave, Jesus tried to be gentle with the priest. "I am very curious to listen to your words, Father."

Justin felt a pinprick. This tramp wanted to have fun at his expense, to mock faith and morals. "Young man, I can see that you don't understand much about religion, and that whoever taught you didn't give you proper Christian instruction. Come back here tomorrow and we'll have a chat."

*

That night Father Justin understood it all. Confused by the culture of materialism and without any moral guidance, these young people had lost their way. And after having been at loggerheads in the city, they had come to the country, like dazed cockroaches. The story of threats to nature they wanted to palm off was another of these modern ideas. Today they would defend nature, tomorrow drugs, and next homosexuality. So much misery in the world and nothing else seemed to matter to them.

If the wolf that he had once killed appeared in front of them one dark night, they would certainly change their opinion about nature. It was earthquakes, floods, droughts, and sometimes wolves that were threatening mankind. And even though they tried to confuse him with the Garden of Eden and the saints, placing plants and animals on the same level as people, it was written in the Bible that God had said, "be fruitful and multiply, and replenish the earth and subdue it."[12] Venerating nature was no more than a form of paganism, worshiping the creature instead of the creator.

Those young people without judgment just needed some good advice before they started to steal corn, too, or from the collection bag.

---

[12].Genesis 1:28.

*

On the following day, Jesus and Magdalene returned to Father Justin's church. If everything were to go to plan, they would not annoy the priest. On the way Magdalene, not entirely sure of how her friend would behave, ran through the advice she had already given.

"As I told you, let him speak, don't contradict him, and above all don't make fun of him. These village priests are very stubborn, they don't accept different ideas and don't have the slightest sense of humor. Agree with him, say amen, and we will have conquered our ally."

"Don't worry. The priest and I are going to get along fine," replied Jesus.

The rising light hit the apse and slid along the roof. The church's shadow flowed down across the courtyard. She stood at the door and he entered. Justin was already waiting for him and wasted no time with small talk or debates about the weather.

"I noticed that you know nothing about religion. I am going to start by teaching you about Jesus; sit down and listen: Jesus Christ is the son of God, born of the Holy Spirit and his mother, the Virgin Mary… and don't go asking how this was possible, because even if I were to explain the divine mysteries to you, you still wouldn't understand. You think that this is like the Internet, that you can click on a button and the answer will appear, but you need to study and have faith to understand religion. So, keep quiet and listen. Now, where was I?" Father Justin paused for a moment and looked to the light of the stained glass windows, trying to find inspiration in the colorful beam crossing the nave and shining on the granite floor.

"Oh, yes. Then Jesus preached love among men, showed compassion for those that suffered, cured the sick and raised the dead. And after a life of doing good and asking for nothing in return, he allowed himself to die on the cross to give us eternal life. Do you understand now, you ignoramus? Have you ever cared about others, helped someone, done something of value in your life? You're lucky I don't know your father. Come, kneel down, repent, and begin to pray. Quickly, so that I can hear your confession."

Jesus followed Magdalene's advice. He did not contradict the priest. Instead, he kneeled down as he had been ordered.

"So, young man, confess your sins and don't try to fool me."

"Please excuse me, Father, but I can't think of any fault worthy of repentance."

"Have you never put your hand in the collection bag?"

"Of course not."

"Have you ever entered someone else's property?"

"No, I have not done that, either."

"Do you covet what is not yours?"

"I don't covet anything."

"Come on, you little devil, confess that at least you have committed the solitary sin."

"I give you my word, that I never—"

"Ah, you believe yourself to be better than everybody else, a saint perhaps. You're worse than I thought."

Jesus made an effort not to get up and leave, trying to convince himself that he had endured greater trials.

Father Justin went on. "You should know that because Eve tempted Adam into eating the forbidden fruit, all their descendants have been marked by the original sin ever since."

"But this story is just a moral parable, created at a time when the unity and survival of a people depended on obeying the commandments."

"Do you dare contradict the Bible?" Justin said.

"Take the example of Lot and his daughters," Jesus said.

The scene of the father with his daughters in the full act of procreation appeared in Justin's mind. If it was up to him, this event would be censored, and made apocryphal like so many others. "That story has no place here!"

"Don't you think that the most important principles of any religion are contained in the call to love among men and that to love thy neighbor is the greatest demonstration of faith? Certain texts in holy books should be seen as the result of knowledge at the time and others as the reflection of the mentality that existed back then. Sometimes they used older myths to make it easier for the communities that already knew them. Even the Vatican recognizes that the creation of Adam and Eve is a religious allegory. Nevertheless, human brotherhood is the only truth that has not changed over time, and is as valid in the past as it is in the future. Love is the light of mankind."

Justin looked at him, puzzled. He looked at Jesus the way he would look at an imbecile who had just demonstrated exceptional judgment. But he quickly found the explanation for talk so inappropriate for a rogue: surely it was the drugs making him say things he didn't understand.

"You think you're a great philosopher, able to correct religions, solve the world's problems and make life a party?" Justin said.

"Believe me, I learned long ago that there's little you can do to change human nature. You pay very dearly for trying. However, as long as a single good man exists on this Earth, there will still be hope."

Justin realized now that another of the evil effects of taking drugs was that it turned people into lunatics. There was no need to waste any more time with this wretch, he had lost the point. So he washed his hands of his fate.

"Fine, I absolve you of all thy sins, my son. Eat well, live a good life, and as for pills and needles, stick to the drugstore. Follow the example of Jesus, go in peace and may God be with you."

*

While she was waiting, Magdalene wandered away from the church, heading along the trail that led to the mountain. The diversity of vegetation fascinated her: ferns, ivy, gorse, heather, pokeweed, purslane, black nightshade, thistles, holly—so many plants that she didn't know the name for, so many new aromas. When she saw the blackberries, she couldn't resist trying one. For the time being, brambles are safe from genetic manipulation. There were black, red, and purple berries—which caused her to hesitate. Were they all edible? Not entirely sure, she reached for the plump black ones. The first berry was placed in her mouth with the care of someone fearing that they are ingesting a poison, but the flavor was so delicious, that she began immediately to pick others. Pricked fingers and blackened lips didn't stop her from climbing right into the middle of the brambles to choose the best blackberries.

She was delighting in their sweetness when she felt the presence of someone at the rear of the church. A man was furtively prowling around the apse. Magadalene interrupted her picking and hid behind a bush. Used to outwitting the police, she squatted down so as to hide herself better. Leaves were grazing her face and thorns hurting her knees, but in that place, every precaution was necessary. Carefully she opened a gap in the branches to spy on the stranger. When he turned around she saw that he was actually a boy. A boy she recognized: the rascal that had insulted them after mistreating the frog.

This kid did deserve a good hiding. Saint Francis of Assisi himself, if he had caught him tormenting animals, would have been able to do the same as his father had done to him when he had sold his shop fabrics at a loss.[13] And she now had an opportunity to teach him a lesson. She might not beat him, but she would scold him for what he had done; this abuser of

---

[13] When praying in the Church of Saint Damian, Francis heard the voice of Christ, warning him of the state of disrepair of the temple. He then sold his merchant father's luxury fabrics at a loss to be able to renovate the church. His furious father accused him of ruining him and chained him up in a cellar. Once his mother had freed him, Francis went to his father, removed his clothes, renounced his inheritance, and left.

nature could be reeducated before he planted GM corn, too.

However, fearing she would disturb the conversation between Jesus and the priest, she decided to stay where she was. Then she could watch the boy and better examine his deviant behavior. She'd make him swallow lit cigarettes if he tortured animals again.

Magdalene then noticed that the frog brute had brought a can of paint with him and was painting something on the granite wall. In red. Although she considered graffitti a right of expression proper to urban culture, done in the countryside on a church, and even worse, by that savage, it now seemed to be abuse. Almost an act of vandalism.

Unaware that he was being watched, the boy went about his task without hurrying, carefully repainting bits here and there. At times, he stopped to examine some detail, as if the quality of the painting depended on this one stroke, and then he started again. The boy seemed versed in the fine arts.

Unable to see the motif that was being painted, Magdalene wondered what had that beast been drawing. Certaintly not doves, fish, or frogs.

With his back to her, the boy now contemplated his work. Finally, satisfied with the result, he grabbed the paint and fled. Magdalene then discovered that the rural artist had painted on Father Justin's church the same symbol with which he had bid them farewell following the frog incident. Not as a tribute to the ancient god of fertility or as an incentive to the faithful to copulate next to the church, but just to take his revenge on Father Justin. Days before, having caught him smoking next to some shrines, the priest had grabbed him by the ears, forced him to kneel down on the gravel, and made him say ten Hail Marys as contrition.

This was an unexpected problem. If the priest saw this, he might think that she had done it, and the plan would fail immediately. In that world, nothing went as planned. So, using a scarf, her own hands, and foliage from some bushes, she cleaned the fresh paint from the wall as best she could, making the red phallus disappear. But she told nobody in the church of what she had done.

*

On the day of Father Justin's sermon against GM crops and in favor of traditional farming, the environmentalists had turned up to witness in triumph the defeat of the multinationals by a provincial priest. Thus, with the city folk adding to the congregation of country folk, it was now the church of St. Martin itself that was pregnant.

The environmentalists were expecting a reaction of fear and revolt from the hillbillies, the dread of hell transformed into the penance of destroying corn, a GM witch hunt that would turn every farmer into an environmental grand inquisitor, and a blazing finale of crops in flames. Nothing short of a green auto-da-fé, an environmental act of faith. Filmed with their cell phones and posted on *YouTube*. Even James and John were now almost convinced that the priest would be able to conquer *Monsanto*.

Prudently they came to a halt in the atrium, worried that the violent farmer and his deranged wife would recognize them and, even in the house of the Lord, peace would not be with them, and they would thrash them mercilessly. Worse still, the other bumpkins would then join in the party and, under the gaze of the seraphic clay saints, martyred without anyone to defend them, either, the *Green Are the Fields* group might become extinct on this day that promised change. Victims of rural terrorism.

However, farmer Joe and Madame Grace, him in a white shirt and her in the black dress that had once belonged to her daughter's employer, had arrived at the church before the environmentalists. They were seated in the front pew, sharing it with the thief who had been punished with sciatica and the girl who had been thrashed, both of whom were praying with their eyes shut.

"Dear Lord, if you cure me of this malady, and if my husband's rod rises once again, I will give alms for the rest of my life."

"Dear Lord, please make that cow of a mother's teeth fall out."

And so, apart from Father Justin, farmer Joe and Madame Grace could see only their fellow parishioners. What's more, having now harvested and sold the leftover corn, their thoughts were occupied with potatoes and onions. As to the incident of their property being invaded, they knew that people, just as animals, learn their lesson after being driven out with clubs and rarely return.

But even in the atrium, this packed rush-hour subway, Judas had to put up with people stepping on his feet and Magdalene had to suffer the protruding paunch of a farmer resting on her rear. And the physical contact was joined by the chemical experience of blended human and animal odors. However, the discomfort of the journey would be compensated by the wonders of the end station; the automatic doors would open, and agriculture would be immune to genetic manipulation. Jesus was spared similar unpleasantnesses because, as if he knew what would happen, he had chosen to wait outside the temple.

Closer to the sky, where there was no new thing under the sun.

As for Justin, he was rejoicing. Seeing as his church could neither house all the people of the Earth, nor could he speak every language of men, there was at least hope for those young people. In the present as in the past, the prodigal sons would always return to their father's house. Some in rags, others in modern clothing. Inside the sacristy, having partaken of an extra glass of altar wine than he normally would have, and putting on the lilac cassock that he wore only at Easter, he felt rewarded for never having erred from defending morals and good customs. Just as rain and snow fall from the sky to fertilize the seeds in the earth, his word would also fulfill the fertilizing mission. Echoing far away, there in modern Babylonia, to bring the lost sheep back to the fold. And these, which he had believed to be just two, were in fact close to a dozen.

Young people reacted like this when they were disoriented. They came to ask for help without really knowing what evil they were suffering from, and the first symptom of being confused was arrogance. It happens to those on the verge of the abyss, wanting to measure themselves by the depths of the cliff. They were therefore delivered to his hands. The wise hands of the sower Justin, fisherman of men, too.

Spying on them out of the corner of his eye from the sacristy, he confirmed that the group of young people really needed spiritual help. "Drugs, homosexuality, and defending nature, of course." In a sudden rush of compassion he was almost moved by these victims of progress. However, as these poor in spirit were so concerned about plants, he would invite them to help in the grape harvest and then to take part in the local religious festival, carrying the litter of St. Martin up to the top of the mountain. Maybe they would then better understand nature and its mysteries. Apart from the fact that the work would help to reeducate those rascals. Penance and atonement would have to wait for later. They had found their road to Damascus, but they still needed to be flung from their horse.

However, as prudence recommended that it was not time to change the usual sermon, the reason behind such an influx of believers in church that day, Father Justin changed very little in his preaching. With the main difference consisting of raising his voice, so that everyone could hear.

And so, to the stupefaction of the environmentalists and to the indifference of the parishioners, having read out part of the *Apocalypse* "...and the great dragon was cast out, that old serpent called the Devil, and Satan, which deceiveth the whole world: he was cast out into the Earth, and his angels were cast out with him."[14] he addressed his words to the young people. "And ye, the youngest, are the greatest victims of demonic temptations, but it is your duty to resist them with all your strength..." Then he quoted the Pope: "And as the holyfather Benedict XVI said, debauchery does not mean freedom, rather slavery and suffering; freedom that goes against truth is not freedom; it is in serving others through charity that we become free." Then he moved onto family advice, "Women should obey their husbands and children should respect their parents"; showing how you achieve harmony in the home, "A slap at the right moment never hurt anyone and an affectionate punch can save a marriage." Suddenly furious, he condemned theft, "and as the seventh commandment says, thou shall not steal..." before he denounced popular beliefs, "And let me warn you again that anyone practicing acts of paganism and idolatry is denying Christian doctrine and has no place in this house." Then he urged everyone to find a new direction. "Examine your conscience, meditate on your faults, don't think yourself superior to others, and repent of your sins..." And finally, in the apotheosis of the homily, he once again addressed the young people, "And remember that God gave you free will to choose between good and evil, and that you may be able to

---

[14] Revelation 12:9

escape the justice of men, but you will not escape divine justice!"

Not a word about GM corn and organic farming.

The rural reeducation had failed.

*

An hour later, a heated meeting took place at the environmentalist camp, during which Judas, with gasoline in his veins, accused Jesus and Magdalene of committing an environmental crime.

"These two traitors sabotaged the plan against GM corn! They are undercover agents working for Monsanto, and have joined forces with the priest to keep farmers in the dark. All the doom that befalls this rural community is their fault. There can be no forgiveness for these people!"

The meeting soon developed into a summary trial in which the examiner paced around the defendants, these two venomous snakes, hurling accusations at them. For its part, the crowd howled insults, demanding justice.

There was no council for the defense. No reptile deserved one. So Mary had already grabbed a stone and John the nunchucks.

It all became even more complicated when Magdalene denied the accusation and tried to explain her own surprise about the priest's preaching.

"You know me, and know this isn't true! I don't understand what happened. He promised that he would help us to put an end to GM crops. He said that he was going to prepare a sermon to explain to the farmers. It's true that to begin with he was suspicious, but afterwards he understood the seriousness of the problem. I explained to him the difference between improvements to plants made by the farmers and the work of genetic engineering produced in laboratories."

"You're lying," Simon interjected. "These provincial priests are horrified by genetic manipulation, by the fact that man can change the work of God. If you had used these arguments, as Judas had explained, he wouldn't have failed to warn the faithful."

"But that's what I said—"

"Liar!" Simon reiterated.

"You've fooled us all," said Mary, before spitting at her.

"Enough talk, let's go and set the cornfield alight!" cried James.

At that moment, in which calls to destroy the crop abounded, Jesus tried to dissuade them from resorting to violence.

"Wait! Resorting to brute force will end up destroying your cause. After all, it's not even certain that the corn is genetically modified, or that it can cause so much harm. And even it were true, you still don't have the right to destroy the work of farmers, to cause them so much damage and a desolation that only someone who works the land can feel."

But Jesus' request for peace among men only works in dreams. And it did nothing to water this dry plant, but only stirred up yet another group that *Greenpeace* would never support.

"Be quiet, traitor! I hope you hang yourself with remorse," screamed Judas, shoving him against his comrades, and then slapping Magdalene.

And so it was that instead of ears of corn, it was Jesus and Magdalene who were subjected to a kind of husking, who almost had the linen torn from their bodies.

If the first *auto-da-fé* had been frustrated, a second had almost been fulfilled. When it doesn't move mountains or corn, faith lets out tongues of fire.

*

Months later, taking advantage of the country folk enjoying the St. Martin festival, tasting wine and dancing, the *Green Are the Fields* environmental group used gasoline to set light to farmer Joe and Madame Grace's potato and onion fields. If at first they were surprised at not finding any corn, Judas soon convinced them that anyone who planted one GM crop would also plant others. And James struck the match.

The environmentalists filmed the fire and posted it on *YouTube*, managing in the process to trigger waves of Direct Action against other targets, apologetic graffiti on walls, and the condemnation of *Greenpeace*.

After investigations had been made, the police dismissed the case for lack of evidence.

Father Justin saw in this a confirmation of his warnings and of papal infallibility.

2

"*And if ye have not been faithful in that which is another man's, who shall give you that which is your own? No servant can serve two masters: for either he will hate the one, and love the other; or else he will hold to the one and despise the other. Ye cannot serve God and mammon.*" Luke 16:12-13

"*And the rain descended, and the floods came, and the winds blew, and beat upon that house; and it fell: and great was the fall of it.*" Matthew 7:27

Guided by the belief that entrepreneurs become rich during crises, Dr. Thomas Alfonso hit the road. He had been looking for a "business opportunity in the tourism area" for some months. In a country where a factory closed every day, which grew olives but imported olive oil, and which wasn't even able to fish off its coastline, tourism was the only industry with any future. Supported by figures published by the *World Tourism Organization*, which showed that the tourism sector that had grown most in the world was Ecotourism, he headed inland. Only in these misty lands, where you couldn't even see your hand in front of your face, was it still possible to find untapped riches.

He was accompanied by his secretary, Miss Barbara, who had made a study into population density in search of lesser-populated areas. A remote area in the northeast revealed the ideal conditions. Nobody lived there. "Wild boars, wolves, and foxes are the only creatures you'll find," his secretary assured him. According to her calculations, they were about to enter a green area, stretching over several kilometers. At a certain point in the journey she instructed the driver to go down a forest road. Gradually the light began to wane, as it does during an eclipse. Dr. Alfonso turned on the headlights, Miss Barbara locked the doors.

But after two hours exploring the misty lands, uncertain as to which way was north and seemingly going round in circles, they had failed to find anything that would merit their trouble. Dr. Alfonso looked through the window and saw nothing but dense trees, rocks, and fog. The land had clenched its fist and not even the sun seemed able to open it. They wouldn't make a penny here. The crisis compass didn't always point where it should.

In the meantime, the weaving journey of curves, bumps, climbs, dips, and sudden braking had begun to disturb Miss Barbara. The worst part was the forest, swallowing them up and making her feel like Jonah inside the whale. The onset of stomach cramps was the warning that she had to get out of there. So she tried to convince Dr. Alfonso to head back.

"Listen, there must be other untapped areas with more promise than this. Mountains, rivers, lakes, caves with pre-historical paintings... There's no natural beauty here, or anything you can use. I know we weren't expecting to find a lost paradise, but this is a real letdown. If you ask me, there is nothing about this place that would warrant any investment in ecotourism."

Getting no response, she tried one last argument. "I know full well you don't believe in such things, but did you know that your Chinese horoscope predicted a bad week for new projects?"

Almost convinced that he wouldn't be doing any business here, Dr. Alfonso was about to turn the car around when he noticed a clearing at the end of the road. Nature had opened a gap and light was pouring into that space. So he slowed down, turned off the headlights, and brought the car to a standstill. "Oooh," babbled Miss Barbara. Before them stood a clearing,crossed by a stream. Flowing down from the mountain, the vein passed unrestrained through the forest. The earth had opened and the vegetation had moved aside to allow it through. Both banks appeared as if creating the antechamber to a sanctuary where water was the god.

Dr. Alfonso climbed out of the car and walked towards it through the bushes and ferns. The air became warmer, the fog lifted. He began to hear buzzing, cheeping, and croaking. Then all of the sounds were dissolved in the gurgling of the stream. The water was clear. The sunlight opened his eyes to the pebbles and caused the foam of the current to sparkle. Dr. Alfonso knelt down, bringing his ear closer as if being entrusted with a revelation, then he dipped his hand in water and freshened his forehead. His ablutions complete, he looked around him: everything was green; hawks were flying in circles up in the sky, and at the depths of the stream he spotted a restless trout. He had found what he was looking for. The compass needle had aligned with the magnetic field of his wishes.

He thus began to envisage a tourism project of great potential. There couldn't even be a single guesthouse within a hundred miles of here; the access roads were reasonable, the exposure to sunlight magnificent. An eco-pool could be made in the stream for canoeing and fishing, a golf course could be created nearby, areas could be established for bird watching, horseback riding, hiking, and extreme sports in the woods. They could set up guided tours to local villages, with wine tastings and regional cooking courses. This space was perfect for building an eco resort, a moneymaking place lost in the mist. The local labor costs were cheap and there were grants for inland development projects. The resort was destined for success. All you'd need was a good advertising campaign with media coverage and a website in several languages on the Internet.

On the following day, Miss Barbara unearthed the number for the municipal council of a place called Vilar de Mochos, of which the piece of land was a part. And then she made first contact.

"Good afternoon, I would like to talk with the Mayor."

"Mr. Mayor is very busy," a woman told her.

"It's an important matter."

"Mr. Mayor is busy with very important matters."

"And when would it be possible to schedule a meeting?"

"There are no openings in the coming months. His schedule is full. Is there anything else I can help you with?"

With no desire to pursue the matter, young Barbara didn't press any further.

Dr. Alfonso was not surprised by the refusal. Whenever you tried to do something, obstacles shot up; this would be the first of many. But nothing was going to put him off. Negotiations with local authorities follow their own set of rules, in a language inaccessible to secretaries or telephonists. Even so, he called again.

"Good afternoon, my name is Thomas Alfonso. I'm an entrepreneur, and my secretary just rang you to arrange a meeting with the Mayor."

"I've already said that he isn't available."

"Listen, ma'am, my intention is to present a project that will develop the town and create lots of jobs."

"Ring back in a few months."

"Maybe you didn't understand me correctly," Alfonso said.

"I haven't got wax in my ears."

"But wouldn't it be possible to schedule a meeting earlier?"

"We don't schedule meetings over the phone."

And she hung up.

Without becoming worried, Dr. Alfonso got in his car and drove towards Vilar de Mochos town hall. The solution was simple, and it all boiled down to a price; there was a market where anyone in power would sell and anyone who wanted to make money would buy. Making things more difficult was a tactic for the vendor to increase the value of the merchandise, but in this case, the laws of supply and demand favored the purchaser. A bowl of lentil stew should suffice.

During the car journey, having passed by the site destined for the resort, he discovered that there were some buildings in the area after all. He felt they were far enough away, however, not to compromise his project. And the quaintness of those "tacky houses" could prove another attraction for visitors; rural culture and heritage also included bad taste.

After driving three hours he reached his destination. A little later he parked in the square in front of the town hall, in a space meant for pregnant or disabled drivers. The council building looked so old that he was convinced time had stopped still in this place. This was a good omen. The more backward and poorer the town, the more authentic the eco resort would be. And if there were barefoot locals, snotty-nosed kids, and sheep depositing their droppings in the middle of the road, the future guests would be delighted. Mass tourism demanded the splendor of major cities, but the elite took pleasure in the exoticism of misery.

He then made his way to the entrance, determined to remove the first obstacle. The public service area was cold and badly lit; a few blocks were missing from the parquet flooring; there were cracks in the wall and the paint was peeling off the ceiling; a musty smell hung in the room. Confident, and with his expectations confirmed, Dr. Alfonso walked up to the counter, a glass partition dirty with fly droppings separating him from a receptionist.

The assistant was crocheting with the help of a lamp. Her bent neck exposed a perm, and this revealed her ears decorated with gold earrings. It took a second knock on the glass for the receptionist to finally put down her needle and lift her head towards the visitor. Dr. Alfonso saw a face with sparkling eyes and pointed chin. The bluish glimmer of her eyes made that woman almost pretty. It was true what they said about tacky women: cleaned and well dressed, they could be very attractive women. Having appraised the adversary before him, he explained why he was there. The woman repeated that without an appointment he would be unable to speak to the Mayor, and then returned to her crochet. Dr. Alfonso knocked on the glass again and passed her a fifty-euro bill. The assistant got up and walked towards a corridor, her broad ass shaking.

*

Mayor Ramsey had been in charge in Vilar de Mochos for almost twenty years and had never faced any problems. People liked him and elected him because he was a good person; he greeted everyone in the street and never did anyone any harm. Whenever he won an election, he held a party for the people, paid for by the council. As for governing the town, Ramsey believed that it was better to preserve the legacy of the past than to ruin everything with "modern eyesores". This resulted in his electoral campaign becoming less and less detailed with each term in office, until finally it disappeared because "what people want is competence and seriousness".

Members of his family held some jobs within the council, seeing as Ramsey only worked with "people he could trust implicitly", and the Almeida Brothers construction company, friends from way back and financiers of his electoral campaigns, always won the public works he was forced to undertake.

One day, after having switched allegiance from the orange party to the blue party and having returned once again to the orange party, he became an independent mayor. Freed from pressure and interests. On the eve of the elections his opponents would write on the walls words like "dinosaur", "Jurassic", and other epithets of a prehistoric connotation, which mattered little to him. Every four years he renewed his term in office.

However, if you were to ask him if he was left-wing or right-wing, Ramsey wouldn't have been able to answer you, because the Left said that it was a friend to the poor, which seemed fine with him, but also intended to revolutionise customs, which he didn't agree with, while the Right proposed to conserve them, which seemed good, but said it was a friend to the rich, which seemed bad to him. As such, Mayor Ramsey had therefore concluded that the best thing, when it came to ideologies and petty politics, was not to get bogged down in such things, as you always ended up covered in mud. "I'm from the center," was the reply he had prepared in case anyone asked him.

And ever since he had made it, he made good on his promise to bring a Brazilian football striker to play for the Vilar de Mochos Eagles; the thirty-year-old from Rio de Janeiro was instrumental in taking the team to the second division of the district championship, and this increased the Mayor's popularity so much that his opposition, fearing for their physical integrity and worried about destabilising the football team, gave up criticising him. The prehistoric lexicon, struck by the meteor of football, became extinct.

Nevertheless, a black cloud was threatening this peace and harmony: the world crisis was drawing close to his town. Lightning had yet to strike in Vilar de Mochos, but you could already hear the thunder in the distance. Not that Ramsey feared economic crises, beneficial to his electoral plan as they were. The problem was the Almeida brothers, greedy and aggressive people who were frightened by the paralysation of the construction industry and demanding "a major public works plan" from the Mayor, while threatening to end their support and even "to make certain revelations". And although the Almeida brothers couldn't reveal anything that everybody didn't already know, Mayor Ramsey valued his reputation.

Lately his moods had changed somewhat. The constant pressure of the builders was starting to rattle his nerves. He was sleeping badly, suffering from heartburn, and had the jitters in one of his legs. His doctor prescribed him some drops, but the remedy to his ailments would never be found in the drugstore.

*

When his niece informed him that a very important man wanted to talk to him, Ramsey immediately grumbled that he didn't want to see anyone. Everyone wanted something from him, almost always money. However, as soon as she mentioned that this man had a big project for the town, his ears pricked up. The chance of some building work being done, thus resolving the Almeida problem, made him change his mind.

The Mayor's office was carpeted and scented with eucalyptus air freshener. On the walls there were photos of Ramsey next to the President of the Republic, kissing the hand of a bishop, in the middle of the Vilar de Mochos football team, and there was also an award from a gastronomic brotherhood. A single cabinet held half a dozen ring binders. On the mahogany desk, between an armillary sphere and a trophy awarded to the municipal trash collection company, lay a pad and a pen. Ramsey was already standing when Dr. Alfonso entered.

Alfonso greeted him with a firm shake of the hand and then introduced himself.

"Mr Mayor, I am a businessman with various interests. I have good contacts with investors and politicians and I come to propose a project that will develop the town: the construction of an ecological resort in Vilar de Mochos."

Ramsey listened to him attentively, put his hand to his chin as if reflecting, strolled around the room, and only then did he speak.

"A resort? That sounds like a good idea, the town needs tourism. And where do you want to build it?"

Dr. Alfonso pulled out an envelope.

"On some land next to the stream. Take a look at these photos."

Ramsey looked carefully at the images, opened a map, traced it with the tip of his finger, and scratched his head.

"Ah, unfortunately it won't be possible on this site. This area has been considered a national ecological reserve by the municipal master plan. And we are very strict in these matters. But there are other interesting places..."

"There are other interesting places in the rest of the country. Here, all that interests me is this wood."

"There is a problem with the trees, doctor—"

"Ahh... the cork oaks."

"They are pine trees, doctor."

"Listen, I'm offering you a chance to develop your town. At this time of crisis and recession, it wouldn't be sensible to refuse it. Eco resorts attract people with a lot of money and bring prestige to mayors. Did you know that ecotourism might grow by up to thirty percent per annum? This is the business of the future. This could be the best decision you make in your life."

"I wasn't expecting your proposal, doctor."

"Did you know that the English love bird watching?"

"There are people who pay to watch birds?"

"It's true. They're fed up with the Algarve."

"This is a delicate matter. The guys from the opposition are a little dull. I need to think about this."

"You're not telling me that a man of your political standing is afraid of the opposition?"

Ramsey puffed up.

"Afraid? Of course I'm not afraid of these good-for-nothings. I'm the one in charge here!"

Dr. Alfonso waited a few seconds before speaking. "Nobody doubts your authority. You were democratically elected and you're doing an excellent job. That's why I came to talk to you."

"I just don't want any scandal in our town."

"Listen, whether there are more pine trees or less pine trees, your town will still be a green zone. There may even be one or two protests, but a year down the line everyone will have forgotten about it. It's always the same."

"You may be right."

"Trust me, I'm experienced in these matters. In our country nobody wants to know about pine trees or cork oaks for nothing. And if municipal master plans were to be fulfilled to the letter, there would be no regional development. What needs to be done is done and then the plan is changed."

"You're quite right, but we have to be careful."

"Do you remember the story of that dam they didn't build because of some prehistoric engravings?"

"I remember," the Mayor said.

"Yeah, and now that place is dead. Did those scribbles create any jobs? Did they bring any money to the place? Are the locals enjoying better lives now? They screwed up and they did a fine job of it. Cultural heritage, environmental heritage, they're all very lovely, but in the end people are forced to emigrate. This isn't what you want for your town, is it?"

"No, not at all."

"Nowadays it is fashionable to defend nature, but people come first. Don't you think?"

"Yes, people come first."

"Very well then, the resort is your dam and you'll certainly make a more sensible decision than the person who stopped the construction of the other one. After all, the forest isn't going to be flooded."

"Let me think..."

"In the future you will be remembered as the man who saved the town."

"It's a risky decision."

"Look, to support the progress of your municipality and compensate for any possible ecological damages, I'm willing to make a generous donation to the council."

Mayor Ramsey tried to look surprised.

"A donation?"

"Yes a donation, as compensation. As you know, it's usual practice in business with local authorities. Both parties profit and the population benefits. For example, no company opens a hypermarket without offering a sports hall, a school, or a health center in exchange. In America they call it lobbying."

"Fine, if it was a donation of social solidarity maybe I would be able to accept. I have to consult the legal department."

"Five thousand euros."

"Five thousand?"

"To begin with..."

"Well, laws can of course be changed, and the price of the land won't be high, but I will make one condition."

"And that is?"

"That the building work be done by locals. There's so much unemployment, you see..."

"If they're competent builders," Alfonso said.

"Don't you worry, the Almeida Brothers are highly competent. They've built things in Paris and in other cities... and as the council will be associated with the project, I will take full responsibility for any problem that may arise."

Dr. Alfonso's mind turned to cheap labor.

"Delays, construction defects, accidents..." Alfonso said.

"Everything. My reputation depends on the success of this project."

"It's a deal, my dear friend. I'll pay you ten thousand euros for the land. Get the paperwork ready within the week."

*

The difficult times in which Manuel and Joaquim Almeida were born did not enable them to benefit from schooling, but it secured them work from any early age. Manuel and Joaquim started pulling oxen and ploughing the earth before they were twelve. Working the land would have continued all their lives if they hadn't been called up to the army to fight in Angola's colonial war.[15] Thus, they decided to flee to another

[15] Unlike other European nations during the 1950s and 1960s, the Portuguese Estado Novo regime did not withdraw from its African colonies, or the overseas provinces as those territories were officially called since 1951. During the 1960s, various armed independence

country. Once they had left, they landed in the shacks on the outskirts of Paris, France, and began to climb the scaffolding of its construction sites.[16]

The move from farming to construction, along with the discovery of liver pâté, the songs of Serge Gainsbourg, and transvestites in the Bois de Boulogne, brought about a great change in Manuel's and Joaquim Almeida's characters and in their outlook on life. They would never be the same again.

After a decade of erecting buildings for others to live in, the brothers, having escaped the slums but not yet past the suburbs, they began the climb up the social ladder. They then set up a home repair company called *Ma Jolie Maison*, doing painting, carpentry, electrics, and plumbing, in any house or shack.

In this enterprise that made them bosses, apart from themselves, they relied on the collaboration of fellow compatriot emigrants. Men of various professions with international practice at being exploited, who only swapped foremen who didn't speak their language for bosses who insulted them in their own. This linguistic harmony, and the practice of using second-hand materials as if they were new, charging high prices for

movements became active in these Portugal-administered territories, namely in Angola, Mozambique, and Portuguese Guinea. Only in 1974 with the Carnation Revolution were the colonial wars ended.

[16] More than one million Portuguese emigrated to France in search of better living conditions during the 1960s and 1970s, and to escape the dictatorship and conscription to colonial wars.Portuguese migrants were sometimes referred to as *Les gens des baraques* (people from the barracks). Most began by working in construction and were exploited.

cheap paint, and similar antics, resulted in the explosive growth of *Ma Jolie Maison*. The profits they earned allowed Manuel and Joaquim Almeida to buy a large house and a car each, despite failing their driving tests repeatedly.

This was when Monsieur Champollion appeared, a competitor of the brothers' in the construction business, and offered them a business partnership to build a 20-storey tower together. Monsieur Champollion would be responsible for the construction of the building, while the Almeida brothers would take on the interior finishes. After a long meeting — featuring a host of "ooh la las" and "oh my goodnesses", of fist banging on tables and calculations on paper napkins, and of Monsieur Champollion's continually referral to his grandfather's involvement in *La Résistance*, to which the brothers replied that Eusébio was the best player of all time — the three finally shook hands.

And so, with each party having deceived the other with exaggerated costs and fictitious expenses, in the end the figures looked as much right for the Almeida brothers as for Monsieur Champollion. So, with the success of the partnership proved, they began to draw up another project, this time the construction of a shopping center. To this end, they opened a joint account in the *Caisse de Paris*.

As he stood before the piece of land where they were going to build the center, Monsieur Champollion praised the homeland of the Almeida brothers and recalled the friendly relations[17] that had always linked it to his own country. He placed it among the nations that guided humanity and discovered new worlds and tried to praise its kings, but the only monarch he could manage to remember was a Spanish one.

Monsieur Champollion may not have been able to transmit a love of culture — nor convince them to visit the Louvre, Napoleon's tomb, or to try mouldy cheese — but, as the Almeida brothers themselves couldn't help but notice, there was one thing that stuck from the deal with their Gallic partner: from then on, in a notable polishing of their mentality and in a gigantic leap in self confidence, they started "to think big in French-style".

However, it wasn't all roses after the brothers' business success. Their first employees accused them of paying miserable wages and of not having paid their social security. Manuel and Joaquim felt offended by those biting the hand that fed them.

Honi soit qui mal y pense.[18]

As such, one Saturday afternoon they went to the Emigrant Recreation Club, where they knew the

---

[17] Napoleon invaded Portugal three times during the *Peninsular War:* 1807, 1809, and 1810.

[18] Its literal translation from Old French is "Shame to be him who thinks evil of it."

slanderers would be playing table football, and proved their innocence with the help of a slap or two. But because they gave as much as they took, with their defence consisting of insults to the honor of mothers, onlookers of the quarrel were unable to establish the truth.

Bitter, the Almeida brothers started that day to imagine returning home. They then received a sign that the time had come to do so. Portugal had joined the European Economic Community. Europe had opened the tap of cash[19] onto their miserable homeland. And to distribute the flood of wealth, many support-fund channels would be created. Diverting some of the flow wouldn't be difficult, meaning that money would be gushing all over the place, falling from the sky, sprouting from the earth — you'd have to be plain stupid if couldn't siphon some off for yourself. These were the thoughts running through the Almeida brothers' minds, revealing in that epic moment more discernment and wisdom than in the minds of the politicians who sat in Brussels, unaware of the banana republic's customs.

Like modern explorers in search of European spices, Manuel and Joaquim packed their bags. And as they were already thinking big and French-style, they took

---

[19] From 1986 to 2011, Portugal received from the European Union more than 80.9 billions of Euros.

all the money out of the joint account with Monsieur Champollion, for whom not even the resistance of his grandfather would help him this time.

Their return to Vilar de Mochos was triumphant, with a crowd coming out into the street to cheer on the local sons who had made good abroad. The Almeida brothers enjoyed the reception, but didn't give out a cent. It had been a struggle to make their money and they weren't going to squander it for nothing on some hicks who had never been to Paris and would do nothing but piss it away in the local tavern. Only the blind guy, who played the concertina — teased by them both during adolescence — started hearing the tinkling sound of coins in his collection box from that day on whenever Manuel or Joaquim saw him.

The money was to be used in a construction company, equipped with the finest machines and run using the same management methods as the healthy *Ma Jolie Maison*. The only difference in this new business phase would be that they would apply for every subsidy and training course paid for with *European monies*, which, according to Manuel and Joaquim's rough calculations, "would be enough for two or three Mercedes Benzes and a jeep." At the same time, they made the resolute decision of never paying taxes. To this end, they would receive the support of their childhood friend Ramsey, to whom they intended to donate a generous amount — this, on the contrary, was money well spent.

And the donation was accepted, under the condition that the works were to be done outside the town. Hand in hand with the power, unhindered by licenses or laws unfavorable to progress, and in a position of an absolute monopoly in civil construction and public works in Vilar de Mochos, Almeida Brothers became a successful company.

Almeida Brothers specialised in the construction of villas with tiled façades, adorned with a garden and fountain — a Parisian style inspiration, the looks of which impressed the locals. At the same time, they convinced Mayor Ramsey to build two sports halls, a cultural center, and public swimming baths; to install a new sanitation network; to create five roundabouts; to tarmac the road where they lived; to erect an Arch of Triumph at the entrance to the town and a monument to emigrants in the middle of the square (designed by Joaquim's brother-in-law, Armindo, who had a knack for making matchstick boats in bottles). Vilar de Mochos thus received a half-baked French makeover.

But, once again, envy raised its head. After one of their *maison*-style houses collapsed one stormy night, with tragedy only avoided by the fact that its owners only lived there during the month of August, the Almeida brothers were accused by the people of Vilar de Mochos of ripping them off by using poor construction materials. It was at this time that they began to call them *Champignons*.

Once again on the cross of thievery, and unable to slap the entire population, Manuel and Joaquim fled to a safe place. Desperate, they swore to their saints that they would never swindle anyone again if they were saved; Manuel to Saint Rita of Cascia, and Joaquim to the Infant Jesus of Prague.

And their prayers were heard, as on the following day, Ramsey, from up on the town hall balcony, assured the people of Vilar de Mochos that the house collapse, "something that happened anywhere in the world", was not the fault of the builders, but that of the engineer, who had made the wrong calculations due to a computer error. And as nobody understood anything about IT errors, or that the engineer was actually a draughtsman who had received a check in payment for promising never again to set foot in Vilar de Mochos, the population more or less accepted the explanation. The competence of Almeida Brothers was resurrected on the third day.

With the dust settled and their promises paid with a donation to the church, for more than two decades they colonized Vilar de Mochos with houses; they laid streets, roundabouts, and a second monument to emigrants (identical to the first), almost meeting the minimum safety regulations.

However, just as the prosperity of the company seemed unshakable, talk of crisis, of recession, of grants, of toxic products, of Madoffs, of bankrupt banks, of austerity, of Mrs. Merkel, of IMF, and other catastrophic words began, putting an end to the sales of their beautiful *maisons*.

Almeida Brothers was once again in trouble and, only the combination of the forces of the Almighty and of Mayor Ramsey could help them.

*

In the meantime, at the end of a journey without destination, stopping here and spending the night there, Jesus and Magdalene found the stream of Vilar de Mochos. Heard from afar, the sound of the current guided them towards the clearing. For a moment they contemplated the watercourse. The flow slid down the mountainside before slowing in that particular area; when the slope ended, the foam disappeared and the surface of the stream began to sparkle.

They made their way to the bank and saw their bodies transformed into patches of light and color, like souls shimmering in the water.

They lay down and drank deeply from the fresh current. With their thirst quenched, they removed their shoes to cool their feet. Magdalene noticed Jesus had a cut on his toe. She took his foot and washed it in the stream, then she dried it and applied a plaster.

They then found themselves surrounded by a line of mist creeping along the ground. The clearing seemed cut off from the rest of the world. It was for them alone. Magdalene saw birds perched on a tree and felt protected, as if angels were watching over her.

"Have we found heaven?" she asked him.

"Yes, we have," replied Jesus.

Unable to resist temptation any longer, she undressed and took a dip in the stream.

A little later they pitched their tent on the future site of the resort.

*

When the licenses for the resort's construction had been obtained, the land purchased, the bank loan secured, and a phone call made to the Secretary of State to ensure a tourism grant, Dr. Thomas Alfonso proceeded to the next phase of the project. Following a visit to the site, an architect designed a tourist complex featuring forty rooms and five suites, an outdoor swimming pool, another indoor one, a gym, two tennis courts, and a mini golf course. The building materials would be locally sourced stone and timber, the heating assured by solar energy, and electricity generated by a micro hydro turbine that would make use of the watercourse. The furniture, textiles, and carpeting would be handcrafted by local artisans, the culinary tasks given to local chefs. The Stream Eco Resort thus came into being.

Dr. Alfonso was so excited that when Mayor Ramsey called to set up a meeting with the Almeida brothers, it already mattered little to him if "these yokels or any others" were building the Stream Eco Resort. He would deal with the rednecks professionally, but with distance. He would greet them, answer any possible questions, and then agree as to the payment deadlines for the work. With negotiations completed, he would take off. From then on, let the architect put up with them. And to get things rolling, he then faxed the plans and the specifications to the Vilar de Mochos council.

Just as he was leaving the office, Miss Barbara called out to him. "I hope the meeting goes well, Doctor Alfonso."

"And what could possibly go wrong? Those people are desperate for work. What could they have against the town's largest development project? Easy business, my dear."

"Yes, but this is the first time you're doing business with a mayor far off the beaten track."

"The difference between inland mayors and coastal ones is that the country folk work out cheaper for me."

But Dr. Thomas Alfonso's predictions were missing one important factor: he was unaware of the reception Manuel and Joaquim Almeida had prepared for him.

Having been warmed by Mayor Ramsey that this was an important doctor, Manuel and Joaquim, aware of the importance of pleasing business partners and wanting to give a good impression of their homeland, were guided by the ceremonial practice they had learned in Paris. So they planned to welcome the visitor in the following manner: first they would attend a Vilar de Mochos Eagles football match — with the attraction of a Ukrainian defender, who was a psychiatrist back home, playing his debut match, then they would take him to eat at Joaquim's house — his wife was a better cook than Manuel's, and finally they would round out the evening in a brothel.

Something in the French style.

In the Almeida brothers' eyes, such protocol would please the most demanding of mortals as it featured everything that really interests all men: football, food, drink, and women. Starting with the smaller pleasures and ending with the greater ones. That doctor from the capital may have traveled a great deal, but Manuel and

Joaquim hadn't the slightest doubt that he would enjoy a nice surprise. Of course, he would already have seen better matches, but as for the roast kid he would eat, and with regard to the horde of women he would be presented with (equally reinforced with Ukrainians and Romanians), he would even be licking his lips.

Once the fly was caught in the honey, the deal would be done without a hitch.

So, fully unaware of the rural pleasures awaiting him, Dr. Alfonso made his way once again to Vilar de Mochos, convinced he would be rid of the Almeida brothers in half an hour. What mattered was that the work would begin without delay. And if anyone appeared who raised the issue of defending the forest, he had the right answer ready and waiting: "Every tourism project has had to cut down trees, dry marshes, and get rid of animals. When man advances, nature recedes. Even so, the environmental impact of this eco resort will be minimal. This is a sustainable development project."

That should be enough to shut up some cocky yokel.

Dr. Alfonso was driving along, planning his meeting when he saw a man and a woman, hitching for a ride. In the light filtering through the trees, he didn't like the look of them. "The walk'll do you good, you hobos," he mumbled, and bid them farewell as he accelerated off. All that was missing were beggars at the gates to the resort.

Jesus and Magdalene would have to carry on using their legs to continue their wandering flight.

"Idiot!" Magdalene shouted at the departing vehicle.

"Never mind, he doesn't know us," said Jesus.

"People are more and more selfish, they don't want to share anything."

"Maybe he had an important matter to attend to."

"With that car, he could only be someone looking for business."

"And what business could you do around here?"

"Who knows, but these guys always discover some way to make money," Magdalene said.

"They are taking advantage of their talents. Is that bad?"

"As they generally exploit people, and destroy nature, it is."

"Well, the next car's sure to stop for us."

"Listen, no one's gonna give us a lift around here. Wouldn't it better to try and look for another road?"

"There aren't any nearby, but we are close to a town," Jesus said.

"How do you know that we're close to a town? I haven't seen any signs yet, no milestone, nothing..."

"A few cars have passed us, they must be going somewhere."

"Yes, but that could be miles away."

"You're right, it was just a hunch. But anyway, we've no choice other than to carry on the way we're going."

"I'm not as used to walking as you are, it would be better to set up camp for the night."

Jesus replied, "Thy will be done."

An hour later, Dr. Thomas Alfonso finally arrived in Vilar de Mochos. Mayor Ramsey and Manuel and Joaquim Almeida were waiting for him at the door to the town hall. The Mayor was wearing his wedding suit and tie, the builders wore grey trousers and floral shirts to show they knew how to follow city fashions; Ramsey had placed his hands behind his back, Manuel Almeida was picking at his teeth, and Joaquim was rubbing his privates. From a safe distance, a few curious eyes spied on the respectable trio, suspecting that something important was about to happen. The stranger's arrival confirmed this.

The rain that had yet to fall now flooded the sky with dark clouds.

When he spotted the reception committee Dr. Alfonso feared that the business might be the harder side of easy, and a larger obstacle than expected. Seen on television, the inhabitants of lost paradises didn't look so threatening: they went on excursions and picnics, and were always cheerful. Now there were ogres guarding the Garden of Eden.

The businessman tried hard to proceed with professionalism and distance, arming himself with an earnest expression, digging in his heels. Manuel and Joaquim Almeida immediately destroyed his pose with two slaps on the back.

"Welcome to Vilar de Mochos, Doc Alfonso!" said Joaquim.

"Today we're gonna party hard!" said Manuel.

"My dear gentlemen, as you know we have scheduled a meeting," Alfonso said.

"This can wait until the night's end, okidoki?" Joaquim said.

"Listen, this project involves a lot of money and I'm a very busy man, so it's better if we get straight down to things. Mr. Mayor, shall we go to your office?"

"Relax, we've got all the figures right up here," Joaquim said. "First you're gonna have some fun and then we'll deal with business."

"I'm sorry, but I'm not used to working like that."

"Oh, Doc Alfonso, we've gone to so much trouble to organize everything for you and now you want to give us the cold shoulder?" Manuel said.

"This doesn't even appear to be from a learned man," Joaquim said.

"I insist that we at least sit down for half an hour to discuss the work schedule. There are very important things that need to be defined. Costing, deadlines, inspections..." said Alfonso.

"Oh, Doc Alfonso, don't talk rubbish. If we don't get to know each other, how can we work together?" Manuel said.

"Look, if there's no trust, this could all go wrong," Joaquim said.

"You see, Doctor Alfonso, they want to pay you a kind of tribute for the investment that you're going to make in the town," Ramsey said. "It's part of our customs to give visitors a good welcome and to repay gifts..."

"Fine... okay, seeing as this is so important, we'll have a drink and then we'll get down to business," Alfonso said.

"It's fine, Ramsey, you can go home, he's in safe hands now," said Manuel.

Dr. Thomas Alfonso was then invited to take a seat in the back of a Mercedes and driven to the stadium of the Vilar de Monchos Eagles, the football club sustained by the patronage of the builders, and coached every Tuesday and Thursday by Armindo.

During the ride Joaquim endeavoured to give some respectability to their family business.

"You see the houses around you? We built all of them. Look at the quality of the materials, at the finishes, at the size of the garden. You can't compare this with an apartment. You can bring your kids up in a place like this, and invite your friends around. We're proud of our work."

"We never take any holidays, Doc Alfonso. We work the whole year through. If everyone worked like us, the country wouldn't be in the state that it's in," added Manuel.

"So, shall we talk a little about the resort?" asked Alfonso.

"Rest assured, a year from now you'll have the key in your hand. We've built bigger jobs than this before and never received a complaint. Building holds no secrets for us," Joaquim replied.

"But you can't do things that fast. The work begins tomorrow; now let's go and watch the footie," concluded Manuel.

As always, the stadium was packed: close to three hundred people were anxiously waiting for the game between the Eagles and Lusitanense to begin. But the Almeida brothers, shoving and elbowing their way through, managed to clear a path through the crowd to ensure Dr. Alfonso "the best views of the match". And the businessman was greeted by a naked pitch, separated from the crowd by ropes attached to wooden stakes, the changing rooms of which consisted of two little brick houses.

"We donated the stadium, Doc Alfonso," Joaquim informed him.

"And we also paid for the new members of the team," added Manuel.

"If we hadn't come back from Paris, this place would be a wreck, Doc Alfonso. You see all these people? They would still be digging the earth. We've built their houses and given them work," Joaquim continued.

"They owe us so much, so much," Manuel concluded.

In addition to the debut of the psychiatrist defender, the game had aroused interest in the fans for three more reasons: firstly because they were playing for a place in the next division; secondly because the Almeida brothers had interrupted the game at the last training session and moved five players' positions; thirdly, because on the following day the discredited Armindo had guaranteed that from then on the team would play José Mourinho style — and to this effect he had appeared in an overcoat he'd inherited from this grandfather and a notepad on which his wife wrote down her cooking recipes.

The visiting team came out onto the pitch first, followed by the home team and finally the refereeing trio. The first were greeted with whistles and jeers, the second with applause and cheers of encouragement, but when it came to the third set of arrivals, the police had to intervene to contain the heckling of the referee. During these displays of football passion, Manuel and Joaquim started to boo at the opponents, clapping and yelling at their team, and then, following the arrival of the referees, to suffer from an attack that caused them to foam at the corners of their mouths, to grunt insults in a mix of languages, and to argue with the police.

However, as soon as the game began, everyone calmed down.

Under the pouring rain that transformed the pitch into a quagmire, Dr. Thomas Alfonso, with a plastic bag on his head given to him by Manuel, witnessed what slanderers of the *beautiful game* would consider simply as twenty-two fools chasing after a ball.

For the first half hour neither of the teams managed to come up with anything that resembled a game plan, with the ball kicked back and forth and out of the pitch, and the fools doggedly chasing after it. The Vilar de Mochos Eagles had a chance to *threaten* by scoring from a corner kick. But, instead of heading the ball, all the Brazilian forward managed was to headbutt the Lusitanense defender on his temple, and both of them fell motionless to the ground, before leaving on stretchers. For its part, all the opposing team could achieve was a single shot that sailed over the Eagles' goalpost. The first half thus ended in a draw, to the great disappointment of the Almeida brothers and the rest of the fans.

During the interval, Dr. Alfonso found himself forced to take refuge in the builders' car. His attempts to broach the resort's construction, "and so, do you already have a quote for the construction expenses?" were met with a toast of cognac pulled out of the glove compartment.

"Have faith in us, man. This is gonna be the best deal of your life," Joaquim replied as he opened the bottle.

"Don't you know that the construction is cheaper here?" said Manuel.

"We're all gonna be rich, Doc Alfonso, drink," ordered Joaquim.

And after two shots he ended up agreeing that the home team was unlucky and that the referee was a thief.

In the meantime, in the changing rooms, coach Armindo, armed with his overcoat, notepad, and a José Mourinho-style look of boredom, gave the players a dressing-down. Then he showed them some cartoon figures scrawled next to a dessert recipe, referring to them as the "winning plan". None of the players understood it, but the Ukrainian psychiatrist could see paranoid delusions in it, as if it were an inkblot test. At the end of the pep talk, completed with the promise of a round of beers, he shoved them back out into the rain. Then he prayed to Saint Rita of Cascia.

When the refereeing trio had returned to the pitch — their changing room was the police jeep — the football match could continue.

In the second half, the home team seemed to have returned with more determination than their opponents, as demonstrated by the daring move by Armindo to replace two midfield players with two forwards. For their part their rivals had also sacrificed two center midfielders, to strengthen the defence. Nevertheless, the tactics did not satisfy the club's sponsors. And Joaquim, in his scepticism, ended up taking things into his own hands.

"That's not how we'll win it. If we'd given the referee a small sweetener we would already be winning by three goals."

"You're not wrong," his brother agreed.

However, the strategic changes brought no advantage to either team. So much so that the two goalkeepers, lacking in work and bored out of their brains, were leaning against their goal posts, the home one having asked to be brought an umbrella, and the away one smoking a cigarette.

It all looked as if the game would end in a goalless draw, when — proving that in football *nothing* is impossible — the defining moment happened. And the ill-fated event took place during a counter-attack by the Lusitanense team, after an Eagles player was sent sprawling by a puddle of water and lost the ball. The rival defence made a long pass to the forward, who took the ball on his chest, bent it to the center, came to a standstill, dribbled past an Eagles defender, penetrated the penalty area and, just as he was preparing to shoot for goal, received a kick in the back, given by the Ukrainian psychiatrist. Peeeeeeeeep! the referee signaled. And the storm kicked off.

The Almeida brothers were the first to invade the pitch, followed at a distance by the rest of the deranged mob, demonstrating unsuspected athletic skills. Of course, they were also the first to hit the referee and any player from the Lusitanense team that came in their way.

Caught up in the tumult, Dr. Alfonso followed the crowd, suddenly finding himself in the middle of a pitched battle. When he felt the baton blow from a policeman he understood that he had made the wrong decision, and that he should have run in the opposite direction. And that's what he would have done if an evil German Shepherd hadn't sunk its teeth into one of his trouser legs, preventing him from escaping.

In the meantime, Manuel Almeida was wringing the referee's neck and demanding to be given a rope, while Joaquim was wrestling with three policemen. One of the linesmen had taken refuge on the top of one of the goal posts and the other was flat on his face in the mud. Players, spectators, and policemen hit out in all directions, oblivious to whom they were actually hitting. There were escapes, persecutions, and savage beatings. Boots, shoes, and broken teeth scattered about the pitch. The cries from assailants and from their victims, the noise of bodies being battered, the sound of the melee over the puddles, and the barking of dogs created a racket that not even the claps of thunder could stifle.

And only after half an hour, with the arrival of police, fire brigade reinforcements, and Mayor Ramsey himself, did the pitched battle come to an end. Seven players from the visiting team, four home fans, and three officers were lying on the ground. Immobile, his arms spread wide and his legs extended, the referee looked as if he'd been crucified on the soil; to his left and right lay the brigands of linesmen, motionless. A German Shepherd had a broken paw and another was missing two teeth.

The Almeida brothers and Dr. Alfonso were arrested for contempt and assault against the authorities. The injured were taken to hospital, and the referee hospitalised with a poor prognosis. Armindo escaped to his father-in-law's house.

But, half an hour later, thanks to the services of Mayor Ramsey with the Police Chief, Mr. McCarthy, the three rioters were released. The sky was now free of black clouds.

Silent until that point, once freed Dr. Tomas Alfonso rumbled with thunder.

"This is outrageous, I demand an apology! I'm leaving right now! The meeting is postponed!"

"I'm sorry, doctor, so sorry…" said Ramsey.

"Oooh, Doc Alfonso, your grace is going nowhere, for fuck's sake! This project is very important for us," said Manuel.

"Oh, you're not fucking going anywhere! We haven't sold a house in nine months," said Joaquim.

"Ramsey's already apologised. But you saw that it was the referee's fault."

"Listen, around here you need to get to know people to do business. The footie didn't go very well, but now you're going to sample Maria Rosa's roast kid. And then we'll discuss the works."

Having thus realized that refusal could jeopardise the project, he gave in and decided not to go against local customs. He offered himself up for sacrifice for the resort. And so, when Manuel Almeida passed him the bottle of cognac again, he poured it down his throat until he felt his stomach in flames. Such a demonstration of alcoholic virility impressed the Almeida brothers, Mayor Ramsey, and Mr. McCarthy, who in the meantime had also been invited to dinner and had joined the group.

"Ah, we have a man with us after all," declared Joaquim.

With the mists of Vilar de Mochos going to his head, Dr. Alfonso stopped feeling threatened by the ogres. They were right. There were much more interesting things than doing business. The money-growing tree could wait. So when the Almeida brothers told him that before dinner they were going to show him the "Vilar de Mochos expo", a development they earned a ton on, he beamed.

*

In the meantime, Jesus and Magdalene had found a group of villas built by Almeida Brothers, in which they sheltered from the rain. Seven two-storey buildings with sloping roofs, tiled façades — in blue, green, yellow, brown — veranda with railings, and a garden complete with granite fountain. Except for the varying color scheme, they were all the same and all of them were uninhabited. The native vegetation was beginning to cover their foreign presence; and where this didn't reach, the sun, wind and damp were doing their own sabotage. There were broken roof tiles, loose wall tiles and shutters hanging from the windows; water seepage blackened walls and ceilings. A few more months of abandonment and the houses would become uninhabitable.

Magdalena took the initiative to open a gate to shelter under the eaves of a house. Even though he doubted the correctness of the act, Jesus followed her. The torrent flowing through the property's access took the morality of the intrusion away with it, too. However, despite being protected from the water, Magdalene did not appreciate the shelter.

"Emigrant houses... they are even uglier than seen in the pics. If there were a prize for bad taste in architecture, these buildings would win. They've completely missed the point. Look at those tiles, it looks like an inside out bathroom. And they still call them dream houses..."

Jesus did not share the severity of her judgment.

"Well, someone must like this style."

"Only emigrants would like this. Living in the slums, building a house became the most important goal in their lives. They took their French and German bosses' houses as a model and tried to recreate them in their village, leading to this beautiful result. They muddle up styles in the same way they muddle up languages," Magdalene said.

"These people emigrated in search of better living conditions, so it's only natural that they tried to imitate the cultures where they prospered. If you had emigrated, perhaps you would have done the same..."

"They were the victims of exploitation in these countries, becoming cheap labor and without any rights to satisfy the needs of civil construction and domestic workers. Why on earth did they have to imitate those who treated them so badly?"

"Maybe they don't see themselves as victims, rather as successful people. Your scenario is different to theirs."

"Successful in earning money. But they returned just as ignorant as when they left, without any political or social conscience. And I'll tell you something else: these houses, child labor, violence against animals and abandoning traditional farming all comes from the same ignorance."

"Are you suggesting an architectural reeducation program?"

*

At the expo Dr. Alfonso tried his aim, throwing darts against playing cards depicting naked women and firing pellet guns at paper tapes, without however winning the prize of a bottle of brandy or a blue bunny. His frustration was eased by some more gulps from the bottle of cognac and by downing some glasses of anisette.

He went for a ride in the bumper cars, and sat next to Joaquim Almeida, an accomplished driver in colliding with other dodgems. Then they went to watch the Wall of Death where two motorcyclists dressed in black leather and red masks defied gravity.

"It's today," said Joaquim.

"You are wrong," replied Manuel.

There was a €500 bet: Joaquim ensured that one of the two artists would fall at the bottom of the well by the end of the year. Manuel advised him to avoid the movies.

With the show over, he copied the brothers when he went up to the blind concertina player to put some coins in his box. And finally he kicked a hedgehog wandering around lost at the expo.

When they finally arrived at Joaquim's house, Dr. Thomas Alfonso burst out laughing, pushed open the gilded gate with his foot, soaked his face in a fountain, where water gushed out of the willy of a *putto*, went in the door without wiping his feet, bumped into a hammered brass pot, gave a kiss to Dona Maria Rosa without introducing himself, went in search of the dining room on his own, broke into laughter again when he spotted a painting of the Eiffel Tower there, sat down at the head of the table, dried his hands on the table cloth, and shouted, "So, is this kid coming or not?"

Across the living room, Manuel whispered to his brother, "Joaquim, he's putty in our hands. He ranted on a bit, but now he's as meek as a lamb."

Joaquim agreed. "These city doctors think themselves very refined, but with us they're fucked."

With the reception plan's success proved, the brothers sat at the table, smiles on their faces. The resort's construction promised to be as profitable a deal as the Paris shopping center. And the new partner was even more of an angel than the one before. The flies may have changed, but the honey was the same.

With Dr. Alfonso sitting at the head of the table, Manuel and Mr. McCarthy sat on the right side, and Joaquim and Mayor Ramsey sat on the left side. Porcelain plates, crystal glasses, and silver cutlery were laid out on the embroidered linen table cloth. A faux Baccarat Versailles-style glass chandelier with twelve bulbs hung from the ceiling.

Then the roast kid was brought out, carried by the hostess. Wearing her best apron, Dona Maria Rosa placed a terracotta tray of meat and potatoes on the table, another of boiled greens, and a large pot of rice.

Instructed by her husband, she tried to be friendly to their guest. "Eat up, Doc Alfonso, you so thin." Having heard her advice, Dr. Alfonso stuck his fork into a piece of meat, the Almeida brothers urged him to fill his plate, while Mr. McCarthy served himself from a bottle of *Veuve Cliquot* resting in a bucket of ice and Mayor Ramsey risked an olive. Satisfied, Dona Maria Rosa returned to the kitchen where she remained, awaiting their request to clear the table.

"She's a bit of a clunker, but she cooks well," said Joaquim in praise.

The dinner passed in perfect harmony: everyone ate the kid with their hands, licking their fingers, smearing the rims of their glasses and leaving circles of fat floating in the liquid. And as is always the case when men come together, the subject of politics spurted onto the table, through the same process that caused food and drink stains to appear on the tablecloth.

Discounting Mayor Ramsey as an "exception to the rule", Joaquim Almeida spoke of the morals of politicians, unloading a truck of rubble on top of them.

"They are a bunch of bloodsuckers and thieves, who entered politics because they didn't have a job. They're completely useless. And they're entirely to blame for all this shit!"

Suddenly he punched the table twice, began to speak louder, and pieces of meat flew from his mouth onto Dr. Alfonso's shirt. Freeing himself of the meat with a flick, the businessman backed the builder's theories. "The less state the better." For his part, Mr. McCarthy, in a bout of nostalgia, recalled other kinds of government. "Say what you like, but today it's daylight robbery. This kind of liberal democracy is only good for thieves."

Mayor Ramsey nodded and focused on his plate. And Manuel, without breaking from cutting a potato, passed judgment.

"Someone should put a bomb in Parliament."

Then, perhaps carried by the blast of Manuel's explosion, war broke out in the conversation. The Police Chief agreed that "a disaster was needed" and Joaquim Almeida, without thinking about the ensuing famine or pestilence, defended its importance for the success of civil construction.

"With this crisis the best thing would be to have a war. Look at the war in Iraq, Doc Alfonso. They did away with all that and now their builders are making so much money that they don't know what to do with it. And with a bit of luck the same is gonna happen in Syria or Iran."

"It's a shame that we didn't have our little civil war. We would have come back earlier and made a fortune rebuilding our country," lamented Manuel, imagining the country in ruins.

"It was indeed a shame, as I had a list of communists to shoot down and afterwards they wouldn't let me," Mr. McCarthy agreed, mournfully, while shredding a piece of meat.

With the dinner livened up, five bottles of champagne downed, the discussions continued. Through Manuel, Dr. Alfonso learned about the Almeida brothers' management methods. Manuel started by confiding something. "Doc Alfonso, all my assets are registered in my wife's name. The houses, the farms, the cars, the money in the bank, everything. If things go wrong, they won't get a penny." Then he revealed a few business secrets. "Firstly you need to have a friend like Ramsey to ensure planning approval and building permits. Then you order some steel, cement and sand, you make the house, you put the money in your pocket, and all the suppliers can wait for theirs." The builder further clarified that such a method requires some legal assistance. "You have to get yourself a good lawyer, the kind who knows how to delay court proceedings, because sometimes the supplier can go bankrupt."

As he sipped the chilled champagne, Dr. Alfonso heard the pop of a cork and wondered if it would hit him. But his reasoning was carried away by the bubbles in the *Veuve Clicquot*.

However, Joaquim, fearing that his brother's words might be misinterpreted, soothed his guest. "But don't you worry, Doc Alfonso, there won't be any problems like that with your hotel. We get along well with the new suppliers. One of them has already been here for dinner."

Satisfied with his brother's contribution, Manuel summed it all up. "That's a lot of experience."

As he sampled Dona Maria Rosa's rice pudding, washed down with a fine Napoleon cognac, Dr. Alfonso became aware that he should say something about the resort. And so he interrupted Joaquim Almeida midway through explaining the "advantages of French women", much to the chagrin of the Police Chief and the Mayor, rapt audience of the builder's *remembrance of things past*. So he raised his glass and proposed a new toast. "To our resort..."

His fellow diners followed suit and Manuel Almeida, remembering the past, added, "And to being able to keep it up forever."

During the libations, Joaquim noticed the terrible state of the businessman's trousers. Demonstrating a rigour with clothing similar to that of savings in steel and cement, he called Dona Maria Rosa.

"Woman, bring a pair of trousers for Doc Alfonso."

A little later his wife appeared with some ironed trousers—wine colored and three sizes too large for the guest. But when she saw that his leg was wounded, a bite the likes of which she had never seen in her husband's construction workers, she volunteered to dress it for him. Armed with cotton, antiseptic, and iodine, she once again contributed to the success of the business evening.

"Don't move, Doc Alfonso, *buge pas.*"

*

Half an hour later they entered the *Folies Bergère,* a nightclub for some, a brothel for others. Or, in other words, a shack lost in the hills that had once been used as a warehouse to store building materials, and which was accessed down a dirt track. The neon silhouette of a female body fixed to the roof served as a lighthouse, guiding the way to terra firma for lost sailors.

The *Folies Bergère* contributed to the sustained development of Vilar de Mochos, in that no tree had been felled during its renovation, the only polluting gas it emitted was tobacco smoke, and it generated little trash, beyond empty bottles, food leftovers, and rubber in the form of condoms.

The Almeida brothers received a bow from the bouncer, to whom they asked the usual questions. "Everything okay? The hookers making money?" Dr. Thomas Alfonso entered clutching the Police Chief, wearing the officer's beret on his head. Mayor Ramsey turned up the collars of his jacket in the hope that no one would recognize him.

Once inside the *Folies Bergère*, Manuel Almeida gave his guest some advice. "Make hay while the sun shines, Doc Alfonso; we all end up as dust for bricks in the end." This was an unnecessary recommendation, as on that night Dr. Thomas Alfonso was enjoying *la vie en rose*, and impervious to thoughts of death or dust. Eros was winning the battle over Thanatos in Vilar de Mochos[20].

On the table before the sofas where they sat down, facing a dance floor with a pole at its center and mirrored balls and red lights twinkling on the ceiling, stood two bottles of fake whisky, a bucket of ice made from well water, and glasses that had been washed in a plastic container. Joaquim Almeida pulled off his shoes, served his friends, and took a swig from the bottle. Then he invited them to choose some of the girls who were leaning against the bar or idling about.

"This is good quality merchandise. I've already tried all of them for a taste of love on the house."

However, seeing their indecision, he specified his preferences.

---

[20] B Freud identified 'instincts' or 'drives' that he viewed as innate. Eros (the life drive/instinct, libido) is concerned with the preservation of life. Thanatos (the death drive/instinct, mortido, aggression) appears in opposition and balance to Eros and pushes a person towards extinction.

"I like the big girls here, but basically this is a beast that moans when squeezed."

And Joaquim's beasts, loose in the whorehouse jungle yet attracted by the owner's presence and curious about his friends, paraded close to the table, shooting lustful glances, moving their hips and pushing up their breasts, in a gestural and lush phenomenon that delighted Dr. Alfonso and caused Mayor Ramsey to blurt out his innermost thoughts.

"Girls nowadays are really well fed."

In the meantime, on the dance floor two dancers had started shaking their stuff, a little ungainly, but well favored by nature's blessings and eating well. The show included a simultaneous striptease number, which the pair had invented after seeing the synchronized swimming event at the Olympics. Rarely did they manage to take off their pieces of clothing at the same time, each of them performed different dance steps, managed to bang heads against each other, and sometimes quarreled during the performance. But none of this lessened the fascination of the audience, who, open-mouthed, watched the feminine performance in a reverential silence of believers before an epiphany. That was the only moment of the session in which the hullabaloo ceased and all that could be heard was an old scratched copy of *Je t'aime, moi non plus*.

Indeed, customers who were noisily bantering, haggling over prices with the girls, confiding their domestic miseries or their professional misfortunes to them, fell silent when they heard the DJ announce that the "never before seen erotic and wild show of Liliana and Ludmila" was about to start. Because the artists, even though they had been on stage for three months and all they had changed was their position from right to left, held this mysterious power of bewitching the patrons of the *Folies Bergère*. A power that possibly came from them being forbidden from dedicating themselves to arts of lust other than those of musical undressing, while the acclaimed erotic and wild show was underway. Therefore, on Friday and Saturday nights the customers' imaginations were driven mad, because of Liliana and Ludmila's wiggles and lack of clothes. One brunette, the other blonde, two peaches.

And even though the fantasies of each customer featured a different technique of wallowing in the flesh of Liliana and Ludmila, they all shared a common desire: "to ride them both at the same time" — a feat that nobody had ever achieved, except Manuel and Joaquim.

The same bestial thought did not escape the Police Chief, a man experienced in taming horses and German Shepherds. As soon as the girls started to shake, while holding onto the pole, Liliana sliding slowly to the floor and Ludmila imitating Cossack dancers, Mr. McCarthy lost interest in Joaquim Almeida's theory on French women, took his glasses out of his uniform pocket, muddled his glass of whisky with that of Dr. Alfonso, and ended up, just like their host, swigging some from the bottle. From that moment on, the fascination of the flesh overcame him, transforming his face; the spell made him stretch his neck, pop out his eyes, bare his teeth, and an idea pounded in his head as firm as the dancers' pole.

Dr. Alfonso whispered something to him about the girls' legs, but he could no longer hear a thing, nor could he see anything else beyond those lascivious bodies. They were two wild animals, two bitches in heat that he would first domesticate and then possess. He wanted to grab his whip, but he had left it in the Almeidas' car. Feeling disarmed before such barbarous creatures, capable of devouring him alive, he hesitated and took another swig from the bottle for Dutch courage.

But when Ludmila dropped her skirt and revealed a pair of generous buttocks on which two butterfly wings seemed sucked into a black hole, Mr. MacCarthy rallied, stood up as if to impose order or shoot some communists, and declared that he was going to "carve them both up." Dr. Alfonso even tried to grab him, but he got away with a kick of his shoe, put his beret back on, and marched off towards the dancers. However, despite his determination, he ended up bumping into another authority: Armando, security at the *Folies Bergère* by night, bricklayer's mate by day and Armindo's cousin.

"You can't touch the girls' behinds, Chief."

"Get out of my way, you idiot."

The uproar that followed, during which the authority of the republic told the authority of the brothel he was under arrest, with the latter having tried to calm the former with the assistance of some customers, ended abruptly with the energetic intervention of the Almeida brothers.

"What is all this shit?" screamed Joaquim

"This isn't a free-for-all," Manuel explained.

The customers were shoved down into the sofas and the guard-slash-bricklayer's-mate threatened with double dismissal. With order restored, Manuel and Joaquim brought Mr. McCarthy back to the table with the promise of going to find the girls.

"Let them go to the bathroom, so they can freshen up, Chief."

Five minutes later, Joaquim Almeida appeared arm in arm with the dancers in skimpy clothing and high heels. Lovely and fresh. After giving them suggestions about etiquette and good manners, "take care, these are gentlemen!" he sent them on their way with a slap on each of their rears.

Frightened like two calves at the door to the slaughterhouse, Liliana and Ludmila prepared themselves to be culled. But there was nothing more than an exchange of kisses on the cheeks and an invitation for them to sit down. The butchering would be gentle after all. The dancers relaxed, crossed their legs, uncrossed their legs, and, little by little, excited chatter started to build up, with plenty of laughter, jesting, and lewd bleating. Toasts with sparkling wine from the shooting galleries at the expo, caipirinha (Liliana) and caipirosca (Ludmila) followed. The Almeida brothers preferred to remain outside the conversation, leaving the honor of the maidens to their friends. Pleased with how the plan was panning out, Manuel didn't forget his protector.

"My Saint Rita never lets me down."

Joaquim disagreed. "No, it was the Infant Jesus of Prague."

Meanwhile, Ramsey was meditating on the meaning of life. Disturbed by the proximity of the girls, the warmth of their bodies, their perfume, and so much flesh on display, he recalled his wife washing her behind in the bidet and cursed his luck—never had the world seemed more unfair and its riches so poorly distributed. The possibility then passed through his mind of experiencing with the Whorehouse Venuses certain practices of which he'd heard talk and which he had never dared proposing to his unfortunate wife. Ordinary, dirty, and dangerous, but which must be a delight. Feeling on the verge of paradise lost, and hoping that a feast always begins with hunger, he puffed out his chest and tried to give off a younger appearance: a goofy smile. However, the dilemma between succumbing to temptation and defending respectability was tearing him apart, in a conflict that generally leads to paralysis or to hesitancy. This is what happened to the Mayor. As soon as he gushed nonsensical praise to one of the girls, he would blush in embarrassment and revert to long silences, leading them to think, each in their own way and in different languages, that there was a perfect moron to be fooled.

None of these problems of moral or hygienic nature assailed the Police Chief. To the girls he boasted of a bullish strength and sought to ascertain the weight, measurements, and specialities of each of them, eliciting loutish laughter from Manuel and Joaquim, even more embarrassment from Ramsey, slight perplexity from Dr. Alfonso, and much indignation in the targeted Liliana and Ludmila. And, not content with the evasive replies from the first of the girls, and those proffered in an incomprehensible language by the second, even after he had shown them a gold credit card, he took it upon himself to find out, measuring them and groping them.

Dr. Alfonso looked on in amusement and, from time to time, passed his hand over the silky thighs of their new friends. However, unlike the reaction unleashed against the Chief, forcing him to remove his hand and threatening to give him a slap, Liliana and Ludmila not only allowed him these intimacies, but also smiled. Encouraging him to carry on his anatomical exploration, and discovery of other secrets. In voices dripping with honey, they spoke in his ear.

"You're gonna build a resort? That's really cool," Liliana said.

"And then you'll let us use the pool, won't you?" asked Ludmila.

Despite occasionally seeing two Lilianas and two Ludmilas, and then eight silky thighs and eight silicon chests, not remembering what he had just said or heard, Dr. Alfonso, who in the meantime had opened his shirt and straightened the folds in his French trousers, began to sniff out a new opportunity. A hardcore opportunity.

And this came about when the Police Chief, afflicted by the ailments of the prostate of an ancient bull, found himself compelled to abandon the girls to visit the bathroom for a piss. He spent no longer than four minutes at the blocked and spit-filled urinal, but when he returned he discovered that he had been betrayed. Liliana was sitting on Dr. Alfonso's lap, Ludmila was clinging to his neck, and he was drinking sparkling wine from one of their shoes. All of them were very excited.

Struck down by the scene before him, like Lot's wife, if she had returned to flesh from her salty form and discovered him with her daughters, the Police Chief, lacking his whip with which to restore morality in this Sodom, immune to raining fire but promising nefarious sins, pouted and demanded to be taken home. The builders did his bidding. As they left they gave new orders to Liliana and Ludmila.

"Take care of Doctor Alfonso and the Mayor. They should want for nothing."

This advice was hardly necessary, seeing as they were all getting along quite nicely, creating fraternal and bovine bonds.

Before the journey began, Mr. McCarthy threw up, supporting himself on a wheel of the Mercedes. Then he lay down on Joaquim's dog's blanket and stayed like that for the rest of the ride. Along the way he barked stammered insults against emigrants, businessmen, and communists. When he reached his destination he opened the door and threw up again. Bolstered by the builders, Mr. McCarthy struggled to get out of the car. "Now, let me be," he ordered, "I'm fine now." He took two unsteady steps and came to a halt. In a tremendous effort he managed to focus on the objects in his field of vision (a house at the end of the road). The hoot of an owl made him turn towards a tree. The light of a lamp pulled the green color of the leaves. A branch shook. Mr. McCarthy took a deep breath and looked at the stars. The laws of the universe had been reinstated. After a while he recovered his poise. He straightened his cap, saluted them, and entered his house without a wobble.

Manuel and Joaquim returned to the *Folies Bergère* half an hour later. As soon as they entered they were confronted with an unexpected situation. Mayor Ramsey was asleep on the sofas, whereas Dr. Alfonso had disappeared. The girls, Liliana and Ludmila, were nowhere to be seen, either. Drinks, snacks, household soap, rolls of toilet paper, towels, bottles of *femfresh*, a tin of creosote, and a silk gown had disappeared from the *Folies Bergère* in the past. But never had human resources gone astray.

When questioned, Armando gave his version of events. "The three of them were doing a slow dance, it was shameless boss, and suddenly they disappeared."

"For fuck's sake, Armando, you're as dumb as horse shit," admonished Manuel.

The Almeida brothers began the search by starting with the most probable place you would find a trio of scamps: the *Folies Bergère* storerooms, a windowless hovel in which six alcoves had been built.

Entering the corridor calling "Oh, Doc Alfooonso," and "Come here, for fuck's sake," Manuel and Joaquim opened the first door they found with a twist of the handle and pushed it wide open. However, instead of Dr. Alfonso, they found an older gentleman in that alcove caught with his trousers in his hand, and a young woman who yawned, dressed as when she entered the world. Frustrated, the brothers slammed the door and continued their search. On their second attempt, a little more cautious this time, they opened the door slowly but found nothing but an empty bed, a sign that the crisis had also reached the brothel. When they reached the third alcove, despite Joaquim having recognized his trousers on the ground, they still couldn't see anybody, naked or otherwise. However, under the sheets something was moving, making the fabric move like the waves of a stormy sea in a theatre play; and in this case it would be a tremendous storm, a storm capable of scaring Christopher Columbus, of intimidating Captain Cook. The Almeida brothers watched the nautical phenomenon and feared getting too close to it, as if Poseidon himself were to erupt from it. Suddenly, as if rescued from a *ménage à trois* with nymphs, Dr. Thomas Alfonso pushed out his dishevelled head from under the sheets. Joaquim then reminded him of his obligations.

"Doc Alfonso, you've already eaten the roast and the hookers, all that's missing now is our check."

*

On the following day, Mayor Ramsey called the population for a meeting in front of the town hall once again. The church bells rang. And from up high on the balcony, flanked by Manuel and Joaquim Almeida, he announced that he had some big news to tell them. The people of the town expected to hear that they would be promised a banquet in the near future. Their expectations were not dashed. In addition to the sausage festival and the fire brigade dance, a third event would reopen the cultural center this year. But before the feast being announced, they were told the good news.

"My friends, a grand hotel is to be built in our town and in the coming years there will be plenty of work for everyone. Tourism will bring work and attract money. Foreigners will come, important people, folks from the television. Progress is coming to our town, development, quality of life... and we owe all this to the wonderful Almeida Brothers."

Straight as plumb lines until that point, Manuel and Joaquim were the first to applaud. The townsfolk followed their example and hailed the Mayor. The blind man played the concertina and some women danced. Ramsey, however, was not happy. Melancholic, with a weary look, he waved weakly at the people, as he was unable to forget Liliana and Ludmila.

*

At the same time, Dr. Thomas Alfonso, following a painful return trip in which he scratched the car when passing under the Arch of Triumph, was in bed with the curtains drawn. The hardcore had been good, but the price far too high. For a week his head and liver throbbed, it still burned when he peed, with Miss Barbara's care helping none. The Chinese horoscope had been fulfilled. However, for the Stream Eco Resort, he would once again lose himself in the mists of Vilar de Mochos.

*

The historic center of Vilar de Mochos had a main square, on which the town hall stood. In this rectangle, punctuated by a 17th-century pillory and ennobled by a monument to the emigrant — a bronze figure with a suitcase on its back — the population was now gathered. Some sat on wooden benches that Ramsey had set up below the ancient oaks, others were in the tavern in front of the council buildings. Four roads exited this square, sticking to their straight trajectory for a maximum of ten meters, only then to suddenly, as if overtaken by folly, contorting into curves and then being joined by other lanes with more curves still, before this serpentine design resulted in something similar to a maze.

As if a road to nowhere, Vilar de Mochos closed in on itself. Locals remarked that this urban layout was the legacy of the era of barbarian invasions and served as a windbreaker. In the present it still offered shelter from the wind, but instead of slowing down ancient barbarians, it attracted modern ones.

Jesus and Magdalene entered the square at midday. They walked around it, looking at its historical heritage, curious about the triple arcade of the town hall, about the pillory with its three-stepped socle, smooth shafted column, and capital with a cross, masks, and gargoyles, bewildered by the monument to the emigrant. Then, they came across people who, wearing grimaces not dissimilar to those carved on the old monument, and as if the intrusion of strangers caused them as much burden as the suitcase on the modern monument, began to gather to watch them.

Not all strangers were welcome in the town, especially young people. A year ago the church had been burgled, months later they had caught a pair of lovers practicing indecencies in the open air, and only weeks ago, a Chinese man had appeared, taking pictures. They would therefore keep an eye on them until they went away. Sensing the tension, the blind man took his fingers off the keys. And the melody withered like a dissipating aroma.

It was then that Jesus and Magdalene, feeling a hunger that only country air and long walks arouse, tried to find out where they could eat lunch. To do so they made their way towards the people watching them. Seeing the two strangers coming towards them, the townsfolk, having already clenched their faces, did the same with their fists, but instead of bad intentions they discovered two smiles in search of a place where they could eat. And as food is a sacred subject in this land, able to unite through the stomach what heads separated, the men and women of the town returned the smile and invited them to try out the snacks in the tavern.

There was no longer any shade in Vilar de Mochos square when they entered the building. The blind man, however, didn't feel like accompanying them. When he heard the voices of the strangers, he decided they were younger than he was, and lost his faith of receiving any coins from them. And he stayed playing alone on a bench.

The tavern had a narrow door, from which plastic ribbons hung, barring entry to flies. It was a single room with whitewashed walls, and with two long tables and benches, a counter with a cracked marble top, the area where the innkeeper moved about (squeezed against three barrels), a hatch to the kitchen, and a cellar in the basement. Sawdust was scattered across the floor, and hanging from the beams supporting the ceiling were hams, sausages, bunches of onions, garlic, chilli peppers, and small pumpkins. Two calabashes were leaning against the entrance to the toilet cubicle. The acidic scent of wine faded only when one stood close to the hanging meats, with their intense smoky and fatty odour.

Seated at the table with the locals, Magdalene and Jesus were treated to cabbage broth, cured ham, cod fritters, black pudding, chorizo, little plates of roast pork, ewe's cheese, bread made with unmodified corn, olives, and white and red wine. An organic feast, achieved without the use of microwave ovens. Healthy and Mediterranean, if eaten in moderation. On the following day Magdalene, having tried something of everything, would weigh a kilo extra, Jesus, thanks to his preference for bread and wine, would weigh the same.

Magdalene was enraptured by the hospitality of the locals. There were still fraternal bonds in this town; the people lived as a community and helped each other, as in an ant colony. Before the curiosity of the townsfolk, she took the opportunity to introduce Jesus and herself, and entered into conversation with several people.

"We are travelers on holiday, and we like discovering inland areas. Some friends suggested we should visit this region, and here we are."

"And do you like our town?" asked a woman.

"Very much so. The heritage is well maintained, nature has been preserved, and there is no pollution. There are few places like this left. I just hope this town stays like this forever."

"Our town is very peaceful and we like it that way. It's the young people who leave it," a man said.

"But they will come back," Magdalene said. "The cities have become dehumanized spaces, where there are no jobs or hope. The return to nature, to traditional activities, and to community living is inevitable. Humanity has no other future."

But she was met with a litany of disparaging remarks about the town.

"Do you think?"

"My son says it's here where there's no future."

"We could use a hospital nearby."

"And a bank."

"And a supermarket."

"In truth, this place is a dump."

"If it wasn't for my rheumatism, I would have left long ago."

"And if I were any younger, I'd be off, too."

"Me, too."

Magdalene looked at her hosts and waited before replying. "What I wanted to say is that if we continue to destroy the planet..."

"Listen, how long are you thinking of staying here?" a woman asked.

"How long? One, maybe two days."

The innkeeper interrupted the conversation. "Stay a week, I've got rooms for rent upstairs."

"Thank you, that's very kind of you, but as I was saying, the abuse of nature—"

"Listen, let your husband say something now," a man said.

"He hasn't opened his mouth once," another woman said.

"Cat got your tongue?" another man said.

"You can see who wears the trousers at home," the first woman said.

"Hey mate, if you want to get a shave and a haircut, you can here, out back," the innkeeper interrupted once again.

Jesus realized that everyone was looking at him. "For we were hungry and you gave us food, we were thirsty and you gave us drink..."

The feast was festive. Excited by Magdalene, the men were trying to guess her measurements, while the women, who didn't see anything in Jesus, pigged out on the food. Toasts to health and happiness followed.

At a certain point the tavern owner feared that he wouldn't have enough wine, such was the thirst of his fellow townsfolk. If they continued to drink like that, downing glass after glass, the red wine cask would soon be empty. This would bring as much shame to his establishment as to his town. In Vilar de Mochos abundance was required, on the plate and in the glass — especially when welcoming visitors. It wasn't his fault, because nobody had warned him that this party was going to take place, but this was no consolation. Worried, he returned discreetly to the cellar to confirm the disaster.

"The wine is finished, what a bunch of drunks!"

It was then that one of the country folk wanted to show the visitors that they did things here as good as anywhere else, that globalization had visited them, too.

"And did you know that they're going to build a luxury hotel here? Maybe the young'uns will come back home then."

Magdalene's ear, sensitive to the decibels of environmental attacks, detected that another crime against nature could be happening, another cause for which it was worth fighting. As green as the corn. She then transformed her cheerful face into a serious and dour look, as if she too wished to compete with the gargoyles for the pillory. Were the emigrants' houses not enough?

The locals were astonished by the girl's transfiguration, confusing the mental arithmetic of those who were delighting in working out her anatomical proportions.

As she was now a self-employed environmentalist — aided by an assistant — Magdalene no longer needed *Green Are the Fields*. She would fight in her own way. Spending time with Jesus she had learned that there are other methods preferable to violence, starting with the word.

She was preparing to question the people of Vilar de Mochos when the innkeeper returned in euphoria, with two tankards in his hands, crying "Wiiiiine!" His eyes were glistening. At the rear of the cellar he had found a cask that he had thought empty, but which was actually full, and wanted to fill everyone's glasses. And the guests, once they tried it, congratulated their host on having kept the best wine till last.

Only then, feigning interest in the development of the town, did Magdalene ask her companions to tell her everything about this large hotel. The temptation to show that something was going to happen in their Eden proved irresistible. The majority bit the apple. However, they knew very little about the subject and each of them added their piece to this tale of the hotel.

The first informant assured Magdalene that she had got it from a good source.

"The hotel is going to be built in the pine grove, it'll have five storeys and a car park."

Her husband, giving her a rap on the head, asserted that she'd got it all wrong.

"You're wasted, woman, it's nothing of the sort. The hotel is going to be on the side of the hill, facing the sun. And as for storeys, there are just two or three because they don't need any more."

In the corner of the table another man gave his opinion.

"Two or three storeys? You're the one who's drunk. They don't make small hotels nowadays. Don't you watch TV? They're all towers."

An elderly man next to Jesus admonished all three of them.

"Why are you talking about stuff you know nothing about? The only person who knows anything is Ramsey and as he never tells anyone anything nor commits himself to anything, nobody will be able to squeeze a word out of him about the matter."

Before you could blink, the brother-in-law of the old guy, over the hill himself, revealed his information. "Oh, I heard that the top floor will have a reception hall with an orchestra."

"Don't talk crap!" his neighbor contradicted him.

The neighbor's wife joined the discussion.

"There's probably some Chinese guy involved somewhere..."

Another woman contradicted her.

"What Chinese guy? The Chinese only have laundries and restaurants, they're never involved in hotels."

Finally the innkeeper, from the high rank given to him by being in charge of the counter, the full casks of wine, and the draught beer machine, and afraid of the competition, passed judgment on the discussion. "The hotel is a hotel like any other and enough said!"

Magdalene also managed to find out that the work, true to tradition, was running behind schedule. She had all she needed to know. A green area was going to be destroyed so that someone could become rich and this was enough for her. Even without knowing the author of the environmental crime, and unable to maintain Christian conduct when put to the test, she already hated him. Someone else in need of having a copy of *Utopia* rubbed in his face and being hit on the head with books by the great masters.

She then recalled a passage denouncing the greed of the rich:

"When every man draws to himself all that he can compass, by one title or another, it must need follow that, how plentiful soever a nation may be, yet a few dividing the wealth of it among themselves, the rest must fall into indigence."[21]

An hour later, they offered their thanks for the lunch and bid farewell to the people. When they had all left they informed the innkeeper that they were going for a walk around the town. Once outside, in the shade of the oak trees, Jesus tried to calm Magdalene.

"I know what you're thinking. The best thing is for us to go to the council offices and find out more information about this hotel."

Magdalena crushed an acorn with the heel of her shoe.

"What for? We already know the important part. They're going to put an end to the forest to build a tourist resort. And it's almost certain that they are violating environmental regulations, as is normal in

---

[21] *Utopia*, p. 38.

this country. I bet you that guy who wouldn't give us a lift is behind this."

"It won't do any harm to go there."

"Okay, but don't expect to hear the truth from them."

"What is the truth?" asked Jesus.

"In this case, I am the truth."

When they came out from the shade of the trees something caught their attention in the sky. Protecting their eyes from the sun with their hands, they could see the commotion caused by two birds in their mating dance. As they pursued each other, the two birds rose up high before descending steeply, swerving to the right before turning left, in a frantic whirl in which space was entangled in their flight paths. As she watched them, amazed, Magdalene said something that surprised herself.

"It's the start of the miracle of life."

"Who would have known that nature could also provoke mystical ecstasies, too," commented Jesus.

"Well, it can, and we don't need to hide away in a convent," Magdalene replied.

Looking towards the sky, Jesus whispered something that she couldn't hear.

"For they sow not, neither do they reap, nor gather into barns."

Magdalene continued to watch the birds. Threatened by the felling of trees, she was obliged to fight for them, too. And the first battle would be to convince the town Mayor to put a halt to the hotel's construction. To make a Mayor aware of environmental issues was as improbable as beating your arms and starting to fly, but she would at least make him listen to her protest.

Jesus and Magdalene were watching the air display when Liliana and Ludmila appeared. Arriving along a lane that opened onto the square, the dancers had risked taking a stroll through the town. Even if they sometimes heard insults from other women — "What are you doing here, hookers?" and "Get lost!" — they'd found spending the whole day in the *Folies Bergère* watching TV, reading magazines, or pedaling an exercise bike was becoming more and more dull. Armando had urged them to exercise in vain, as even without any exercise they still had the best legs in the joint, squeezing themselves into the hot tub with their bosses provided enough gymnastics. So, once again they dared to go down into the town, ignoring Armando's advice and disregarding the bosses' orders. It was such a lovely day. After all, getting a slap now and then was part of the job — and both of them were safe from harder whacks that could compromise the show.

Jesus caught their attention. Ludmila, with the eye of a hawk, was the first to spot him.

"Look at that guy over there."

"Mmm, he is handsome," agreed Liliana.

"He's never been up to ours, has he?"

"Not him. Apart from that other one who said he was a businessman, we only get fat lumps and old farts."

"By his skin he must be a foreigner, but he's not from my country. They're not so dark there," Ludmila said.

"He really does have a fine face, well maintained hair, delicate hands, you can see he comes from a good family. It's a shame there's someone with him," Liliana said.

"So what?"

"Don't forget that our bosses have your passport," Liliana said.

"You're right..."

"But there's no harm in looking at him, though."

"I'd give him one for free," Ludmila said.

Jesus saw them before Magdalene and immediately lost his interest in the birds. On Earth there were more interesting creatures, with skin instead of feathers, and which, instead of soaring to the heights, eyed him as if he were a piece of meat. The silhouette of those women fascinated him: long legs, narrow waists, full breasts.

And their faces, of both the brunette and the blonde, seemed equally beautiful. It occurred to him that he had found two pagan goddesses. Seeing his interest, Liliana gave him a wink and Ludmila passed her tongue over her lips. The two of them were now swaying their hips, in a preview of the wild and erotic show. The pagan goddesses seemed to want to initiate him in a Dionysian ritual. Jesus was ready to give into temptation and go and talk to them when the absent-minded Magdalene noticed the harassment.

"What do those hookers want?"

Surprised by the accusation, Jesus tried to defend his admirers. "How do you know they're prostitutes? They look like any other girls to me."

"Surely you can see they're women of easy virtue. Look at those miniskirts and those high heels. And the lipstick and mascara, so over the top! They're not fooling anyone. The inland areas are full of brothels exploiting women like them. They must be immigrants sent by human traffickers. It's all so degrading!"

"More victims of capitalism?"

"These aren't victims of anything. They are two shameless hussies chasing clients. But they won't find any business here. Come on, we have to talk to the Mayor." And she pulled him away by the wrist.

Lamenting their luck of being stuck in Vilar de Mochos, a place where there wasn't a single man worth taking advantage of, Liliana and Ludmila watched on as they departed. Without Jesus noticing, Magdalene, pretending that she was doing her hair, stuck her arm out backwards and saluted them with the gesture she had learned from the frog torturer.

*

When they entered the council hall they were barred by the receptionist, who was busy making another piece of crochet. To begin with she ignored them, but when she was forced to assist them, she made her usual reply. "Mr. Mayor is very busy."

Without offering her a single penny, or tips on knitting, another attempt helped Magdalene equally as little. "We want to look at the resort construction file."

The assistant raised her voice. "That's impossible!"

Magdalene shouted even louder. "I demand to see this information!"

In response, the assistant pointed a needle at her. Magdalene thumped immediately on the glass window above the counter. A neon light flickered and a tile rose on the floor.

When Jesus had managed to bring peace between them, Ramsey appeared. As he was not being greeted by well-dressed and important people, he was swift. "Out! Get them out of here immediately!"

"You corrupt man! Aren't you ashamed of destroying your town? How much did they pay you?" Magdalene said.

"Get out, or I'll call the police!"

"You're a prostitute and a pimp at the same time..."

Magdalene would have continued to revile the Mayor if Jesus hadn't pulled her by the arm. In the meantime, the Mayor's niece came out in defense of her uncle and threw them out of the building with jabs from her needle in their rears.

The light flagellation didn't bother Jesus, but it made Magdalene even more furious. Once again the persuasion method had failed. And as she couldn't string up Ramsey on the pillory, and whip him with a pine branch that she'd intended to rip off, she would set fire to the peaceful nature of the people of Vilar de Mochos. Igniting the revolt against the resort. Saint Francis of Assisi may not have been able to use such radical methods, but he certainly wouldn't have stood by and done nothing before such an attack on the creator's garden.

"This isn't over yet. Now we're going to sort this my way. There's a time for talk and a time for action."

The match would be lit by telling them, "You are being robbed!" a warning that would startle the most humble of men. Then she would fan the flames, by explaining to them that the hotel's construction would destroy what belonged to everyone in order to make a few rich. Without the forest, the town would lose its charm. Nobody would ever come here again and they would be forgotten and abandoned. All that would be left would be misery, famine, and, worse still, TV crews would come and show everything to the world. It would be a tragedy, a scandal, and bring shame on the community. The construction of the hotel would therefore be the greatest disgrace that could ever happen to Vilar de Mochos.

However, despite having formerly threatened to cast fire on the Earth, Jesus wasn't going to acquiesce to another blaze. Vilar de Mochos would not be transformed into a burning bush. So, in light of Magdalene's fury, and her determination to rouse the people against the Mayor and the resort, he poured water on her fervor.

"Wait, let's not rush this! We still know practically nothing about the project. We just heard hearsay. It may also be an investment that would benefit the town without harming nature. It may have advantages. Whatever the case, it should be the locals who decide on the matter."

"Exactly, they will be the ones to decide, but first they need to be well informed."

On that same day they began to make their way through the town, knocking on doors to talk with the people of Vilar de Mochos about the construction of the resort. However, Jesus and Magdalene didn't exactly say the same things.

And the result was that at nine in the morning on the following day, Vilar de Mochos' main square was full of very agitated people, without the slightest doubt, armed with hoes, forks, rakes, and large bottles of red wine. An anthill in fury.

None of the five hundred and two inhabitants of Vilar de Mochos was missing from that meeting in the square — not even the Ukrainian reinforcement, though unarmed. The sun was unable to break through the dense forest of their bodies and reach the ground. The square only seemed to exist above their heads, as if part of the façades and of the pillory had been cut off. However, as each of them had a different opinion about what was happening, the people of Vilar de Mochos were arguing with each other in a great tumult. The blind man had put down his concertina and was brandishing his cane.

This wasn't a flutter of butterfly's wings in Tokyo setting off a hurricane in New York. The cause and consequence were in the same place. What Magdalene hadn't reckoned with was the extent of the chaos. The fire had spread too fast. From one house to the next, it had spread through the town, and was now concentrated in the square. And if it had been easy to find a match, it was no longer possible to find a hose.

In vain she climbed the steps of the pillory and tried to organize the unbridled masses and command their wrath. After five minutes of screaming out and shouting, "Wait...listen...this is important..." Magdalene, already hoarse and exhausted, understood that nobody was interested in what she was saying and so eventually shut up.

Sensing the start of a tragedy in the swell of popular fury, like an embryonic leviathan in the belly of the town, Jesus decided to act. It was imminent, the stoning of those who wanted to adulterate Vilar de Mochos. But he did not propose to them, *he who is without sin among you, let him be the first to cast a stone,* nor ask them to turn the other cheek or exhort them to love their enemies. He climbed the steps of the pillory and, without having to scream or lift his hands, or to hurl *Utopia* at them, he grabbed their attention by speaking in the following way:

"Dear friends, I ask you to calm down before you make any decisions, and to try and get more information about this project. Listen to the people who are developing it, consult specialists, discuss the matter in another venue, carefully examining the benefits and possible harmful effects, as you certainly still know very little about this project. And only then, when the light of enlightenment illuminates you, will you be able to choose the solution that best protects your interests and defends the future of your children."

The townsfolk fell silent and looked at one another. Something was moving within them. They felt the vibration and planted their feet firmly on the ground. But the rumbling soon died out, without leaving a single crack. The danger had passed. Recovered from the shock, they began to argue among themselves, to dally about in opinions and make judgments, why yes, why not, it's like this, it's like that, let's do this, let's do that.

A stray dog approached Jesus, sat down at his side, and they both watched the human chaos. While he caressed the animal's fur, he let out what his soul was feeling. "Why don't these people ever understand me?" And the dog gave him his paw.

As soon as he had heard the cry, "This is shameless, Mr. Mayor," Ramsey had ordered the doors to the town hall to be locked and had refused to face the crowd. The bawling increased, dust rose, there was some banging on the door, but they eventually gave up. Unable to speak to the Mayor, the people decided to march to the resort's construction site, where the Almeida brothers' employees were clearing the trees and leveling the ground. The long march of two kilometers lasted no longer than twenty minutes, without Magdalene managing to assume the post of Great Helmsman or of Liberty, guiding the people, with one breast out, or both covered up.

On the contrary, both she and Jesus were behind the crowd, pulled by the human mass. But when Magdalene discovered that the resort was going to be built on *her* paradise, in the waters of which she would not bathe again, she became furious once more.

By this time, Ramsey had already phoned the Almeida brothers — who were at the work site — and Dr. Thomas Alfonso — who was in bed with the Miss Barbara — informing them of the people's revolt and of his suspicion that they were being manipulated by two strangers. The builders prepared themselves for a pitched battle, the businessman prepared himself for psychological warfare.

*

The pitched battle never took place because the employees of the Almeida Brothers' construction company, as soon as they heard the threats from the rabble, dropped their tools, abandoned their machines, and fled — the promise from their bosses to double their wages if they fought the intruders helping little. Manuel and Joaquim, not budging an inch, now faced the insurrectionists, argued, insulted them, and were insulted, but, when they felt the sharp prongs of the forks on their backs and the iron of the scythes over their heads, they eventually left, too. However, as they were leaving, they appealed to Saint Rita of Cascia and to the Infant Jesus of Prague to avenge the strangers that had conspired against them.

Jesus, Magdalene, and the Ukrainian psychiatrist watched the discussion from a distance without knowing for sure what position to take. Before this legion of the possessed, Jesus couldn't resort to pigs; having suffered rural fury, Magdalene feared the implements; after also having received a beating from the police, the psychiatrist was convinced that he had emigrated to a dangerous country.

As for the psychological warfare, it was about to begin because Dr. Thomas Alfonso, leaving Miss Barbara snoring in bed, got up and went to his office. He then began to hatch a plan to convince the people of Vilar de Mochos to accept the Eco Resort. A local election campaign held a few years ago and a scandal circulating on the Internet served as inspiration. In less than half an hour, he had already found a solution for the problem of the hillbillies of Vilar de Mochos, as well as another for the strangers that had led them to mutiny. To calm the former he would have to loosen his purse strings — the account would then be endorsed to Mayor Ramsey; to be free of the latter, all that he needed was for them to send him a photograph of the ringleaders.

*

Three days later, a large truck packed with televisions, battery operated radios, clocks, alarm clocks, lamps, screwdrivers, pliers, plates, cutlery, ashtrays, slippers, bars of soap, washing detergent, shampoo, bath gel, razor blades, nail clippers, toothbrushes, toothpaste, plungers, cotton wool, antiseptic, alcohol, batteries, grease, brooms, mothballs, dolls, phone cards and plastic Christmas trees — everything purchased at the Chinese shop for €800 — was sent by Dr. Thomas Alfonso to Vilar de Mochos. The cornucopia would be delivered to the Town Hall, in the care of Mayor Ramsey.

When he saw the delivery, Mayor Ramsey took fright. He immediately called Dr. Alfonso and was then instructed on how to proceed.

"Ramsey, listen carefully."

"Yes, Doctor Alfonso."

"Put this junk in some boxes and say it came from the resort developer. Give it to the people to shut them up."

"As a proof of goodwill..."

"Exactly, as a proof of goodwill and the desire for good relations."

"Doctor Alfonso, and what criteria should I use to distribute the goods?"

"Make sure every family receives a hamper filled with presents of the same value. Give the televisions to the poorest, give the dolls to those who have children…"

"And then…"

"Firstly, tell them that there had been a misunderstanding about the resort. Few pine trees are going to be felled, and those won't be missed at all. Then, ensure them once again that the project will bring progress and development to the town and that everyone will benefit. Look serious when you're saying all this, swear on your honor, make promises."

"I'm sorry, Doctor Alfonso, but do you think this plan will work?"

"Everyone has their price, and theirs shouldn't be more than this."

"You may well be right."

"Isn't this how politicians win elections?"

"Well, not all of them."

"Got any better ideas?"

"Okay, tomorrow I'll start handing it all out."

"Hang on a sec, I've also sent you a parcel in the post, with posters in it. Just put them up around the town."

"Posters about the resort?"

"Posters *in favor* of the resort."

"Don't worry, Doctor Alfonso, I'll take care of everything."

"Just one more thing. Who is this man and who is this woman who want to put a halt to the resort's construction? Are they your enemies?"

"I've no idea, Doctor Alfonso, no one does. It's as if they just fell from heaven."

Two days later, Mayor Ramsey received a box in which he found copies of the front page of a well-known newspaper, featuring pictures of Jesus and Magdalene. It was dated from a year ago and the headline read *"Drug traffickers escape prison"*. A brief account followed, outlining their criminal activities.

When he had recovered from astonishment, Ramsey surmised that this was a trick by Dr. Thomas Alfonso. Although the scenario was different, urban instead of rural, that was indeed the portrait that he'd asked to be sent to him. A novice when it came to the mysteries of computers, he did not come to the conclusion that the image had just been *Photoshopped*. But how it was managed was of little importance, there was no way he'd let those two strays prevent him from solving his problem. What people wanted was competence and seriousness.

A prudent man, Mayor Ramsey decided to involve the Almeida brothers in the distribution of the hampers and in putting up the posters of Jesus and Magdalene — now transformed into delinquents. As soon as they were told of Dr. Alfonso's plan, Manuel and Joaquim sniffed a great opportunity, in one fell swoop, to solve the problem of the resort and to restore their good reputation. Their prayers to Saint Rita of Cascia and to the Infant Jesus of Prague had been answered once again. Nevertheless, Manuel understood that the divine wrath was weak.

"Yes, indeed, but just in case, we'll send round some guys to break their legs, too."

"No, don't do that. You'll give the town a bad name and harm the resort," warned Ramsey.

"But they want to destroy our livelihood," Manuel insisted.

"I know, but we have to handle them differently," Ramsey said.

"If this were France," Joaquim said, "that's how the matter would be resolved. Two blows on each of them and the deed would be done. They don't mess around there. But okay, whatever Doc Alfonso says, goes."

Like summer Santa Clauses, they would be the ones handing out presents to the people in their sleighs without reindeer, where they usually transported sand and bricks. Without the people of Vilar de Mochos having hung their stockings over the fireplace, Manuel and Joaquim — switching white beards for stubble, red suits for gray trousers and shirts, and sliding down the chimney for knocking on the front door — would fill them with presents. And in the end, they would all eat Christmas cake, roasted chestnuts, and eggnog in the resort. For the Almeida brothers, it was very important that the left hand always knew what the right was doing.

As for putting up the posters with the newspaper photograph of the drug traffickers, Manuel and Joaquim, subverting the Christmas spirit of summer, remembered to turn them into another present. Dr. Alfonso's plan was perfected: tame the people with the trinkets and anger them straight afterwards with the posters.

The result of handing out so many Christmas presents exceeded all expectations. There were apologies and hugs for the Santa Clauses. The men called them *compadre*, the women kissed their hands, and the children asked if there were any mobile phones or tablets. The happy recipients also felt obliged to thank Mayor Ramsey, although Manuel and Joaquim had not associated him with the gifts.

On the following day two neighbors, one armed with a Christmas tree and another with a plunger, got into a brawl because they both claimed the ownership of a hamper found in the street containing two radios and an alarm clock. "It's mine, you bitch,"; "It's mine, you cow." Ending up shattering the presents during the melee, they now demanded justice. The Almeida brothers called their husbands to their office, rebuking them for not being able to control their wives, but ended up giving them two cases of sparkling wine from the expo stalls. And nothing more was said about the incident.

However, despite the happiness and plenty, nobody forgot that two dangerous bandits were in the town and that they had taken advantage of the villagers' good faith. And this was unforgiveable. More than the drug trafficking, or the tavern bill that they would have to pay, what really infuriated them was having been hoodwinked. The party was over. The time for justice had arrived.

To this end, after thanking Ramsey for the presents he hadn't given, the people began to discuss the scandal of the two drug traffickers.

"They never had me fooled."

"I had them sussed from the start."

These were the comments heard the most.

But there were some who ventured other theories.

"They wanted to stop the hotel's construction because that's where they were trafficking drugs."

"There must be drug plantations hidden in the woods."

"And trucks probably come at night to fetch it."

"Planes."

However, when an unfortunate fellow expressed a different opinion, "I've heard that hotels are often built to launder drug money," going against the popular tide of Christmas fraternity, he was given two slaps. With the official truth imposed, the minority who suspected that there was some discrepancy held their tongues and remained as silent as trees.

In the meantime, Jesus and Magdalene returned to the town after their daily visit to the woods to assess the environmental damage caused by the project. They weren't too worried, because efficiency was not the main quality of the Almeida Brothers construction company. Indeed, apart from the thirteen felled pine trees, a burnt thicket, and thirty abandoned stout bottles, everything was just as it had been.

When they came across a repeat performance of the gathering that had led to the resort's embargo, they interpreted it to be the result of progress in negotiations with the council. Maybe they were about to announce that the project was to be shelved. The pressure from the locals had worked, the almost nonviolent resistance had proved victorious, and Vilar de Mochos would remain intact.

"Hey, I think we've managed to avert an ecological disaster," said Magdalene.

"And without having to resort to violence," said Jesus.

"Yes, but we still needed to shake them a little, didn't we?"

Expecting good news, they walked toward the people to share in the common joy without noticing the strange signals the Ukrainian psychiatrist was making at them. Magdalene was holding a daisy that Jesus had given to her.

Close to the mountain, the sun turned red. The mosquitoes awoke. The birds turned in.

Five minutes later the two of them were tied up and placed in an oxcart.

The people of Vilar de Mochos watched them closely, scrutinizing their faces to delve into their soul, like physiognomists from the nineteenth century examining those condemned to deportation. And there they saw, written all over them, all the unmistakeable hallmarks of the worthless: eyes radiating evil, mouths twisted with hatred, the brows of scoundrels and the hands of murderers. There wasn't the slightest doubt that these two lazybones really were drug traffickers.

They then felt really proud of their feat, having risked life and limb in capturing the dangerous foreigners. Nobody could mess with the people of Vilar de Mochos. If there were more people like them in this wretched country, then the rebelliousness would end in an instant.

At this, the police patrol arrived.

Noticing the fuss, the patrol stopped the jeep and demanded an explanation.

"What's all this, then?" an officer asked.

"We're the ones who do the arresting around here," said another.

The people felt as if the authorities had caught them in the act, as if at fault, without actually knowing why. They then tried to justify their actions.

"They're the drug dealers, we've caught them."

In the meantime, the three officers surrounded the oxcart. Two on the left side, one of the right. The crowd moved back to allow the authorities do their work. The sound of boots could be heard crunching in the sand.

"You're under arrest!"

Now they did have the situation under control. It was all over.

"On your way, on your way!"

With the experienced eye of the law, physiognomists of another calibre, it was now their turn to appraise the captives, they too convinced, given the strangers' appearance, that these were suspicious people.

"They've certainly been up to something," said one of the officers.

"And if they haven't done it yet, they were getting ready to do something," added the second officer.

"It's best if we take them to the station," the third decided.

They shoved Jesus and Magdalene into the trunk of the jeep without untying them and put the papers that the people were calling evidence of their guilt into the pockets of their uniforms. Then they set off for the station, sticking to the speed limits imposed by the Highway Code.

On the ground lay a daisy crushed by a boot.

The police station was a yellow painted shack with a green barred door. Once through the entrance, there was a hallway, a waiting room on the right, an office on the left, and a kind of storeroom that held a changing room and bathroom, finally a cell with space for no more than three people. When the neon lights were turned on, the walls took on the frozen hue of snow and the ground took on the dark hues of a steely sky. Inside the station winter had a permanent home.

In the office, the two senior police officers were forced to interrupt their game of dominoes because of this unexpected and inopportune arrest. Lined up on top of misdemeanor proceedings initiated against stallholders selling fake goods, the tiles followed a pattern of broken lines similar to a swastika. The game was locked in a tie.

The elder of the two rose to reprehend his subordinates. "This isn't the time to be arresting anyone."

The younger of the two took steps to return order. "Go on, put them in the cell. And be quick about it!"

Annoyed, saying "this is getting worse every time", and "tell me about it mate", they continued their game. They would question the captors about the offense committed by the detainees and analyze the evidence collected afterwards. At the moment, they had other priorities. There was a €50 bet resting on the outcome.

And the game continued, now arousing the interest of their subordinates, fascinated by the unpredictable decisions of their senior officers: placing this domino with that one when they could very well place it with the other; if it was them playing they might risk another go, or maybe not; dominoes was a complicated game, and not for everyone, for goodness' sake.

Nobody wasted another thought on the prisoners, proponents of a tedious investigative game where there were no rules and the turns were made in the dark. And during this process of capture, incarceration, and oblivion, started by the sanhedrin of Vilar de Mochos and continued by the domino players, Jesus and Magdalene, pawns lost in a cell, didn't protest once. She, from shock, he, out of habit.

In the meantime, the people had arrived at the police station and were demanding justice. Armed with hoes, forks, rakes, and large bottles of red wine, they promised not to budge. Instructed by Manuel and Joaquim, Armando and Armindo hollered the most.

"You should tie them to a pine tree and set them alight!"

"Hang them by their ears!"

His cane in the air, the blind man supported the torture.

The racket broke the players' concentration and forced a new interruption. One of the senior officers sighed with relief because the other had been preparing to end the match; the almost-winner slammed his fist down on the misdemeanor proceedings and set the domino tiles flying; the spectators were devastated.

At last the senior officers analysed the evidence and, after examining the photo, reading the article, and associating them both with the prisoners, they looked at each other and cleared their throats. There was no agreement as to the probative value of the paper.

"It's strange," said one.

"It's very strange," said the other.

In doubt, they followed one of the house rules that said it was better to arrest an innocent person than to set free a guilty one, and another that said you had to ask the chief before you did anything stupid. Following the rules led to a phone call to get instructions about what to do with the prisoners.

Seated on a sofa, before a stool on which he had set up a chessboard, Mr. McCarthy was playing against himself. Neither the gulps from the whisky glass, nor the scent of stew from the kitchen could distract him from commanding his white and black pieces. These were under threat of losing a bishop, but the others could well be forced to move their rook; should he exchange the bishop for a rook or give to the white queen as bait? Chess was even more complicated than dominoes, for goodness' sake.

But when they informed him that a horde had circled the station to bring justice to a couple suspected of drug trafficking, he used a strategy that defeated the blacks and the whites at the same time. With his boots put on, he also kicked the stubborn queen, who had refused to eat the bishop.

Sober, Mr. McCarthy did not tolerate anarchy in any circumstance. Order was the supreme value of existence, without which all the others would be in ruins. All you had to do was look at nature, from the changing seasons to the organization of beehives, to understand that everything was perfectly ordered in the universe. Man alone, this unpredictable creature, disturbed the universal balance by contesting authority. This was the cause of the world's disgrace, with society thrown into chaos. It was therefore a duty to put the rioters back into order, using the only language they understood. In former times, his colleague Judge Roy Bean had known how to set the example.

However, when he saw the swarm in front of the police station, he suspected that facing that mob was going to be harder than having his way with Liliana and Ludmila. This reminded him of the riots of the revolution, with lunatics bawling that all authority was fascist, that power was of the people and suchlike nonsense. Pranks were resolved at the time by arresting the instigators and teaching them a good lesson. However, now the case was more serious. This wasn't about half a dozen communists anymore, but about the entire population of Vilar de Mochos. The barricade had grown and everyone had transformed into the judge of the revolutionary tribunal.

And as he didn't have a battalion armed with tear gas, rubber bullets, and the desire to crack heads, he resigned himself to the idea of having to use different weapons. Persuasion, this tactic of the weak, was unfortunately the only one that might work. As such, while he would have liked to pass through the crowd whipping and kicking, he thought it more sensible to greet the people of Vilar de Mochos and not shove anyone as he entered the station.

"A very good evening to you, ladies and gentlemen, please allow the authority to pass."

On that chessboard, the police station was a king under check, without having enough pieces to defend himself.

Inside, while the subordinates showed him the evidence for Jesus and Magdalene's guilt, without even knowing that they came from the traitor Dr. Alfonso, he screwed them into balls and netted them in the wastepaper basket. His subordinates closely observed the elliptical trajectory of the evidence ball, but weren't convinced of the innocence of the detainees. Their sentimental nature easily fell for guilt. However, the Chief didn't order the immediate release of the prisoners, because if he did so, he would reveal weakness and fear to the populace. Neither did he request backup, as this would show that he was incapable of controlling the situation. So, just as a captain of a ship does not leave as it sinks, a police chief never asks for backup. With the difference that one drowns, while the other learns to swim on his own.

"What do we do, Chief?" one senior officer asked.

"Nothing, you idiots. You've already caused enough trouble," Mr. MacCarthy replied brusquely.

"It wasn't us who arrested them chief, it was them," said the other senior officer pointing at the three petrified officers.

Fifteen minutes later, he went himself to fetch Jesus and Magdalene from their cell. The woman was a stranger, but he felt that he had seen the man somewhere before. He asked them if they had been well treated, but didn't ask them if they were guilty of anything, or if Jesus was some sort of king. Then he asked them to accompany him outside. In the middle of the two, his face gilded by the dusk light, and his hair fluttering in the breeze, he headed towards the people.

"Citizens of Vilar de Mochos, here is the man and the woman. What accusations have you to make to them?"

From within the people someone replied: "Chief, if they weren't wrongdoers, we wouldn't have delivered them to the police."

"But I find no basis for a charge against them."

"They are bad people, they have brought disgrace to our town. Enforce the law, Chief."

"What law are you talking of?"

"We have just one law, and if you release them, you are not our friend."

The Police Chief looked at the people. All of Vilar de Mochos' energy was concentrated in that mob. The spark that would set off the explosion might be a word, or a gesture; and the blast wind would only run out when a tragedy had taken place. Without riot police at his disposal, he decided that the only way to avoid checkmate was to do the will of the people.

"After all, doesn't democracy consist of respecting the will of the masses? In the power of the people, by the people, and for the people?" the Chief brooded, discovering now that not all democratic principles were invented to conspire against authority. At the end of the day, Roy Bean himself ended up dismissed. He therefore felt worthy of his position and satisfied with himself. It was time to go home and have his way with the stew.

Meaning that Mr. McCarthy, without even being asked to release a Barabbas and to put the prisoners on a cross, also washed his hands and handed Jesus and Magdalene over to the people.

And the people let out a cry that could be heard all the way to the *Folies Bergère*. Then they bundled them once again into the oxcart and proceeded to pass beneath the Arch of Triumph, before expelling them from Vilar de Mochos with the threat of breaking their legs if they ever dared return.

*

A year later, the Stream Eco Resort was opened.

Six months later the ceiling collapsed in the dining room, almost killing twenty people.

The Almeida brothers fled to Angola, where they forged a partnership with a member of the government and discovered the real meaning of thinking big, French-style. And faith in Saint Rita of Cascia and in the Infant Jesus of Prague flourished in the tropics.

Dr. Thomas Alfonso was charged with malpractice.

Miss Barbara underwent breast enlargement surgery.

Mayor Ramsey never won another election.

Liliana and Ludmila, with the *Folies Bergère* closed, opened a massage parlour — with Ramsey becoming their best customer, with access to the wild, erotic show.

Mr. McCarthy tried to have the parlor closed, but as he was unable he become a customer, too, although he always paid above board and never managed to have his way with them both at the same time.

The Vilar de Mochos eagles, replacing Armindo with the Ukrainian psychiatrist, became district champions.

3

RACE

"But I say to you which hear, Love your enemies, do good to them which hate you, Bless them that curse you, and pray for them that despitefully use you. And unto he that smiteth thee on the one cheek offer also the other; and him that taketh away thy cloak forbid not to take thy coat also. Give to every man that asketh of thee; and of him that taketh away thy goods ask them not again. And as ye would that men should do to you, do ye also to them likewise." Luke 6: 27-31

Saint Augustine versus Rousseau

Is man born evil or is it society that makes him so? Did Hitler and Stalin, who in all likelihood were born cute, chubby, and rosy-cheeked, and who then went on to become the greatest murderers that humankind has ever produced, come into the world with their evil already preloaded or, on the contrary, were they pure and innocent and was society to blame for turning them into monsters?

Saint Augustine, whose godly condition afforded him information unavailable to ordinary mortals, assured us that children were born with evil already in their bodies; the result of *Original Sin*, which manifests itself through the misuse of free will granted by God.

But Rousseau, whose reflections led to the defense of equality between men, countered that man was born pure and that the social environment corrupted him, causing some to become bad people or proper scoundrels.

There are therefore two theories to explain the phenomenon of evilness and the consequent tendency that certain humans feel: the compulsion to steal, harm, and kill others.

Following the philosopher's line of thought, it's not difficult to see that a child whose family lives from crime is shaped by this bad example, if not forced by those villainous people to become criminal.

But, returning to the saint, how is it that those born to so-called good families, educated at the finest schools and surrounded by good examples, stumble into wrongdoing, commit crimes, and sometimes end up by stealing from their own kinsfolk? It is assumed in these cases that these creatures really were born with evil in their bodies, full of original sin, and that they lost interest, as soon as they were allowed, in the possibility of using divine free will to do good.

Rousseau is now in trouble, but not entirely defeated.

Because if the illuminist did not notice that certain people, to whom society has offered everything, pay back the gift by preying on what belongs to everyone else, just as he was unable to discern that there were thieves and murderers in the most primitive of communities, living in nature untouched by urban vices, good, pure, and cannibalistic; neither did the saint take into consideration the fact that God's grace does not always withstand the torment that devastates the lives of many unfortunates.

It seems likely therefore that the truth does not lie somewhere between the two, but moves restlessly like an atomic particle from one to the other, from free will to the social environment, from the social environment to free will, while never accepting that one part or the other could take hold of it.

But, as surely both Saint Augustine, despite having advocated violence against the heretics, and Rousseau, despite having placed his children in an orphanage, went to heaven, it is highly likely that they have since met up there and are still passionately discussing the nature of evil.

Therefore, as the two were very stubborn, let's hope they don't lose their heads for failing to convince the other of the veracity of their arguments, and start hurling accusations: "You, sir, are a religious fundamentalist", followed by, "And you, sir, are a cruel parent", and end up fighting. Because, just as Saint Augustine is now unable to slap Rousseau, invoking the theory of original sin, Rousseau is unable to excuse pulling Saint Augustine's beard for having been corrupted by their celestial surroundings.

*

A new housing development was created following the expansion of an old council estate designed by an architect, who, because of an *Athens Charter*,[22] believed

---

[22] The Athens Charter is a document from 1933, drafted and signed by great architects and urban designers, including Le Corbusier. The Athens Charter set forth, in social terms, that each individual should have access to fundamental happiness, to wellbeing at home and to beauty of the city.

that architecture could change the world and improve people. It was called the neighborhood of New Europe. Locals were joined by black families and gypsies who lived in shacks. Poor gypsies, blacks, and whites thus began to live in a new suburb of Athenian inspiration. Or in other words, *metics*. The three races lived peacefully together for years, until one day a war began — though not similar to the Peloponnesian War.

*

According to the gypsy community, it was the blacks who started the riots.

A gang of adolescents, who liked to harass gypsy women and to scrawl graffiti insulting the virility of the men, entered the gypsy café and, after refusing to pay for their drinks, smashed up the furniture and stole the takings from the till. Knowing that calling the police would only cause more problems, the gypsy community was forced to solve the problem on its own, to dispense their own justice. A meeting was held in the patriarch's house and it was decided to retaliate that very day, "because with us it's an eye for an eye, a tooth for a tooth, and no one laughs at the gypsies for long." They then went after the assailants. And it wasn't hard to find them, as they were celebrating the raid in one of their houses, in euphoric fashion. The gypsies weren't the first to shoot, however, because bullets began to fly as soon as they rounded the corner of the road in which the gang was lurking. From that night on, the blacks started to attack any gypsy; even women and children weren't spared.

Questioned on what had happened, Dona Eufrásia, a gypsy in her sixties, who sold designer clothes at the market, said the following: "Of course they're the ones that started it. Who else could it have been? These blacks are bad blood! They leave their children on the street and the girls will do it with anyone. They sell drugs and rob people. I've never seen one do a day's work. Do you know what they want? They want to kick us out of here and take our houses. They should stick them all in a boat and send them back to where they came from."

According to the black community, the whole thing happened differently.

No robbery took place at the café, and no one caused any damage to the premises. It was a Saturday evening and the boys had decided to have a beer and chose this place by chance. They entered in an orderly manner and politely asked to be served. But the café owner replied, "We don't serve blacks here, each to his own." At that very moment, the gypsies got up from their tables and started to shove them outside the establishment. Still not happy, outside they set about pummelling them with punches and kicking them. In the end they chased them away, forcing them to take refuge in a house nearby. It was then that some of the gypsies pulled out their pistols and began firing at the windows before others arrived with shotguns, adding to the fusillade. The young men's reaction was defensive; if they hadn't fought back they would have met their maker, as the gypsies were preparing a raid on the house.

A witness to the event, Lourenço Marques, godfather of one of the victims and retired builder, got his feelings off his chest. "Everyone knows it was the gypsies who attacked us. We are a serious people around here, we don't want trouble with anyone. But, with the gypsies it's impossible, man! They think that this place is theirs, they don't respect anyone, they threaten you and pull out their weapons for the slightest thing. Robbery and drugs are their main source of income. Have you ever seen them working or picking up rubbish? Of course not. These problems will only come to an end when they are all thrown into prison."

For her part, another resident, Dona Lurdes, housemaid and white — but whose dark complexion and curly hair seemed to want to deny her Caucasian status — also gave her opinion of the facts. "Whose fault is it? It's both their faults. It was peaceful here before all these blacks and gypsies got here. Everyone knew and helped each other, the neighbors were like a family. If you needed a bay leaf you just knocked on your neighbor's door; people looked after other people's children. But after they arrived our neighborhood became hell, what with stealing, drugs, fighting, shooting. You can't sleep at night for all the racket. It's scary around here. It's enough to make you sick with worry. And the police don't lift a finger. If it was up to me, I'd send them all back to where they came from."

*

From then on, the neighborhood of New Europe became a war zone from which the police knew to keep their distance, held to the north by the gypsies and to the south by the blacks. Getting rid of the rival ethnic group was the goal. There was sporadic shooting, started by one side or the other. Lacking in strength, neither side dared to invade enemy territory, so there was almost a truce.

Like two armies facing each other, without attacking, contained by commanders experienced in the art of war, blacks and gypsies waited for the right moment to advance. Until that moment they maintained their position, watching the enemy's movements from a distance. Their castles were their homes, from which they tossed Molotov cocktails, strongholds against the collision of cars transformed into battering rams.

On the gypsy side the commander was an old guy called Honório. Sporting a white beard and always dressed in black, he was highly respected by the entire community. His long experience of life led him to make sensible decisions, such as only firing on the blacks from the top floors of buildings with the lights off.

On the side of the blacks, the chief was a young man nicknamed Pelé. Sporting close-shaven hair and always dressed in a tracksuit, he was highly respected by almost the entire community. His short experience of life led him to make sensible decisions, such as wearing gloves when grabbing a gun to shoot some gypsy.

If Honório and Pelé were to be asked just why the two ethnic groups were at war, they would reply, much like the residents who have already spoken, that the reason lay in the impossibility of living together in the racism of blacks and in the racism of the gypsies. Any act of aggression against one of their members implied an act of aggression toward the whole community. Not seeking revenge would be considered a sign of weakness, the result of which would be the contempt of others and the derision of their own people.

For this reason, even those who tried to avoid resorting to weapons when the fury spread through their community ended up grabbing pistols and joining in the shooting; they found themselves isolated and understood that in times of war you were either with your people or against them. Some of them proved so committed that it seemed it was their idea to shoot their rivals dead. This radical change of attitude took place in women in particular, as once they realized that reconciliation was impossible, they became warriors of greater courage than their male counterparts.

*

When the unrest in New Europe was caught on camera and then set loose on television, not only the whole country — which lamented the poor aim of those involved — but also Jesus and Magdalene saw these images, too.

For Magdalene, so disappointed with the eco battles and the mentality of country folk that she couldn't even stand talk of soy milk, this was another opportunity to contribute to a better world, the construction of *Utopia*. She would do this by defending society's outsiders — other victims of this same capitalist system, which, in addition to modifying corn and building resorts where you shouldn't, was creating the social and urban conditions that led to the fratricidal struggle between blacks and gypsies. She then recalled another passage from the book, which could easily be applied to the current leaders that had created these ghettos:

"For one man to abound in wealth and pleasure, when all about him are mourning and groaning, is to be a gaoler [jailer] and not a king."[23]

And surely in that concrete jungle, mothers weren't flogging their children in the street, and kids weren't torturing frogs or pointing catapults at people. Nor was there wine in baby bottles.

Jesus, for his part, although he didn't have much faith in being able to pacify the two warring communities, understood that the presence of them both would not make the conflict any worse. Maybe the attempt to bring peace to the men at war would result in something as obliterated as a bombed house. Even so, he had never stopped believing that among the ruins something can always be found that has escaped destruction, or that from the rubble you can construct a new building once again.

Both in agreement, they decided they would try to enter the neighborhood of New Europe.

*

---

[23] *Utopia*, p. 26.

Life was going on almost normally in each of the zones, provided that nobody dared cross the line demarcating their territory. Nevertheless, just as the Red Cross is allowed to move about during a war, there was one person who was authorized to move with complete freedom, welcomed by the gypsies, carried on the shoulders of the blacks, and there were even moments of ceasefire when rumor had it he was out in the streets. One time, on one of the occasions in which rivals came across each other outside the neighborhood and the immediate provocations deteriorated into violence, when a black man and a gypsy were already dancing the first steps that precede the mortal embrace of a stabbing, a yell from that voice was enough to bring an end to the choreography, for the knives to return to pockets, and for each of them to go on his way.

An honest fellow, he had never taken advantage of this privilege for any personal gain that wasn't related to his profession, such as, for example, reselling the cornmeal cake baked by Lourenço Marques' wife to the gypsies at an inflated price, or smuggling Dona Eufrásia's clothes into the black zone, also at a scandalous profit.

We are, of course, talking of Professor Kacimba, who did unto others as he would have done unto him.

African healer, master of Voodoo, expert in cowry-shell divination, in tarot readings, in palmistry, while also endowed with powers of telepathy, clairvoyance, and dowsing — he has not however mastered Chinese astrology. And for this very reason, he is able to solve problems concerning health, love, impotence, work, money, and to undo the work of other healers, such as the evil eye, curses, enchantments, and other evil witchcraft. In high demand, in addition to consulting in his surgery, he also went to people's homes and offered a remote service. And as he never failed, Professor Kacimba not only stopped being poor, but also gained the respect, and the fear, of everyone living in the neighborhood of New Europe. In addition to having put on twenty-five pounds.

Thirty-five years previously, when known as Raimundo dos Santos, Professor Kacimba fled his country, just as the civil war had begun. Like many of his compatriots, he had been welcomed by relatives living in shacks in the suburbs of Lisbon and he had started to work in the building trade as an apprentice bricklayer. This was his profession for twenty years. Moving from site to site, perching on scaffolding, he contributed to the construction of the buildings, bridges, and viaducts that made the city grow and he was never short of work. With no other qualifications, without the means to set up a business, and with no chance of returning to his country, Raimundo resigned himself to being a bricklayer for the rest of his life. The mortar holding the bricks together also held him to the building trade. But he didn't fear the economic crisis or any competition from new immigrants because he had built up a reputation as a competent worker and honest person. He never missed a day of work, and never turned up drunk or got into a fight.

One day, after his club had been thrashed once again by its rival from the north, he bought a sports paper and came across a page full of ads from clairvoyants, sorcerers, astrologers, tarot readers, fortune-tellers, folk healers, warlocks, and wizards. He had seen these ads before, but never so many of them. He was amazed that such people could guarantee to solve every problem known to man, and yet more amazed that there were, from all appearances, so many people willing to put their faith and money in them. Just like the girls in sex line ads, people working with the occult had the wind in their sails — never before had flesh and spirit been so valued. Strange things were afoot in this country, and not just in public works or in banks.

Unable to get the idea out his head, he spent weeks ruminating on it. Society was building an urbanization with unknown materials, under the command of improbable master builders, and neither the quality nor the height of the buildings were subject to restrictions or inspections; the sky was the limit.

Chatting with his friends, he found out what he needed to know. Raimundo's biggest surprise didn't come from them telling him that their wives were using these professionals — while omitting that they themselves went there, too. This he already suspected. Rather it came from hearing the prices charged for each consultation.

"I don't believe in these sorcerers; my wife goes there from time to time though."

"Me neither, but I have heard that they do actually solve some problems."

"Yes, they do. One guy I know was diagnosed terminally ill by doctors, but now he's as right as rain."

"So, what do they do, actually? How do they cure people?" Raimundo asked

"Well, they have powers, they do magic, that sort of thing…"

"You're not supposed to ask them, they don't like that."

"No, it's secret."

"And how much do these consultations cost?" Raimundo asked.

"It depends."

"Thirty euros."

"Fifty."

"There's one that takes a hundred."

As soon as he heard these figures Raimundo's practical mind understood that there were people who, without being doctors, engineers, or footballers, were earning more money in a day than he did in a month, without having to risk their lives on scaffolding or lugging bricks about.

So, tired of so much hard work and little money, made even less by a hernia he had developed on the job, and with the rest of his body just as pummelled by the grindstone of the building trade, Raimundo dos Santos decided that is was time for a change of life. And so the bricklayer Raimundo, without recourse for magic arts or artifice, transformed himself into Professor Kacimba.

He recalled having been present at ceremonies at which the tribe's healer, to the sound of chanting and drumming, put on a mask and thus was transformed into a *muzhik* possessed by a spirit that endowed him with supernatural powers. He then began a frenetic dance and spoke in tongues. During this trance state, he would banish evil spirits, pass judgment, heal the sick, make women fertile, and force the clouds to burst with rain. And when none of this worked, it was because even more powerful spirits had interceded.

This was the model Raimindo chose for his metamorphosis into Professor Kacimba, adjusting it to the society in which he now lived. The *muzhik's* mask was not necessary, and neither were the fetishes studded with nails. But he had to arm himself with other props, because no great professor can turn up empty-handed.

He began by buying some outfits and a red cap from a fancy dress shop, necklaces, and bracelets from street sellers and statues of saints from a saint statue shop. Then he bought some books about the occult, an astrological map, a stuffed owl, and made use of a fish bowl that, when turned upside down, was transformed into a crystal ball. And unable to find mandrake root at the market, he decided that cassava root would have the same effect.

The friends who visited him were intrigued by the accumulation of strange objects.

"What do ya'll want those for?"

"Are you going to sell these knickknacks at the fair?"

"This lot'll get you plenty of crates of beer."

Raimundo felt that they weren't ready yet for him to reveal his change of life. And for the time being he didn't have the magic to stop them from bursting out in laughter. The forces of the occult were ruthless with anyone who was exposed to ridicule.

"Decoration, merely decoration," he said.

He began to practice consultations with imaginary patients. The secret was to console people. The most wretched of people that came to see him would have to leave the surgery full of hope. A little theatrics, a touch of pantomime, and the promise of happiness. Priests did the same, and some doctors, too. When he had received what he was actually looking for — some attention and a little comfort — the wretched soul would pay any price.

So he perfected a formula he believed would work, with varying degrees of modification, for every case and for every future customer. And the final result was the following: he would start by saying, "I can see from your face that you have great problems..." then he would pause, during which time he would place both his hands on his temples and close his eyes for a few seconds, before finishing with "but I have a solution for your case".

Seeing as health and *Masterchef* were in fashion, Kacimba also decided to make some dietary recommendations to his patients. Having seen a scientist on the news explaining the benefits of red wine, revealing remedies called *resveratrol* and *flavonoids*, he would recommend a glass at dinner time. As to health-giving foods, to avoid cancer and encourage bowel movements, he chose broccoli. So that when the consultation came to an end he would recommend they "drink red wine and eat some broccoli salad". They could certainly not do anyone harm.

Finally, he went in search of a place in which to carry out his new profession, which should have two conditions: cheap rent and nobody knowing him in the neighborhood. After looking all over the place and being refused because of the color of his skin, he ended up having to settle for a small apartment in the neighborhood of New Europe, which also contained an African hair salon. There was little magic in these premises, the supernatural powers would certainly feel timid, but for the start of his career it would have to do.

However, when negotiating his rent, Raimundo felt discriminated against once again. Not for racial issues, but due to a clash of cultures. The owner feared that the reliability of the tenant was as volatile as ectoplasm.

"So you're going to open an astrology office?"

"A center for the study of occult sciences, to be more precise."

"Fine, you can start by paying four months' up front."

"Four months? But that's illegal!"

"My dear friend, it's we who make the laws around here. Take it or leave it."

In his surgery, where the hair dryers blew like trumpets from the great beyond, he decorated the walls with the astrological map, some black and white pictures of some unknown people that he had found in an antique shop, and a color poster of Dolly the sheep. And the effect of this syncretic décor was such that some of his patients took the people — one the foreman of a coffee plantation in Guinea, the others his employees — to be great sorcerers of the past, and Dolly the sheep for the goat that symbolizes the devil. Even so, a devout patient advised him to put a prayer card of Saint Rita of Cascia on the door.

"With the saint on your side, Professor, you'll be able to cure everything."

But how did Professor Kacimba, born in Africa, much more black than white, a great fan of *Kizomba* and *Kuduro* music, goat and chilli *moamba*, gain the trust and respect of the gypsies?

He achieved this with proven results, by clearly demonstrating his powers in solving problems where doctors and his professional colleagues, science and magic (other "healers") had failed. Miracles impress the most sceptical of people, whatever their ethnic background. In addition to this, Professor Kacimba would accept payment only after the problem had been solved, leaving it up to the patients to decide how much they would pay.

One night, one of the forty grandchildren of the patriarch Honório fell ill, the victim of an unknown ailment that left her bedridden with a terrible fever.

The doctors were unable to cure her and said that it was a virus, but the medicine didn't return her to health. The woman that read palms paled when deciphering her fate line. An amateur sorcerer was chased off. A Brazilian magician, who wanted to be paid in dollars, ended up being beaten. Nothing seemed to help. Desperate, the gypsies didn't hesitate in calling Professor Kacimba.

"Oh, my daughter is dying," the mother of the child told him in tears.

"Save her, save her!" implored other women.

"How old is she?" Kacimba asked, not used to child cases.

"Thirteen."

"Thirteen? I'll see what I can do," said Kacimba, not that certain of his craft.

As soon as he entered the girl's room, he told everyone to leave — there were ten people there mourning her; he smoked the space, smoked the child, uttered prayers in tongues, performed *muzhik* dance steps, let out three yells to frighten off evil spirits and, finally, already perspiring greatly, examined Honório's granddaughter by placing his hands on her burning forehead. Terrified, the girl let out cries and lashed out. Unperturbed, Kacimba continued his examination. After her forehead, he took her pulse and finally opened an eyelid. "Aaah!" he then exclaimed. There wasn't the slightest doubt, the young thing had been the victim of the evil eye.

He called the family back to the room, presented his diagnosis, and explained the method of treatment. "You need to cut the neck of a black cockerel, right here."

"Professor, we've only got brown and white hens at the moment," said the grandmother.

"No problem. Bring two fat ones."

"And then, Professor?" asked the mother.

"Then you need to mix the blood with bristles from Honório's beard, as the work of magic was done to reach him indirectly."

"I knew it, the girl never did anyone harm," said an aunt.

"And I did?" said Honório, enraged.

"If you didn't, you were going to," replied the grandmother (his mother-in-law).

"Listen up. Then you add some powdered cassava root, mix with a hand blender for two minutes, leave it to rest, don't rush it or you'll ruin everything, and in the end, cover the patient's body with it."

"And that's it, Professor?" the mother dared to ask.

"And if the girl took some paracetamol along with her medicine, Professor?" the aunt suggested.

"Don't even think about it. It would immediately stop it working," Kacimba replied peremptorily.

Even though Honório had been hesitant as to believing in the effectiveness of the cure and had thinned his silver beard reluctantly, what is certain is that on the following day the fever began to fall, the girl's appetite returned, and she managed to get out of bed. Two days later she was fit as a fiddle once again, helping her parents at the fair: "Get it here, get it here". Her illness left no aftereffects, unless you count hiding whenever she saw the healer, or developing a great dislike for broccoli.

From that day on Kacimba definitively established the reputation of a great professor, and celebrated the feat on the following night with spicy grilled chicken for his friends.

*

Apart from Professor Kacimba, there seemed to be no chance of agreement between the gypsies and the blacks; the animosity had not lessened. Ridden by the horsemen of hatred, their instincts had conquered the badly defended territory of reason. However, they hadn't been able to take on one particular fort, one that proved impregnable. There inside, Romi and Julian were safe from the violence of New Europe.

Abandoned by his mother at the age of fifteen, and never having known his father, Julian, now sixteen, he had been welcomed by his aunt and uncle who lived in the neighborhood of New Europe and began living in the same house as his cousin Pelé.

At that time, weeks before the conflict between the two communities began, when children played together on wrecked swings and played ball in the middle of the potholed road, when black and gypsy teenagers would gather at *Hip-Hop* festivals and the adults almost always got drunk in the same bars, Julian quickly made new friends, irrespective of ethnic background. He did use, however, another kind of segregation, making use of a different system meant to separate the races: he avoided the company of those who boasted about shoplifting or committing violent assaults on passersby.

When their only attempt at initiating him in their art failed, they would then leave him in peace.

"Come with us. Sneakers, good clothes, mobile phones, whatever you want…"

"It's not my thing," he responded.

"Okay, go and work on building sites, you jerk, and see if cement is your thing."

*

It was at one of these *Hip-Hop* concerts in the summer holidays that Julian, to the thundering chorus "police kill us, yoh, police kill us, yoh" of rapper *Kid Tuga*, that he discovered Romi in the middle of the dancing throng. The gypsy girl Romi, sixteen years old, and the eldest granddaughter of Honório.

Maybe because she preferred *Flamenco* rhythms to *Hip-Hop* beats, songs sung in Spanish, the "*aiiii, aiiii, aiiii*" to the "yoh", Romi was not enjoying the concert, and instead was scanning the room. After passing her gaze over the heads of the audience several times, staring momentarily at some of the faces but not dwelling on any of them, she finally noticed that a black boy was watching her. Romi enjoyed knowing she was being looked at. Julian thought that looking was something very easy.

He was mistaken.

Then started that game similar to the children's one, where you try to surprise your friend with an imaginary shot, with the difference that the goal here was to shoot glances without being seen, or to catch your opponent in the act of looking at you, the high point of the game, ensuring victory to the astute observer. After half an hour of shooting quick glances, sloppy dodges, and ridiculous disguises, Romi, more experienced in the warring arts of seduction, ended up surprising Julian, who was gazing wide-eyed at her. She stared fixedly back at him, forcing him to lower his face, put his hands in his pockets, and pretend he was dancing. With her shot right on target, she had won the first battle. And he had gone home with a wounded heart.

On the following day, Julian entered into careful investigations to find out the girl's identity. He had been unable to find out who she was from his black friends, and was thus forced to question his gypsy friends.

But, as necessity is the mother of invention and inventiveness soon outweighs cowardice, Julian went up to two gypsy boys. Questioning gypsy guys about the girls in their community didn't usually work out well, either in terms of information, or in terms of the physical integrity of the person asking. However, as they wanted information, too, it was possible to start negotiating.

"I'd like to ask you something..." Julian began.

"Fire away."

"Who was that girl with you at the concert?"

"And what do you want to know for?"

"No reason, just curious."

"Go and be curious somewhere else."

"Get out of here!"

"If you tell me, I'll get you the mobile numbers of my cousins that you like," Julian said.

"Those two hot mulattos?"

"They're the ones."

"Tell us what she looks like."

"She's tall, with long hair, and she was wearing a red blouse."

"Give us the numbers."

"Nine two, seven seven..."

"It's Romi, Honório's granddaughter."

If on the one hand Julian was thrilled, on the other, at discovering the lineage of his muse, he understood that there was a problem.

As for Romi it was all a lot easier and less risky as the female system of information, whatever the ethnic group, has more advance methods, with more efficient agents and a permanently updated database. As such, all it took was to ask some friends during the concert who was the boy staring at her to know that it was Julian, cousin of the awful Pelé. Such kinship didn't frighten her. A teenage girl who falls for a cute guy fears nothing, except putting on two hundred grams or discovering a spot on her face.

As the first, short step had been made, the problem now was to make the second one, a little longer, without breaking their legs. The rules of engagement between sexes prevented Romi from taking the initiative of introducing herself to Julian, while the ineptitude of Julian hampered his courage to approach Romi. The solution was therefore, and once again, the use of third parties. However, just as she couldn't get any of her friends to introduce him to her, he wouldn't dare ask the same thing of his gypsy friends. And so Julian, whenever he saw Romi, began to feel great joy, which was then transformed, by the chemical reactions of passion, into great suffering. When Romi saw Julian, she smiled and began to sway her hips, more given to the physical than to the chemical. But the weeks passed and the deadlock continued.

The teenage boy, who at school notched up girlfriends to win bets with friends, and who even tried his luck with a trainee teacher, discovered that relations with the opposite sex are based on the paradox of the intensity of affection being inversely proportional to the ability of taking the initiative. In other words, translating this logarithm of emotions, the more he liked her the less he felt able to tell her. He didn't imagine covering her with petals, kissing the ground she walked on, or facing dragons to save her — reveries that can also occur to a *Hip-Hop* fan. The dream of going out with her was enough. He just didn't know how.

Little by little, Julian began to lose his grip on reality.

"Why aren't you eating?" his aunt would ask him at mealtimes.

"I'm not hungry," he would mumble.

"Come on, we're going out," his friends who appeared at his house would insist.

"I don't feel like it," he would tell them, showing them the door.

"I'm a coward," he would admit to himself.

In the solitude of his darkened room, he tried to dedicate a sonnet to her, but the first verse came out sounding so silly that he immediately ripped up the sheet. Then he tried to sketch her face and ended up with something that looked more like one of the characters out of *South Park* — and he ripped up that sheet, too.

He then decided to predict the future, by resorting to astrology. His searches online gave him plenty of information, though not coinciding with his sign. An astrologer said that the next week would be good for undertaking projects and making dreams come true, if he was committed and he persevered. Another predicted the arrival of difficulties and unexpected problems that would scupper the fulfilment of those projects and the realization of those dreams, no matter how much commitment he placed in his actions. And a third gave a mix of the two previous predictions, saying he would achieve some success, but on the other hand suffer setbacks, too. Julian thus understood that the stars weren't going to help him. He therefore didn't get around to opening the Chinese horoscope page and as a result didn't find out that, although he belongs to the sign of charm, of intelligence and people who get along easily with others, as well as being very careful when it comes to money,[24] the current year would be very extremely unfavorable for him.

It was at this time that he discovered he could die.

Until then, death was something that didn't exist or at least was a problem other people had to deal with. Every now and then an old person would die, he would hear news on the television of some famous or unknown person dying, but he had never thought the same thing would happen to him. For him, nothing was deader that death itself. But now, as if his grave had opened under his feet, he became aware that he could lose his life at any moment. These weren't eschatological concerns that worried him, they weren't concerns about knowing whether he would enjoy celestial pleasures to the sound of angels singing, or suffer the torment of hell prodded by the pitchforks of demons. Possibilities of reward or punishment were the last things on his mind, as nothing had the slightest importance before the threat, in this world where love is covered in kisses, of never seeing his dear Romi again.

At the same time, he stopped recognizing his body: he thought he was too thin, with skinny legs

---

[24] Characteristics of people born in the year of the rat.

disproportionate to his torso, his arms lacking in muscles, his hands feminine, his ears wonky and his neck covered in veins. And as to his face, his discovery was even more sinister: he was frighteningly ugly. He couldn't put his finger on the reason if someone were to ask him, unable to place the blame on any particular feature, on the color of his eyes, on the shape of his teeth, on the shaven hair, or on the combination of all these features. He didn't need such explanations to prove the disgusting image that the mirror had begun to show him.

The worse thing, however, was when he discovered that he was unable to remember what her face looked like. The delectable moments of projecting his loved one's face, making it appear whenever he wanted and taking it with him wherever he went, this amazing enjoyment of having her within him and being able to contemplate her whenever he wanted was suddenly interrupted by a cruel loss of memory. Bringing her face to mind degenerated into the appearance of dozens of different faces, each with a vague resemblance to a given characteristic — her hair or her mouth — but each different from the rest. And the more he tried to get her back, pulling her from any point on which he could lay his hand, the more he deformed the outline, ending up envisioning another stranger. Thus Romi evaded him in his mind, too, her image proving as fleeting as her body.

This was all killing Julian. Fighting against himself, with one leg wanting to move in one direction and the other walking in the opposite, he ended up tearing himself in two.

Concerned, his aunt tried to discuss her nephew's problem with her husband.

"Listen, he's so thin, has dark rings under his eyes, he never talks, maybe he's depressed."

"It's all the jerking off he does."

His uncle passed judgment without even lifting his eyes from the newspaper he was reading.

This was therefore another case that only Professor Kacimba could solve.

Following a sleepless night, Julian, joining the gathering of sufferers from the neighborhood and of patients from further afield, entered his surgery, sat down, and waited his turn — entertained by the show of styling difficult hair taking place in the same waiting room. To his surprise there were more whites than blacks and gypsies waiting to see the Professor. And even a man of Chinese extraction was there, sitting discreetly in a corner in socks and flip-flops. Julian counted ten people, old and young, men and women. All different and seemingly strangers, they were united by a common feeling: distress. The rough hand of suffering pinched each of their faces, deforming them; the pressure was exerted with greater intensity on their mouths, but the sum total of this pinching was concentrated in their eyes. As such, none of them said a word, or had the strength to look up.

Seeing so much pain, so much despair, Julian started to reflect that maybe his problem wasn't that bad after all. In truth, he wasn't suffering from some incurable disease, he wasn't in need of cash as he had never had any. He had two legs, two arms, and two eyes in his head, a voracious appetite (until a week ago, at least) and plenty of friends. Looking at these people afflicted by unknown ordeals, carrying crosses that would certainly crush him, crucified by lives that he would never have to live, he came to realize that his problem was nowhere near as bad as he had thought.

Just being in Professor Kacimba's waiting room was proving beneficial for Julian. The flames of his humble hell didn't go out, but their ardor became easier to deal with. A fan spinning on the ceiling must have helped, too.

"What are you doing here, my child?" an old woman with an eye patch asked him.

It was then that Julian almost felt ashamed to be there. Sharing that space with those people, he felt embarrassed by his presence. An imposter in a sanctuary for the wretched. Uncomfortable, he thought about leaving. But the brute force of desire violently drove out any such idea.

*

On that day Professor Kacimba was very tired. He had already seen nineteen patients and solved some complex cases. A cheated wife had managed to get her husband to leave his lover, the lover of a married woman had been saved from being shot by the betrayed husband, a bankrupt tradesman would soon see his creditors excuse his debts, a failed football coach would go on to lead the championship, a widow had spoken with her dead husband, a bald man had felt some hairs growing on the nape of his neck even before using the cassava lotion, and only a gentlemen looking for the magic formula to seduce the ladies wasn't entirely satisfied with the advice given, to start by shaving off his moustache.

In brief, a day like any other in Professor Kacimba's consulting rooms. The paranormal routine.

When it was Julian's turn, as this was a teenager, Professor Kacimba thought that he was dealing with someone tormented by the usual problems that the rare patients of this age told him of: fights with their parents, a pregnant girlfriend, the police after them. He was astonished then when Julian only asked him for help in meeting Romi. He hadn't hit his mother or his teacher, he wasn't going to be a father, he didn't want to be rich. He was just in love. He was sorry therefore for having said, "I can see in your face that you are going through great problems...but I have a solution for your case", and the ideas hadn't crossed his mind to summon positive energies, chant prayers in tongues, do his little dance steps, throw cowry shells onto the table, play patience with cards, or scrub Julian with magical cassava oils — but wine and broccoli wouldn't do him any harm. Before what he had just heard, Professor Kacimba, at that moment, became Raimundo dos Santos again.

And so Raimundo, as if he were the boy's father, listened intently to Julian's story and offered him a tissue when the first tear appeared. Then, aware of the boy's tragic tale, he told him stories of his own love affairs and amorous misadventures, showing him that he had been through the same thing. As he couldn't give him the fish, he tried to teach him how to catch one.

"It's not in my hands to make her like you, but rather in yours. Only you have this power and nobody else. Go and see her and tell her that you want to get to know her. It's easier than you would think. And the magic will happen."

"And then? What do I say to her?"

"Well, boy, you say the same things you've already said to other girls, just with more tenderness."

"But it doesn't work with all of them. Some of them run off, others start laughing."

"It'll work with this one. That I can guarantee you."

Nevertheless, for a moment Professor Kacimba reappeared, when Raimundo advised Julian to prepare at home how he would approach Romi. A little theater, some pantomime, and the confession of love. He just didn't recall, having treated so many patients, that a few years back he had also saved the muse of his new friend from a terrible illness — he remembered the grilled chickens, but not the sick child. It was certainly already written in the stars that the fate of the two lovers would have to pass through Kacimba's hands, or that the Professor's would intercept it.

Advised by his friend Raimundo and by Professor Kacimba, as soon as he got home Julian rehearsed ways of seducing Romi, forcing himself to cut down on the poetry. "Hey, how's it going, I'd like to get to know you." "Hi, all right, I'm Julian and I'd like to get to know you." "Hello, you into *Hip-Hop*? I'd like to get to know you." Then he created imaginary dialogues on a series of themes: computer games, music, TV shows. And finally he dared to risk a kiss on his pillowcase — cotton lips and body turned into flesh. For people in love, a pillow can become the most important thing in their lives, a value they do not give to hot water bottles. He didn't have any lustful thoughts (not thrust onto the pillow), tenderness surprising them with open arms. Because the love that awakens in teenage hearts tastes the apple but does not commit the sin.

That night he dreamed of her and when he woke he hadn't the slightest doubt that he would seduce her in five minutes. *Yoh*. He had a shower, put on some cologne, dressed in his best clothes, and went out to look for her. Full of beans. Now he could see her face again, playing with the image effortlessly. Giving once again into poetry he daydreamed that getting to know Romi would be as natural as breathing, as natural as the blue sky and the pale moon. It wouldn't take long for the love affair to begin.

But the poet Julian forgot, as often happens to anyone floating in the clouds and leaping over the moon, to return to Earth. Where would he find Romi? And he became aware only that he hadn't taken into account the possibility of her not being in New Europe after he had made three trips around the neighborhood, going in and out of cafés, studying the face of every gypsy girl he saw go by, and finally being questioned by the kiosk owner.

"Hey, are you looking for someone?"

It wasn't the question that struck him down, but the abrupt answer he gave to himself. "She's left; I'll never see her again." With the same certainty that he had had of finding her just an hour previously, now he had no doubt that she didn't live there anymore. Like betrayed lovers, who go from the lyrical confession, "you are the love of my life" to the zoological sentence, "you are a fat cow" (or a fat pig), Julian was unable to produce any other logical conclusion other than extremes. The more unlikely, the more credible.

Heartbroken, he stopped in the middle of the road, forcing passing cars to honk so as not to send him skyward once again. The noise brought some residents to their windows, more women than men. Romi was one of them. He didn't see her, but she felt a shiver. "What's he doing there?" She quickly understood why. So she went to the mirror to fix herself up, let her hair down, spray perfume on her neck, neckline, and wrists, and put on her high heels. She then went to meet him.

In the meantime, a cloud let loose some drizzle.

When he saw her crossing the road and coming like an arrow right at him, the target, Julian forgot Raimundo's advice and couldn't remember any of the words he was going to say to her. Instead he had to suppress the urge to run away, and the desire to hide behind the rubbish container.

"You're looking for me, aren't you?" Romi asked him after trapping him against a wall.

Julian, caught with his heart in the rain, still tried to make excuses. "Me? I was just going for a walk."

But Romi didn't let him shake his feelings to the ground. "I know full well that you like me."

Unmasked, Julian made his first confession. "You're pretty."

Satisfied, Romi grabbed him by the hand and took him to the courtyard of a building away from her house.

In the sky, ardent rams pulled off the wool with which ecstasy is woven.

*

The start of the war between the blacks and gypsies separated them. Romi was prevented from leaving her territory; Julian was unable to enter hers. She was given a warning from her father. "Talk to that black kid again and you'll get the strap."

He was given some advice by his cousin Pelé. "Forget the gypsy girl, man."

They kept in touch, in secret, through their mobiles, chat sites, and emails — in a writing system that shrugged off any rules governing syntax and semantics — but, since then, they hadn't met up. For the time being the vigilance of Romi's brothers and cousins, opponents of racial interbreeding and critics of female emancipation, nixed any plans they had to meet up outside the New Europe neighborhood.

Even so, between promises of love and sighs, Julian proposed ways of meeting up. One day, in the middle of the afternoon, Romi's phone rang.

"It's me, can you talk?"

"Make it quick."

"I've had an idea."

"What is it?"

"We'll run away."

"Where to?"

"We can go wherever we like."

"Stop being an idiot, I've got to hang up."

At midnight, Julian came up with new plans.

"It's me again."

"Quick."

"What if we buy some bulletproof vests?"

"Don't be dumb."

"What if we disguise ourselves?"

"As idiots?"

Frustrated, Julian once again sought refuge in his bedroom and tried once again to compose poems and to draw Romi, this time her whole body — exaggerating the size of her chest a little. He thus ended up once again filling the bin with crumpled up pieces of paper. And when he tried to get help from Professor Kacimba, Raimundo, very seriously and in a tone of voice that seemed more like an order, advised him to have patience and to keep quiet if he wanted to stay alive.

Now, not even the Infant Jesus of Prague, nor Saint Rita of Cascia were of any use to Romi and Julian.

*

Jesus and Magdalene then arrived in the neighborhood of New Europe.

Even though the color of their skin should have enabled them to move about in the black zone and in the gypsy zone, the intrusion of strangers in the neighborhood wasn't usually well received. They would need to come up with a good reason to ensure they were accepted by the residents, and to be granted the right to pass through the outlawed territory; permission for an entry visa. And the people in charge of granting visas, the maximum authorities of local power, were Honório and Pelé. Nevertheless, permission was dependent on meeting bureaucratic norms, which varied from day to day, depending on the moods of the bosses and the amount of money the tourist was willing to pay.

Magdalene was going to try to get around the rules. Remembering that in the *favelas* of Rio de Janeiro, traffickers sometimes allowed students and researchers to live for a time in the heart of the community in order to carry out field work and to denounce the excesses of the police. She would use exactly the same argument to convince the leaders of the neighborhood. A white lie, therefore. As such, as Jesus never lied, it would have to be her to deal with the matter.

In this way, thanks to Magdalene's powers of fabrication and practical sense, they became two sociologists who were doing research for a piece on stigmatized communities. She supposed that through showing an interest in the neighborhood's problems, making it worthy of a study, material with which to write a book, they would become popular with the residents. Worthy of an entry and residence visa.

Once they were convinced that they weren't undercover cops or drug dealers, the leaders of the neighborhood, interested in being talked about, quite simply warned them to take care.

Pelé gave them one piece of advice.

"If there are any shots, throw yourself to the ground, and don't move! It doesn't usually take long."

Honório foresaw other consequences.

"Watch out! You're not going to get yourselves killed in my street. We've enough problems as it is."

As they made their way through the neighborhood of New Europe they were greeted by a drab, dirty, and rundown place. The walls of the buildings were cracked and smudged with graffiti, which either insulted the blacks or insulted the gypsies, and was also enough room to call for death to all police; the ground was littered with rubbish and dog excrement, the sidewalks were cracked, the road riddled with potholes, the streetlamps broken; all that could be recognized in the children's playground were the iron swings; packs of dogs scratched away at plastic bags releasing unholy stenches; from verandas and windows clothes were hung out to dry, as if executed; different sources of music, all at full volume, fought for airspace in a deafening cacophony.

Magdalene was shocked.

"This is a ghetto where society has dumped the excluded and unwanted. Before they were shipped off to Africa, now they deport them to the suburbs. Low-income housing estates are a legal form of ethnic cleansing. They've cooked up some social engineering to purge the city and then they're surprised when the pressure cooker explodes."

Jesus agreed in part with the diagnosis. "This place is horrible and it certainly worsened the problems it proposed to resolve. All the same, every person that lives here is still responsible for their own actions."

Irate, Magdalene raised her voice.

"The people responsible for this were the politicians who rehoused them in this isolated neighborhood, without cultural services, leisure facilities, or decent transport services. How could you not rebel when you discover that your place of residence prevents you from getting a job or from entering entertainment venues, and makes you a suspect of crimes you can't even remember doing?"

"These people have plenty of reasons to feel humiliated and it's natural they feel resentment, but—"

"But nothing. What would you do if you were accused of threatening the public order, when you were innocent?"

"As we know, it's outrageous to hear unjust accusations," Jesus said.

"When social integration policies are adopted that avoid these ghettos, then all ethnic groups exist in peace. If this is not the case, feeling like foreigners in their own country, they start to fight for the only territory left to them."

"And do they really have to fight with weapons?"

"Don't you see that this is about a protective instinct, the type you see in someone who feels harassed? Even the most civilized peoples have a past of violent struggle in the defense of their land. Look at the history of this country…" Magdalene said.

"Until now non-violent fighting has not proved that successful. But I agree with you, these people were dumped here."

"And when the apocalyptic future of *Blade Runner* becomes reality, when the planet becomes uninhabitable due to pollution or to some nuclear war, they will also be the ones left on Earth, while the elite colonize new worlds. Just like geneticist J. F. Sebastian[25], they will be second class citizens."

"At least they don't live in emigrant houses," Jesus said.

"Forgive him, Lord, for he knows not what he says."

While they were chatting, a group of men leaning in the doorway of a café watched them suspiciously.

"What do those two want?"

"They must be from the police."

"The cops don't care about us anymore."

"I heard that they are studying the neighborhood."

"They must have nothing better to do."

"If she was my wife, she would already have been given what for."

"Hey, if they get shot in the ass it'll do 'em good."

*

Having received permission to enter the neighborhood, nobody asked the strangers why they were there. On the contrary, instead of posing

---

[25] In the film *Blade Runner*, J. F. Sebastian is a genetic engineer who suffers from a degenerative disease causing premature aging. Due to this problem, he is considered an inferior human and prevented from leaving Earth.

questions, it was the residents that started being questioned. In the gypsy zone, although they received more than one version of the events, with time, place, and culprits varying, the conclusion was always the same: it was the blacks' fault, the gypsies were good and honorable people; they didn't get into trouble, but they knew very well how to defend themselves if they were disrespected.

After many trips around the area and many similar replies, some offers to buy drugs — which Magdalene thought was a good price but didn't dare buy, they decided to ask Honório himself about the reasons behind the conflict. They found him seated at the door to his house in the company of other gypsies. Honório understood what they wanted and signaled to them to come closer. The other gypsies moved away, watching them from a distance. The patriarch was barefoot. His feet were enormous and swollen, his nails twisted like talons.

"You don't know what it is to be a gypsy! Our people have always been maltreated and excluded. Nobody wants us to be nearby; nobody employs a gypsy, not even a girl as a servant. Have you? Would you trust a gypsy? How many gypsy friends do you have? They say that things have changed, but they're wrong. We are still treated like dogs. Gypsies aren't the ones who don't want to integrate into society. No! It's you who won't let us! That's why they put us here with these blacks, who are even more racist than you white people."

In the black zone the attempt to extract information from passersby produced the same effect of version multiplication, warm as loaves of bread but without the miracle of obtaining another conclusion other than it was the gypsies' fault, because the black community was good and honorable, didn't get into trouble, but knew very well how to defend themselves if disrespected.

So they went in search of Pelé, receiving new offers to buy drugs along the way — at prices that Magdalene thought inflated — to hear the explanation from the leader of the young blacks. They found him playing pool in a smoke-filled café. Pelé saw them coming, but didn't stop playing his game. Only after he had missed a shot and had thrown his cue onto the green baize, did he give them his attention. His bull's neck seemed ready to break the gold chain around it.

"You got any idea what it's like to be black and poor? You were born with everything in place. But I never had any opportunity in life. You get it? And do you know what happened when I was a good little boy and followed all your rules? Nobody respected me. They called me nigger, they brushed me aside. One day some skinheads got me and broke my arm and two teeth. You see this scar? I s'pose you haven't got any? But now, nobody messes with me. Do you see my gun here? Now I'm in charge! And you better believe that the gypsies are gonna be taught a lesson because they're even more racist than you guys."

Finally they asked the whites why they thought the neighborhood was being torn apart. Looking from side to side before answering, as if even the walls had ears and could rat on them, they confirmed the relationship between the ethnic groups and the interpretation of events.

"Do you want to know the truth? The blacks and the gypsies are all a bunch of criminals."

"There are no innocents in that lot of dark folk."

"This is all about race; it's in their blood."

"Look, this war is almost a good thing, because they'll end up killing each other off and the neighborhood will be clean."

And the drugs they tried to sell them were the cheapest of all (but also slightly impure).

After listening to the residents, it was clear to Jesus and Magdalene that the responsibility for the acts of violence in New Europe lay with the blacks; it also lay with the gypsies and the whites. It lay with everyone and with no one.

The difference between what they knew before and after they had entered New Europe was they had discovered that a mass of poisoned air had settled over the neighborhood, sending out bolts of lightning and rolls of thunder to those who breathed it in. And there seemed to be no Zephyr with enough breath to blow it away. Blowing Venus to Earth in a scallop shell seemed easier than blowing hatred away from men. And both Jesus and Magdalene doubted if they would be capable of setting such a gale loose.

They urgently needed an ally. They didn't know it yet, but their ally could be no other than Professor Kacimba.

The following morning, they were wandering through the neighborhood when they began to hear a strange noise. Guided by their ears, they walked in the direction of the sound. The brutish noise was initially refined into a thunderous roar and then into two distinct growls. An animal fight was about to take place.

"I've heard that they have dog fights in these neighborhoods," said Magdalene, feeling uncomfortable.

"Who would organize such savagery?" Jesus asked her.

"No idea. There's talk of clandestine betting, mafias, some police involvement. They sometimes manage to film it on TV but no one has ever been caught. In the end, the dogs turn up at the vet's, their lives in the balance."

Jesus quickened his step without saying another word. Magdalene found it hard to keep up with him.

They then discovered that the racket was coming from the courtyard of a building. They passed through a small tunnel and entered this enclosed space. Before them, two boys and two dogs. Facing each other, as if this were a duel in which the dogs had replaced the weapons, they were holding their beasts at a short distance from each other while provoking them. There was no one around them; the concrete courtyard was empty. Magdalene understood what was happening: this wasn't a fight with betting yet, just a training session. As two competent trainers, the boys were preparing their dogs for the major event. And what better way of preparing a fighter than forcing it to fight?

"Stop this!" she cried.

The boys looked up at her.

"Shut up, bitch, or I'll sick my dog on you," one of them threatened.

And they went back to concentrating on their task, now slapping the dog's backs. Suddenly they moved away and the animals launched themselves at each other dementedly. The clash took place with their front paws, which were wielded as their mouths tried to sink their teeth in their necks. One of the dogs managed to bite the side of the other's snout, while the other went for its jawbone. Both fell back to the ground bleeding, looking like Siamese twins joined at the head. And the intense growling was transformed into a furious whining.

"Wait here," Jesus told her.

And Magdalene once again spotted the authoritarian look on his face that had frightened her in the dream about the laboratory. Jesus then began to walk towards the center of the courtyard, making the ground reverberate with every step. As soon as they realized that a stranger was approaching, the boys prepared to face him. One pulled out a knife and the other grabbed the brass knuckles he had in his pocket. "Get out of here, or else..." But the moment they looked up at him they were left even more frightened than Magdalene. Before Jesus was even five meters from them, they had begun their flight, leaving their dogs behind them.

A resident loomed in the window of an apartment, before immediately losing interest in yet another disturbance in the neighborhood.

One of the dogs, a *Dogo Argentino* crossed with a *Bull Terrier*, had its paws on its adversary, a purebred *Rottweiler*, and its teeth dug into the skin close to the other's neck. As one was white and the other black, both were dyed a rusty color.

Jesus stroked their fur very softly, caressed them behind their ears, but the dogs continued to fight. Then he moved his hand to the scruffs of their necks and started to try to pull them apart. With energetic tugs he made the dogs shake and shiver without managing to separate them, however. He got as far as lifting that mass of self-devouring flesh up to shoulder height, but to no avail. On the contrary, his intervention provoked them even more. The *Rottweiler* managed to seize the paw of the *Dogo Argentino* in its mouth, and looked as if it were about to rip it off.

"Let me help you!" cried Magdalene from far away.

"Just stay where you are," he ordered.

Jesus then let go of the dogs' scruffs, lifted his arms, clenched his fists, and brought them down on their heads. There was the sound of bones cracking, and the animals fell down, seemingly struck dead. The white dog had fallen on its side and black lay with its paws in the air. The concrete was splattered with blood.

Magdalene came running up to him. "Have you killed them?"

Instead of replying, Jesus knelt down and placed his hands on the animals again; this time on their chests, close to their hearts. He remained thus for a few seconds and, suddenly, the dogs jumped up and shot off, their tails between their legs.

"They were just stunned," said Jesus.

"I didn't know you practiced martial arts. You could have done that to Judas."

"It was just a tap, to get them apart."

"And you're covered in blood, you look like Christ," Magdalene said.

Jesus then entered a café to wash off the blood and animal drool. Even though she had not been defiled by the fight, Magdalene also felt the need to wash herself. Her clothes were stuck to her with sweat.

The café was packed. Sitting on metal chairs with foam seats, wandering among the faux granite-topped tables, the customers spoke noisily. When Jesus and Magdalene entered silence fell. A fly could be heard being electrocuted. "Hello," they both said as they made their way to the washroom — and nobody replied. When they came out, their hands still wet as there'd been nothing to dry them on, they went to the counter to get something to drink. Two men moved out of their way. A third turned his back on them. Anticipating their order, the café owner placed a beer and an orange juice on the countertop. "On the house." The beer was warm and the juice hadn't been strained. In the meantime, the customers had started talking again, not concerned about their presence anymore —

sooner or later those intruders would end up leaving. It was then that Magdalene and Jesus heard the name of Professor Kacimba for the first time. Because everyone was talking about him.

"Man, if Professor Kacimba were to leave, it would be misery for all of us."

With such a catastrophic possibility spoken, some of the customers became afraid, others reproached the ominous voice, and a lady even crossed herself. Thus began a discussion about Professor Kacimba, where each person tried to outdo the other in extolling the healer's merits.

"Oh, Professor Kacimba has already saved many people in my family."

"He cured my aunt's rheumatism in her knee."

"He made my husband come home."

"He lifted a curse from my family."

"My nephew was in prison and they let him out early."

"If it wasn't for him, many people wouldn't be here today."

"The neighborhood would already have been bulldozed."

Any recrimination of bad practice, criticism of negligence, any gibe about him being a sham, or even the slightest doubt as to Professor Kacimba's methods, were never uttered or heard in the neighborhood of New Europe.

For Magdalene this provided more than enough to form an opinion on the man, to define him and rate him: he was a charlatan, a con man, a crook taking advantage of the naivety of residents — who now seemed similar to country folk to her. When they left the café, with a taste of bitter orange in her mouth, she could no longer contain herself.

"Son of a bitch! I can smell con men like that a mile off. You see stuff in the paper every day about the elderly or the illiterate being the victims of some scam or other. I'm not so bothered when they cheat rich people. But the main victims of these crafty characters are those excluded from society. These people here. Did you hear how they spoke about him? This guy is a pro. Listen, if it was down to me these dodgy dealers who get rich at the expense of other peoples' misery should all be arrested. This sort of behavior can't be forgiven."

Jesus listened to her without interrupting, recalling that he had once been the victim of similar accusations. But when she had finished passing her judgment, he disagreed with his friend.

"I don't know what this man does, but maybe he can tell us something we don't know yet. As you said yourself, no one should be excluded. I think it's important we hear what he has to say. Who knows, we mind find a pearl of great value?"

His suggestion disconcerted Magdalene. How could someone so level-headed have the nerve to suggest they visit that con man? How could he suppose that that guy, one of the links in the chain choking the residents, could actually be the one to free them? This was worse than eating genetically modified corn or sleeping in a resort built in an environmental reserve.

"Instead of pearls, you'll find a big fat pig. Don't expect me to be a part of this farce. I refuse to enter this den of exploitation."

"Would you prefer to look him up on Wikipedia?" Jesus asked.

"I would prefer hell to truly exist, which would be the only just punishment for this creature."

"Maybe he's already met it in this life."

"But now he's in heaven, with angels all around him."

"This is your chance to send him to purgatory. Direct Action."

"You're against violence, aren't you?" Magdalene asked.

"Fine. I'll go alone."

Jesus went back into the café to ask where he would find Professor Kacimba's surgery. The café owner sniffed out a smile; even sociologists went to the healer.

"It's easy. Go out, turn to your right, walk about fifty meters, then turn to your left at the first crossroads, and go straight ahead. After five minutes you'll come across a sign for a hair salon. You should go in there."

At a table to the side, an elderly woman who had heard his question interrupted the conversation.

"Have faith, have faith young man, it'll all work out fine."

While on his way, Jesus saw a woman trip on something at the end of the road and sprawl onto the pavement. The fall must have been a bad one, as she didn't get up, and she was rubbing her ankle as if she had twisted it. As he was running to help her, Jesus saw a man walk by her without stopping, and a woman, equally indifferent to the fate of the helpless lady, until finally, when he was just about to reach her, a guy with a big hat came out of a building, put his arms around her, and led her into the edifice.

Jesus then knew he had reached his destination.

In the meantime, Magdalene was wondering around the neighborhood, kicking the litter she found on the pavement. Without noticing, at a certain point she entered the gypsy quarter. A stronger kick on a sardine tin caused the packaging to twist along the cement in successive pirouettes. The metallic clatter caught the attention of a girl who was arriving home. She put down her shopping bag, turned, and stared at the stranger. Out of embarrassment, Magdalene spoke.

"Sorry if I scared you."

"You did nothing of the sort."

"What's your name?"

"Romi."

"Magdalene. Do you know I'm doing a study of the neighborhood?"

"Everyone knows."

"Ah…"

"But it's not going very well, is it?"

"People aren't used to these surveys."

"And what did you expect? There are no intellectuals here."

"Can I ask you some questions?"

"Fine."

"Have you ever been discriminated against for living here?"

"It was worse when we lived in the shacks."

"There are many preconceptions regarding gypsies: the men steal, the women read palms, the children don't go to school—"

"I'm going to take a vocational course."

"Are you going to be a beautician, a hairdresser?"

"IT, Java programming."

"Ah, that's great."

"Why on earth would I have to be a beautician or a hairdresser? Have you ever thought about following those careers?"

"Sorry, it was an unfortunate question."

"Maybe you'd have more luck as a hairdresser than a sociologist."

"You've got a sense of humor, that's good. So, do you like living in the neighborhood?"

"Until the shots began, it was good…"

"But don't you think that these rehousing programs alienate you from society?"

"I was already alienated, now I live in a house," Romi said.

"Yes, but you could live closer to the city center."

"And one day I will live there, without anyone's help."

"It's not help, it's part of the social contract of any decent society."

"I know, but I like to take care of myself."

"Fine. And can you tell me what you think about this conflict?"

"What do you want me to say? There are good and bad people on both sides. Listen, if it was up to me, I would end the fighting right now."

"Don't you hate the blacks?"

"I don't hate anyone."

"And do you have black friends?"

"More than you have."

"Don't get offended, I'm on your side," Magdalene said.

"You waltz in here without asking permission, and you think you're on my side?"

"I'd like you to trust me."

"Trust you? This is nothing more than work for you, but no matter how many questions you ask, you're never going to understand who we are and how we live."

"So tell me what I should do."

"To start with, you could stop bothering people. Not even the most annoying hairdressers ask that many questions," Romi said.

"I'm going to tell you something. We're here to try and put an end to the violence. This is our mission. Do you want to help us?"

"You're not right in the head, are you?"

"If you want to show solidarity you can't be right in the head, so, no, I'm not."

"Nobody can help you, much less me."

"You seem different. Maybe you have an idea."

"Do you want me to tell you my idea? Get out of here while you still can. Go jump in a lake somewhere else," Romi said.

*

Jesus was reading a sports newspaper in which football seemed a sacred matter and the future of the country depended less on the Government than on referees, when Magdalene entered the waiting room. Contrary to the expectations of the real hairdressers, who judged her to be a customer in need of having her blonde mop permed, she sat down by his side. Sulkily she picked up a gossip mag and pretended to read. Hairdryers trumpeted in her ears.

Finally she decided to explain her change of heart.

"Did you think I was going to leave you alone with this delinquent, with all his tricks?"

"Great, let's save him from hell."

"But I'm not going to shake his hand," said Magdalene as she placed on her headphones and turned on her iPod.

"*Noli me tangere*[26]," said Jesus, without her hearing.

Nick Cave was now singing *The Witness Song*: "*...who will be the witness, when you're all too blind to see...*"

In the meantime the door to the consulting room opened and a smiling woman that only Jesus recognized came out.

After waiting two hours, during which time Jesus discovered that football is more of a religion than a

---

[26] *Latin for "Don't touch me" or "Don't tread on me", words spoken by Jesus to Mary Magdalene when she recognized him after his resurrection (John 20:17).*

sport and Magdalene had confirmed that famous people go to a lot of parties, travel all over the world, and suffer terrible heartbreak, it was their turn to be seen. Having seen a Pacific island in the magazine on which a famous couple had chosen to marry again in a ceremony held by a spiritual healer, Magdalene also tried to avail herself of magical powers and send Professor Kacimba there, too. But despite her efforts, she couldn't manage to budge him an inch.

Nevertheless, after the person concerned asked them to enter, the magician's apprentice discovered a new target at which to aim her kinetic fury. If Jesus hadn't been with her, she would have grabbed the owl, the Dolly the sheep poster, the plantation foreman, and the aquarium, and thrown all that junk out of the window; she would refrain from chucking the hat-wearing crook out after them, however, because even that creature had a right to life.

As his day was going really well — he had treated three new patients, recommended by former ones — the Professor decided to add a pinch of fantasy to his reception formula.

"I can already see that you have marital problems, that you are going through a difficult patch, that your mother-in-law is no help, and I can tell that there isn't enough money left at the end of the month and there are bills to pay, but you need to relax because you are young and love conquers all."

Suddenly he fell silent and stared at Jesus. At first he was perplexed. His smile twisted into a grimace beyond astonishment, his eyes glazed over like a doll. Then he became panic stricken. One of his legs escaped him and made him take a step back. Looking for strength in Raimundo, Kacimba managed with great difficulty to control himself. He was now sweating and his heart was pounding. He then asked Jesus to take a seat and, terrified, approached to take his hand. Kacimba opened his mouth but was unable to say a word. An unknown tongue was forming. Suddenly, with his voice altered, he began to talk.

"I feel an intense energy, it's something so strong! I have never experienced anything like it—"

Bewildered, Kacimba paused for a few seconds. And then resumed speaking.

"...There is a great power within you! This isn't normal. You won't believe it, but death plays no part in your life, it was beaten long ago... and... and you even seem to have two lives. How strange! I don't know what I'm saying... How old are you, friend? Where were you born? Who are your parents? I admit that I'm lost..."

All of a sudden, Kacimba closed his eyes and spoke like a possessed *muzhik*.

"I see... I see you come from afar, you've suffered greatly — betrayal, tremendous injustice — many evil and malicious people have crossed your path, they were also in conflict with your father. And now I feel that you did something extraordinary... yes, something truly amazing... but I can't make out what it was. I can just see that there are many people waiting for you, for so much time... How very strange! My God, who are you actually?"

Jesus answered him. "I am a man like any other, of flesh and blood."

Professor Kacimba knew that this wasn't the case, but at the same time he couldn't find any other explanation and he didn't have the courage to express the suspicion going through his mind, so crazy did it seem to him. A double miracle had taken place. For the first time he had truly experienced all the energies, extrasensory powers, and visions that he proclaimed to possess, and sensed them much more powerfully and frighteningly than he'd ever imagined possible. And stranger still, he knew he was standing before someone who appeared to be not of this world. Respectfully, as he felt unworthy to welcome him in his place, he removed his hat from his head and confessed his impotence.

"Sir, there is nothing I can do for you. In fact, you don't require help from anyone."

"Yes, I might not need it, but the people of this neighborhood do. Help us to help them."

Professor Kacimba was struck dumb once again.

"Me? But how? I'm surprised they haven't even shot me yet."

Magdalene now saw through the trickster's mask. She didn't see a con man anymore, but just a poor devil trying to survive. So, she let go of the urge to throw things out the window. She then approached him and looked as deeply as she could into his still fearful eyes, trying to find the malevolent focus she imagined to be lurking there. But she couldn't find even the tip of the tail of this venomous snake. The straight line guiding her feelings about Kacimba had become twisted again and now it changed direction; what she had just seen on the left was on the right, what was in front was now behind, and with lightning speed it guided her to this man, who seemed at that moment as fragile and as equal as all the other residents.

"Sir, Professor, you must know these people well. They confide in you, get things off their chest, entrust you with their secrets. Maybe you know of something that both communities share, a common desire, the point to start to unravel this tangle."

Professor Kacimba looked hard for the point, but this was beyond him, his nails were too short to loosen the knot. "Let me think, let me think."

Magdalene questioned him again. "And no one ever asked you to put an end to the conflict?"

"No. My patients have asked many things of me, to bring people back from the dead and everything, but none of them has ever spoken about this. They have more serious problems."

"Sometimes problems bring people together. They've lived together in this neighborhood for so long and have never established any relationship? There has to be something that unites them," Magdalene said.

"Truly, there's nothing that I can see," the Professor said.

Jesus intervened.

"Maybe a passion."

Kacimba raised his arms.

"Yes, a passion, that's just it. It may seem impossible, but there are two teenagers in love. He's black and she's a gypsy."

Professor Kacimba began to tell the story of forbidden love between the two teenagers of different ethnic backgrounds and family members running the neighborhood. He didn't tell it in its chronological order, as he didn't know it. He invented some situations he deemed plausible, and at times he veered from the subject to describe the living conditions of the residents. He skipped the advice he had given to the boy, but in the end he painted a reliable portrait of the passion uniting Romi and Julian.

"There's hope after all, because if a black boy and the gypsy girl I just met can love each other in this tumultuous suburb, then maybe the other blacks and gypsies don't necessarily need to crack each others' skulls," thought Magdalene, passing her finger over a scar on the back of her neck.

Jesus was also amazed by the story, as only kindness and love among men managed to surprise him now. However, he was more cautious as to the possibility of this miracle being able to bring about another. "It's wonderful that the seed of love has sprouted in a soil parched by hatred. But don't affections tend to lock themselves in the hearts of lovers, refusing, unlike hatred, to spread to other people? And don't some human beings become hostile when faced with the happiness of their fellow man, as if wanting to destroy what they do not have, because they are unable to cope with it in others?" These were the thoughts running through his mind, but he didn't want to destroy the illusions he had seen in Magdalene's face and the glimmer of hope sparking in the now fearless face of Professor Kacimba.

Magdalene, moved by the passion of the teenagers, began to hatch a plan, favoring intention over originality.

"What about organizing a reconciliation party?"

"A party, just like that?" countered the pragmatic Professor Kacimba, as Raimundo once again.

"Well, there's always a reason to throw a party," insisted Magdalene.

"Nobody here goes to parties without good reason."

"We could contact some cultural entertainers, I know a few."

"The last one here got shot in the leg."

And thus they continued trying to discover the good reason they would need to throw a party — Magdalene tried to recall a passage from *Utopia*, but was unable to find any that would serve the purpose, rejecting those promoting that a case of beer has great festive potential or those guaranteeing that when the food is free, everyone comes. New Europe wasn't Vilar de Mochos.

They were about to give up, when Jesus, as if recalling what he had said about Caesar or about the stallholders he expelled from the temple, about the great differences between the kingdom of Heaven and the kingdom of Earth, while also disproving his supposed ignorance of matters financial, pronounced a magic word.

"Money."

Magdalene and Kacimba looked at him in astonishment. Magdalene was astonished with indignation, as she felt money was always a problem.

Kacimba was astonished in admiration, as he knew that only someone from another world would be able to resolve such serious conflicts with such simple answers. So much astonishment rendered them both silent.

Jesus, seeing astonishment similar to that revealed by the apostles when a disconcerting decision was announced to them or some behavior contrary to good sense was suggested, quickly explained what he wanted to say with such a cursed word.

"The ties of love are very strong but they unite only two people at a time; this affection can't be transformed into a web linking the community. Even if the lovers were to speak the language of angels, this wouldn't be the solution. This power, and it pains me to say this, is reserved to money, as it is only through trade and business that man truly unites, as it is in everyone's interest. *Pecunia regina mundi.*"[27]

Magdalene was so surprised with this unexpected facet in her friend that, for a few moments she imagined him dressed in a suit and tie, presiding over the board of directors of a bank, preaching, "It's easier for a camel to pass through the eye of needle than for a tax inspector to discover our offshore accounts."

As for Professor Kacimba, whose takings for that day had been particularly good, and who had also

---

[27] Money rules the world.

discovered that he could speak Latin, he understood that they could only attempt a reconciliation between blacks and gypsies through money. Good accounts make good friends.

"You're right. The residents will listen to someone who reminds them that the conflict only does them harm and that reconciliation will allow cafés, shops, and grocers to buzz with customers again. I will speak to them."

However, seeing the disappointment on Magdalene's face, Jesus added something to what he had said.

"But don't get me wrong, I also believe that the passion between Romi and Julian bodes well for the reconciliation between blacks and gypsies." Thus he saved one cheek instead of turning the other.

Under Magdalene's reproving eye, Jesus then told Kacimba how he should proceed.

"Professor, first go and whisper the word money in the ear of Honório and Pelé, how much they've already lost and how much they could earn, and let human nature do its work for a few days."

"And then, sir?" asked Kacimba.

"Then, when the ointments of temptation have softened the crusts of hatred, you can then convince them to negotiate peace."

At that moment, Magdalene butted in. "Hey, have you ever heard of dog fighting here in the neighborhood?"

Kacimba was surprised by the question and became embarrassed.

"The fights aren't here. And the majority of people betting are from elsewhere — many immigrants appear during the summer, but you're right, there are some residents involved in this."

"Does this mean that the dog-fighting business is part of the money they will make after they reconcile?" asked Magdalene

"I'm not sure. As I said, the gamblers don't live in the neighborhood. I, like everyone who loves animals, am against these fights. I will also try to convince them to stop doing this, but it won't be easy."

Like a UN mediator, Professor Kacimba was now invested with the mission of convincing the blacks and the gypsies to stop behaving like Israelis and Palestinians. He therefore had to defuse the bomb without being blown apart, an ethnic cluster bomb, whose mechanism contained wires, charges, and detonators that appeared impossible to disarm. But once again, Professor Kacimba wasn't going to turn his back on difficulties, even if they caused him to explode.

On the following day, Kacimba placed a sign on his consulting room door, saying: "Closed due to *force majeure"* and headed to Honório's house, hoping that the advanced years of this man would translate into good sense. Honório stopped playing with his grandchildren to listen.

"I come to ask you to make peace with the blacks."

Good sense took its time to reveal itself. The gypsy chief first showed surprised, then indignation, and finally the onset of fury, the consequences of which, if it hadn't been Professor Kacimba, would be quite different from fading wrath. His left eye was closed, and a vein pulsated on his neck.

"You what? Are you mad, man? Leave me in peace before I—"

However, as money has the gift of returning reason to the most irrational of men, good sense reared its head, swept twice through Honório's, and with his mind clear and sparkling, he said: "It's a deal. Let's see what we can do."

Professor Kacimba then made his way to the café where he knew he would find Pelé, aware that the young age of this man meant he would likely possess good, but youthful, sense. However, youthful good sense is a mystery yet to be fully understood. They are attached together with parts destined for other functions; some of the screws are actually missing, and it takes a good many whacks with a sledgehammer before the first hint of good sense appears.

Pelé interrupted a business deal to listen. His pupils were dilated and a blood vessel had burst in his left eye.

"We're going to put an end to this war, I've already arranged a meeting with Honório."

Pelé's good sense had to work really hard to emerge from the deep well in which it was imprisoned, forcing Professor Kacimba to fight with Pelé, too, while his friends hurled abuse at him.

"Traitor!"

"You've sold your race to the gypsies!"

"You're gonna be sliced!"

But as Professor Kacimba once again became bricklayer Raimundo — pumped up in building site gyms — he threw two attackers straight to the ground, thus bringing some sense to the rest of them. As a result, the good sense of preserving the body allowed Professor Kacimba to explain to them the financial benefits of peace with the gypsies.

The meeting between the Israelis and the Palestinians of the neighborhood of New Europe took place in Professor Kacimba's consulting rooms, with the afro hair salon having closed on that day. The host understood that the meeting would require a befitting atmosphere, conducive to the envisaged peace: he placed a jar of wisteria flowers on the table, lit some incense sticks and, just in case, he summoned the benevolent spirits by performing a *muzhik* dance. If any of his old patients were to enter the room they would note that something had changed. An aura of harmony was emanating from the enclosed place, overlaying the old aura of mystery, since even the cocoa plantation foreman seemed less dour and the servants more eager to work; and as for Dolly the sheep, this retained the same air of ovine imbecility.

The first to arrive was Honório, an hour earlier than arranged, as he believed it fundamental to know the lay of the land he shared with the enemy, even though he had already been in Professor Kacimba's rooms. Without meaning to show any mistrust for the mediator, just another side to his good sense, he inspected the site, imitating the procedure he had seen the police carry out so many times when they had entered his wife's tent. The owl was scrutinized as if its feathers might conceal a blade.

"No offense, Professor, this is just to make sure that everything runs smoothly. They've tried to kill me so many times..."

But while he was inspecting he began to be taken in by the atmosphere of peace created by Professor Kacimba; the last vestiges of suspicion disappeared, and Honório, definitively pacified, even felt the desire to give the host a hug.

Two minutes prior to the agreed time, when Kacimba was already beginning to fear a no-show, Pelé appeared, a revolver in his hand. And he also began to investigate the consulting rooms. The backs of the photo frames from Guinea were carefully examined.

"I'll warn you that I'm prepared for any trap they've set up for me."

Neither Kacimba nor Honório were surprised by this reaction. After all, they were still at war. However, the effect of the wisteria, of the burning incense, and of the benevolent spirits summoned by the magician didn't take long to also sweeten the impetuous Pelé. And so, as if a host of cherubim had delicately taken hold of his weapon, while another host of seraphim were singing him celestial *Hip-Hop*, Pelé placed the revolver down on the table and shot out, "Let's get down to business". However, as the atmosphere enjoyed in business deals is not made of peace or of spirituality, a deluge of tales, losses, and damages thrashed down on the environment of mystical harmony, flooding the wisteria, putting out the incense, and almost certainly shocking the spirits. Because before agreeing to return to business, Honório and Pelé, as if ripped off by a private bank, demanded recompense. This was a problem with which Professor Kacimba had not reckoned and which must also have escaped Jesus. (Magdalene, as she continued to think that money only brought problems, didn't even think about the matter again.)

Each had compiled a list of the debts that the other owed them, which included broken glass, doors riddled with bullets, walls smeared with graffiti, flat tires, scratched, burnt-out and vandalized cars, stolen motorbikes, bicycles, tricycles, skateboards, roller skates, mobile phones, and iPads, a destroyed clothesline, two poisoned dogs, a cat that had gotten its whiskers chopped off, and bills from the hospital, from the Red Cross, and from the chemist's that frightened even Professor Kacimba. But as he had laid the foundations for the reconciliation of them both on financial grounds, he felt like a foreman with no authority to scold them.

So, he left them to negotiate the losses in loud protests.

"That door was already ruined!" Pelé said.

"That car wasn't even worth scrapping..." Honório said.

"The gypsies stole that bike."

"The blacks stole that mobile."

"The whites must have robbed that shop—" Pelé said.

"The whites must have set fire to that motorbike," Honório said.

"My cousin has been left with a limp..."

"My brother-in-law has been seeing a shrink for ages."

"My mother-in-law has become a stutterer," Pelé said.

"You never liked her, anyway," Honório said.

And on the rare occasions when they asked him to pass judgment, he would say only "maybe", or "there's something in that" or "I'm not sure", thus not daring to cross one group or the other.

Then at the end of three hours of compensatory wrangling, Honório and Pelé agreed that the fair solution would be for the gypsy chief to hand over a *Rottweiler* puppy to the leader of the blacks, and in exchange to receive a *Pit-bull* puppy — and in the heat of discussion the whiskerless feline was forgotten. In the neighborhood, dogs, especially if they bit, were more equal than cats, even if they scratched.

"We actually get on quite well, don't we?" said Pelé.

"Every family has its problems," said Honório.

"Quite true…"

"I'll tell you a story: a white guy, a Chinaman, and a black guy were on a plane..."

"I've got one, too: a white guy, a Chinaman and a gypsy were on a train..."

With the sensitive issue of compensation now sealed with jokes, Professor Kacimba suggested a great party to celebrate peace between the blacks and the gypsies.

However, he too was sensible enough neither to mention the romance between Romi and Julian, nor to broach the delicate subject of dog fighting — he would speak on this matter at a more appropriate time.

"This celebration will be like the dawn of a new era in which people of all ethnic backgrounds can learn to live together, accepting what separates them and resolving differences via peaceful means. And then united, can discover the wonderful miracle of existence."

To Honório and to Pelé, Professor Kacimba's words sounded like those of the city councillor who visited them every four years around election time, or those of the evangelical pastor who had never managed to open a church in the neighborhood. Accordingly, false and also nonsensical. However, as neither of them wanted to play the role of the black sheep who spoils the party, so favorable the climate now established with the benevolent spirits, and the scent of wisteria and incense, they agreed to Kacimba's suggestion.

"Well, yes, a party..." Pelé said.

"A party is always a party," Honório said.

And when they were about to enter another argument about who would pay for this party, with one claiming he would hire *Flamenco* musicians and the other *Hip-Hop* legends, Professor Kacimba opened his arms.

"Be quiet now, I'll pay for the party."

And they both obeyed him.

"Very well, Professor, be my guest," said Pelé.

"And that's the last of the matter," said Honório.

If Raimundo had been great at cementing bricks, Kacimba was even better at cementing reconciliations.

The news of the end to the conflict between blacks and gypsies was received by both parties — and by the whites — with distrust, scepticism, and even with a sense of betrayal.

"They almost killed my son and now I'm going to eat with them?" protested Dona Eufrásia.

"This isn't a Hollywood war," warned Lourenço Marques.

"I've more to do here," said Dona Lurdes.

However, as this was an order given by the neighborhood authorities, which, when it came to internal regulations, were more conservative than a club for English lords which doesn't accept women or Indians as members, the residents were left with no other choice but to obey. And so they were forced to reconcile. Because anyone who dares go against the powers of New Europe will not only be thrown out of this club where poker and beer replace bridge and gin, but also may have to leave the establishment — connected to a resuscitation machine.

Gradually the residents began to talk about the matter with greater enthusiasm; they admonished those who still grumbled. And then they convinced themselves that even if there was not going to be a reconciliation, they would at least have a great party. The fact that it was a reconciliation festivity was now irrelevant. However, among the variety of suggestions, a veritable miracle took place between blacks and gypsies: they agreed on what food should be served. And the whites were in agreement, too.

A multiethnic group of residents took the initiative to choose the dishes.

"We'll vote on what food we'll have: it'll be grilled sardines and pork steaks."

"Of course! It's tradition."

"It can't be anything but this."

Despite the racial agreement, on the following day a group of two black men, a gypsy, and a white man protested the choice.

"Sardines are hard to digest and cause heartburn. We want grilled chicken, too."

Some ladies (also from every ethnic background), perhaps benefiting from a leak of information that Professor Kacimba was footing the bill, contested this demand and made a new proposal.

"Chicken contains growth hormones. Grilled rump steak would be best."

And from the gastronomic clash between multiculturalism and tradition came an unexpected victim: the pork steaks.

Nevertheless, in spite of the progress, a decision was still to be made between *caipirinha* and *caipirosca*. And the surprising offer of cornmeal cakes from Lourenço Marques' wife complicated matters further.

As to the choice of music, there appeared to be no possible agreement.

"That's not music!" proclaimed gypsies and blacks when they heard, respectively, *Hip-Hop* and *Flamenco*.

"Not music? So young gypsies don't listen to *Hip-Hop*?" the blacks reminded them.

"Ah, yes? And there aren't many blacks that like our guitar music?" countered the gypsies.

These arguments only entered their ears when repeated by Professor Kacimba. Two styles of music would be heard at the party therefore. Even so, the choice of which one would open the dance would have to be decided by a draw.

Had the residents of the neighborhood of New Europe seen *A Clockwork Orange*, they might grow to like the classical music of Beethoven. In that way the matter of music would be easily overcome, with *Hip-Hop* singers and *Flamenco* musicians replaced by an orchestra that would close the party with the *Ninth Symphony*, with no need for ultra-violence.

Preparations for the racial reconciliation party began on an open field. The first job involved unloading a van of all its containers holding food, drinks, plates, cutlery, and glasses. The second, more complex task involved getting in order the huge pile of tables and chairs that every family had brought along. The third involved making the food. And the fourth was decoration.

The sun blazed down and the wind whipped up balls of dust.

Following a custom shared by every ethnic group, the women did the work, a few men gave the orders, others watched on, and more still went off to the bar. Gypsies, blacks, and whites who hadn't exchanged a word in months, and who had even stoned each other, had come together in a highly productive workforce where there was plenty of good cheer, camaraderie, and opportunities to catch up. And not even the dust or the heat could dampen their commitment to work.

For their part, the gypsy, black, and white men who were supervising the setting up had also joined forces in a directive team that required the strict compliance of the plan they had hatched. In the end, they concluded that in the future, the women would have to improve their productivity.

"They have to work more and speak less."

As to those who sat watching, they got up from time to time to pee against the lamp post before taking their place again. And those who had gone off to the bar, when they returned, the first thing they did was to go and pee against the post before taking a seat, too.

Finally, the party setting was complete. Order was born from chaos, under chains of colored lights and little flags of every nation of the world. The gardens of New Europe didn't exactly match those of Versailles, but Madame Pompadour couldn't have done any better.

By late afternoon when the residents of New Europe were all at the reconciliation party, half of the beer barrels had been emptied and the limes for the *caipirinhas* (which had won out over the *caipiroscas*) had all but run out; they started grilling the sardines and the green peppers. It didn't take long for the effluvia released from the coals to dispel any remaining wisp of racial fog. The thought of some delicious sardines and some fine red wine removed any unhealthy ideas from the mind of the most savage of men, even if he had a pistol in his pocket.

Reverence for Professor Kacimba and each person's personal style ensured that everyone made a real effort in choosing what to wear. The men came in outfits of jeans and t-shirts, black suits and white shirts. The women showed more taste and creativity in their choice of clothing, with Dona Eufrásia, in a fake Chanel suit, the lady who stood out the most.

In addition, at least during the first hour of the party, nobody dared to spit on the ground and the litter bins received the leftovers they were intended for. English lords dressed in smoking jackets and armed with glasses of gin couldn't have done better.

The sardine and pepper grillers were faced with a long queue of men, women, and children, who, with plate in hand, waited to be served the delicacy; and in that anxious wait, where all the residents mixed and nobody dared jump the queue, you could already see the racial harmony that the party aimed to celebrate. Even those who had complained about the fat in the sardines were unable to take their eyes from the sizzling fish on the coals. For their part, the owners of the African hair salon had managed to find another reason for satisfaction in the cloud of smoke that would work its way into clothing and hair, predicting a packed salon once again on the next day. Never had New Europe seen so many people happy at the same time.

The sun cooled and the wind died down. Mosquitoes buzzed in the air.

At this moment, Professor Kacimba appeared, and those who were about to be served moved aside, giving up their place to the ethnic peacemaker who was paying the bill. Professor Kacimba refused the courtesy gently but firmly and purposely went to the back of the queue. But humility got him nowhere, because a woman immediately took him by the arm.

"Get out of the queue, Professor. That's no place for you."

Then along came another, running with a plate heaped with food.

"I picked out the best ones for you, Professor, they're nice and hot."

And finally the rest of the residents almost forced him to sit down and eat.

Having kept their distance, observing these first tentative steps towards each other, the only positive thing that they finally managed to achieve (God takes his time, but doesn't fail), and feeling happy though also left out, as if attending a party to which they had not been invited, the freeloaders Jesus and Magdalene were called over by Kacimba.

"Sir, miss, please sit."

"We don't want to bother you," replied Magdalene.

"This is your party, too. From today onward, you are also part of the community of New Europe."

"But there's a girl over there who doesn't much like me," Magdalene said.

"Who?" Kacimba asked.

"That gypsy at the back there. Do you see?"

"Yes, I think she's a beautician or a hairdresser. But you know these kids, they're never satisfied with anything."

"Maybe it's my fault because I didn't know how to talk to her," Magdalene said.

"Think no more of it. Not everyone is able to understand others as you do."

While Magdalene and Kacimba were talking, Jesus felt something rub against the back of his legs. Something warm and fluffy. He turned around and saw the two dogs he had separated, once again joined at the head. They were biting each other, but there was no blood in their lustrous fur. They were playing. And the beasts immediately sprawled at his feet.

It wasn't long before two plates overflowing with food appeared. And, even though they weren't hungry, they had no choice but to eat what they had been given — not as varied, but just as delicious as the delicacies of Vilar de Mochos. Together again, Jesus, Magdalene, and Kacimba confirmed that sometimes solving great problems doesn't require prodigious powers or miraculous solutions. The knots that men create, no matter how tight they become, can be untied with good sense and sardines.

A little while later, Honório approached, greeted Kacimba, and turned to them.

"Have you already finished your study? I hope you tell the truth and speak well of the gypsies. This country owes a great deal to our people. And don't forget me, because if it hadn't been for me, this party would never have happened."

He then squeezed Jesus' shoulder and left.

As soon as Honório had left, Pelé followed his example.

"So, when does the book come out? It was about time someone said that the black community has suffered in this neighborhood. This is what you're going to talk about, isn't it? Don't believe what the gypsies say, they're liars. And if you want to know more about my life, I can give you an interview."

Having said this, he ran a finger through Magdalene's hair and walked off.

Kacimba had no idea what study or book the neighborhood's leaders were talking about, but he didn't dare ask more questions. "A *caipirinha*, and make it a strong one," he said to the lady in charge of the drinks. And he drank it down in one gulp. Certain mysteries should be left to float in the ether, like ice cubes in a glass.

In the meantime, as the revellers served their food, they moved from the queue to the tables, undoing the ethnic togetherness. Because blacks, gypsies, and whites sat down at separate tables, forming three distinctive areas. Honório and Pelé raised their glasses in honor of the celebration, twenty meters away from each other. The dust that was raised in this instant interrupted the toast. And as they gulped down their drinks they were left with an aftertaste of earth in their mouths.

In each of these racial enclaves there were loud voices, laughter, drinking, and eating, the like you would expect at a festive event. In excess. As the menu was the same for everyone, the conversations in each of the demarcated zones resembled each other, too, in recalling old stories, praising the host of the party, and discussing politics.

"My granddad once took me to the island of Luanda."

"My daughter doesn't mind marrying her cousin anymore, ever since I consulted our friend..."

"All governments are corrupt."

Far from the party, Romi and Julian, burning over coals much hotter than those of the sardine grill and seasoned with the spices that only penetrate the flesh of teenagers, were eating the sardines without tasting their flavor; they ate the steak as if swallowing medicine. Having failed as yet to exchange a single word, even though the messages originating from their eyes and telegraphed by their eyelashes had managed to compose a series of love declarations, they were waiting for the crowds to stop stuffing themselves, and for the dance to begin. But deep are the stomachs of people when food is aplenty.

At around this time Kacimba began to get worried. Ever since Raimundo had broken that bone he could detect changes in weather, and once again he felt the pain that announced a storm brewing. Suddenly, a flash of lightning. As if he were possessed once again, he began to hear a voice that nobody else could.

"If water has the ability to adapt to any shape, hatred has the gift of hiding within other emotions. It becomes see-through, odorless, tasteless and intensifies the feeling in which it is housed. So the happiness of those who hate each other can seem more sincere than that of those who love one another. But like the virus that annihilates the cell on which it feeds, the time comes in which the guest devours the host. Seventy percent of the human body is made of water, the remaining thirty is hatred."

Then a roll of thunder. Instead of a lively party, Kacimba then started to see something else: the knives and forks weren't utensils for eating, but tools for digging trenches; blacks and gypsies were entrenching themselves as if expecting an invasion, using all their strength in this defensive task. Then Kacimba also saw that, once the trenches were dug, the knives and forks were now being sharpened as if swords and daggers, destined to cut through enemies. And in the dogs salivating under the table for the next piece of meat, he spotted angry beasts, ready to tear each other apart as soon as the fight began. Finally, a hedgehog appeared, just like that.

This vision was so clear that he hadn't the slightest doubt that it revealed reality at its purest, and that until now he had been in some kind of dream or delusion. And not even the discovery of platters of broccoli and plenty of red wine could calm him. Because no amount of food could mitigate the serious threat to the health of these people, invited to climb badly assembled scaffolding.

Kacimba heard and saw but said nothing. He was no Pythia of Delphi from whom you accepted the prediction of tragedy; his reputation was based on solving woes and preventing disasters, and nobody expected him to be a bird of ill omen. What's more, an old custom of getting rid of bad news might be taken up again by the residents of New Europe, who on hearing his message, much like kings to whom it was communicated that the queen had opened her chastity belt, would decide to kill the messenger. And so, Kacimba decided to keep his mouth shut.

And then the dance began.

According to the schedule, picked from a hat as neither side would give in, highly respected *Kid Tuga* was to kick the singing off, inviting those who were moved by the hammered poetry of *Hip-Hop* to get up and dance. He did so with the hit track, very fitting for the occasion, *Police kill us, Yoh.*

"I didn't do nothing!
I stole nothing!
But the police are watching.
And the bullet's on its way.
Police kill us, Yoh.
Police kill us, Yoh."

And as feelings for the police force were shared by the blacks, the gypsies, and the whites — ethnic cohesion before authority — the young bodies immediately rattled in jolts and jerks. Pelé's gang, Honório's dozens of grandchildren, and just as many white teenagers were taken by a writhing dance. Even the woman who had twisted her ankle seemed to be fully cured.

Now no one could be in any doubt as to the success of this reencounter of estranged brothers. Cane inviting Abel to dance on the hot tiles of hell, Abel forgiving the aggression that had robbed him of his life.

Even the pessimist Kacimba, no matter how much he focused on the prophesized doom or how much his tibia hurt him, could see no other reality than the happiness of youth. Under the strings of colored lights and the little flags of every nation of the world, these Israelis and Palestinians seemed very much different from the others. Kacimba saw it and almost believed it. He blamed the drink for the hallucination he had had, and tried to have fun, too.

And so, they were all in agreement that police kill people and that if police kill people the best thing is to kill the police, too, so that the police can't kill anyone else, and of course, at that moment no one was thinking that after killing the police the people might then kill each other, because, after all, some were people, while others were no more than animals. Either way, at this encounter between everyday brutality, lyrical ballads, and taxonomical precision, there was always someone who died and someone who invented songs.

At last it was time for new music, for *Flamenco* — passion according to the gypsies.

Neither *Manitas de Plata* nor *Paco de Lucía* had been able to make it to the New Europe neighborhood party. However, the group hired in the neighboring country, *Los Bravos Gitanos*, didn't want to leave their unknown credits to someone else's hands and ears. Especially after the resounding success of the minstrel, *Kid Tuga*. They were going to show this amateur just what real music was, how the guitar was played and the castanets clacked, and most importantly that great dancers prefer ankle boots to sneakers.

So, as soon as the first bars of the soundtrack of the film *Les enfants d'Hipollyte*[28], two gypsy snakes burst onto the stage, shaking their arms and hips, waving their hair and fluttering their eyelashes, and there was no one, apart from the astonished *Kid*, who could resist the lustful temptation of *Flamenco*. The gypsy soul brought to life.

The party was a success.

Magdalene looked like a blonde gypsie, Professor Kacimba adapted his *muzhik* moves to *Flamenco*, and Jesus discovered that dancing was more difficult than walking on water. Nobody was seated (the *Kid* had left). And the flow of blacks, gypsies, and whites mixed the choppy estuary of the dance floor to such an extent that no one would be surprised to find Romi and Julian pinned to each other. She prancing gracefully, he totally unhinged. A perfect pair. But the party was about to end.

A blood-colored full moon was rising on the horizon.

*

Nobody knew how it all began.

Some said it was a black man who pushed a gypsie, others were certain it was gypsy who stood on the foot of a black man, some said they saw two blacks groping

---

[28] Film about the life of gypsy musician Hippolyte Baliardo, brother of Manitas de Plata.

three gypsy women. Others countered that it was three gypsies groping two black guys, while someone asserted having seen a black and gypsy kissing. It was also said that the Chinese had infiltrated the party, that someone had thrown a whiskerless cat into the crowd, and there were others who blamed the architects.

But the black box of the reconciliation banquet of the residents of New Europe was never found. And if it had been, nobody would have been able to decipher its recordings.

When the police arrived, the shooting forced them to keep their distance for almost an hour. They formed a barrier to stop anyone from entering the party. But what actually happened was the crazed flight of dozens of people who wanted to get away. Screams and moans opened the gap through which the deranged rush of women and children passed. They couldn't untangle the blacks, the gypsies or the whites, because besides the blood and the earth spotting their faces and plastering their hair, they now all belonged to that human species that horror carves and standardizes.

There was therefore no man or boy among the fugitives, as in the neighborhood of New Europe, men never run away and are afraid of nothing.

Suddenly silence fell.

A last shot fired out, to which no one replied; in its place a tension remained between the police officers that the roar of armed fire had kept dormant. A bubble blown from hell hung above their heads. Not a word was spoken lest it burst.

They advanced in silence, like spectators making their way to a hanging, until they reached the site of the neighborhood residents' reconciliation party.

Then the bubble popped.

There were survivors crawling under the tables, bodies that were still writhing, and many dead. The sardines were now swimming in puddles of blood. To start with, the police officers were also unable to associate the bodies with ethnic backgrounds because, thanks to God, there are massacres to show that all men are equal.

The dogs licking the injured and weeping for the dead, growled at the officers. But there had been enough violence, even for the Pit Bulls and the Rottweilers.

The reconciliation between the blacks and the gypsies had finally happened. As proof, there lay the body of Julian embracing that of Romi.

*

At last the ambulances arrived, letting out blue flashes to show the moon that in a contemporary tragedy, illuminating the scene with spectral lights is not enough. The dead and the injured demanded filmic lighting on their wide eyes and gaping mouths so that the spectacle of their misfortune could be appreciated by the public in newspapers and on television.

*

Only a few minutes after getting up did Professor Kacimba understand that he was alive. Unscathed. Without a scratch.

But he didn't notice that no bullet had injured him. Because every single shot had hit him and because all those people had been killed by him.

Therefore, he was dead after all.

Raimundo dos Santos also died that day, buried in the rubble of the work he had failed to build.

And no officer of the law dared to detain death when he turned around and disappeared from New Europe.

Pursued by the finger of the moon.

*

Magdalene died of a shot to the head.

Maybe fired by a black, or by a gypsie or by a white. The bullet had opened a hole in her temple, from which blood was still flowing when one of the medics knelt down before her body. But death couldn't rob her of her beauty, leading the medic to ignore other bodies and to forget the dying to remain with her.

He took her hand and looked at her.

He seemed to see a light that wasn't coming from the ambulance.

Then he began to stroke her bloodied hair and caress her trodden-on face.

Then he kissed her, in the hope of resuscitating her.

But Magdalene was no longer there.

She had left with Jesus for somewhere far away from the neighborhood of New Europe.

Certain that this time she would find Utopia.

The journey took longer than usual because they didn't want to leave without saying goodbye to Professor Kacimba.

João Cerqueira

Abelheira, Viana do Castelo, September, 24, 2014

joomcerqueira@gmail.com

João Cerqueira has a PhD in History of Art from the University of Oporto. He is the author of eight books. Blame it on to much freedom, The Tragedy of Fidel Castro, Devil's Observations, Maria Pia: Queen and Woman, José de Guimarães (published in China by the Today Art Museum), José de Guimarães: Public Art.

The Tragedy of Fidel Castro won the USA Best Book Awards 2013, the Beverly Hills Book Awards 2014, the Global Ebook Awards 2014, was finalist for the Montaigne Medal 2014 (Eric Offer Awards) and for The Wishing Shelf Independent Book Awards 2014 and was considered by ForewordReviews the third best translation published in 2012 in the United States.

The second coming of Jesus (A segunda vinda de Cristo à Terra) won the silver medal in the 2015 Latino Book Award.

The short storie A house in Europe won the 2015 Speakando European Literary Contest, received the bronze medal in the

Ebook Me Up Short Story Competition 2015 and an honorable mention in the Glimmer Train July 2015 Very Short Fiction Award.

His works are published in The Adirondack Review, Ragazine, Berfrois, Cleaver Magazine, Bright Lights Film, Modern Times Magazine, Toad Suck Review, Foliate Oak Literary Magazine, Hypertext Magazine, Danse Macabre, Rapid River Magazine, Contemporary Literary Review India, Open Pen Magazine, Queen Mob's Tea House, The Liberator Magazine, Narrator International, The Transnational, BoldType Magazine, Saturday Night Reader, All Right Magazine, South Asia Mail, Linguistic Erosion, Sundayat6mag, Literary Lunes.

www.joaocerqueira.com

49241012R00194

Made in the USA
Middletown, DE
10 October 2017